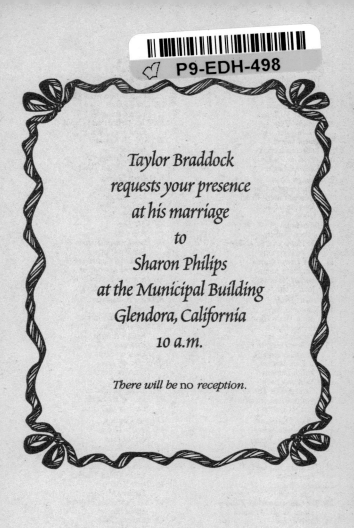

P9-EDH-498

Taylor Braddock
requests your presence
at his marriage
to
Sharon Philips
at the Municipal Building
Glendora, California
10 a.m.

There will be no reception.

Ranch Rogues
1. *Betrayed by Love*
   Diana Palmer
2. *Blue Sage*
   Anne Stuart
3. *Chase the Clouds*
   Lindsay McKenna
4. *Mustang Man*
   Lee Magner
5. *Painted Sunsets*
   Rebecca Flanders
6. *Carved in Stone*
   Kathleen Eagle

Hitched in Haste
7. *A Marriage of Convenience*
   Doreen Owens Malek
8. *Where Angels Fear*
   Ginna Gray
9. *Inheritance*
   Joleen Daniels
10. *The Hawk and the Honey*
    Dixie Browning
11. *Wild Horse Canyon*
    Elizabeth August
12. *Someone Waiting*
    Joan Hohl

Ranchin' Dads
13. *Rancher's Wife*
    Anne Marie Winston
14. *His and Hers*
    Pamela Bauer
15. *The Best Things in Life*
    Rita Clay Estrada
16. *All That Matters*
    Judith Duncan
17. *One Man's Folly*
    Cathy Gillen Thacker
18. *Sagebrush and Sunshine*
    Margot Dalton

Denim & Diamonds
19. *Moonbeams Aplenty*
    Mary Lynn Baxter
20. *A Home on the Range*
    Judith Bowen
21. *The Fairy Tale Girl*
    Ann Major
22. *Snow Bird*
    Lass Small
23. *The Countess and the Cowboy*
    Linda Randall Wisdom
24. *Heart of Ice*
    Diana Palmer

Kids & Kin
25. *Fools Rush In*
    Ginna Gray
26. *Wellspring*
    Curtiss Ann Matlock
27. *Live-In Mom*
    Laurie Paige
28. *Kids, Critters and Cupid*
    Ruth Jean Dale
29. *With No Regrets*
    Lisa Jackson
30. *Family Affair*
    Cathy Gillen Thacker

Reunited Hearts
31. *Yesterday's Lies*
    Lisa Jackson
32. *The Texas Way*
    Jan Freed
33. *Wild Lady*
    Ann Major
34. *Cody Daniels' Return*
    Marilyn Pappano
35. *All Things Considered*
    Debbie Macomber
36. *Return to Yesterday*
    Annette Broadrick

Reckless Renegades
37. *Ambushed*
    Patricia Rosemoor
38. *West of the Sun*
    Lynn Erickson
39. *Bittersweet*
    DeLoras Scott
40. *A Deadly Breed*
    Caroline Burnes
41. *Desperado*
    Helen Conrad
42. *Heart of the Eagle*
    Lindsay McKenna

Once A Cowboy...
43. *Rancho Diablo*
    Anne Stuart
44. *Big Sky Country*
    Jackie Merritt
45. *A Family to Cherish*
    Cathy Gillen Thacker
46. *Texas Wildcat*
    Lindsay McKenna
47. *Not Part of the Bargain*
    Susan Fox
48. *Destiny's Child*
    Ann Major

Please address questions and book requests to: Silhouette Reader Service
U.S.: 3010 Walden Ave., P.O. Box 1325, Buffalo, NY 14269
Canadian: P.O. Box 609, Fort Erie, Ont. L2A 5X3

WESTERN *Lovers*

DOREEN OWENS MALEK

A MARRIAGE OF CONVENIENCE

Published by Silhouette Books
America's Publisher of Contemporary Romance

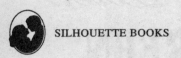

SILHOUETTE BOOKS

ISBN 0-373-30155-3

A MARRIAGE OF CONVENIENCE

Copyright © 1989 by Doreen Owens Malek

This edition published by arrangement with Harlequin Books S.A.

Visit Silhouette at www.eHarlequin.com

Printed in U.S.A.

Chapter 1

"Tell him I'll be there around five, if he can wait for me," Sharon Philips said into the phone. She listened to the response and nodded.

"Okay," she answered, concluding the conversation, and hung up thoughtfully, staring out the window at the full, newly blooming trees.

The appointment was to discuss her father's will with his probate lawyer. Her father had just died on the West Coast, leaving instructions forbidding a funeral or memorial service of any kind. His passing seemed unreal to Sharon, who had never had a chance to say goodbye.

The house line buzzed on her phone. She picked it up distractedly.

"How about dinner tonight?" Pete Symonds said.

"Pete, I can't," Sharon replied. "I have to go over to Charlie Crawford's office and discuss my father's estate. Charlie's being very mysterious, refusing to talk about it over the phone." Sharon had been dating Pete, her colleague in the Philadelphia district attorney's office, for several months.

"Maybe your dad left you an emerald mine in South America," Pete said lightly.

Sharon smiled. "I wish it were that simple. I'm sure it concerns the ranch, and what I'm going to do about *that*, I haven't a clue."

"You'll resolve it," Pete said confidently. "Selling it is probably the answer."

Sharon didn't reply.

"How's the trial going lately?" Pete continued. "Still think you haven't got a chance?"

Sharon sighed. "No chance at all. Closing arguments are day after tomorrow, but it's over right now. I'm certainly not helping Desmond's reelection campaign with this debacle."

"Nobody could have won that case," Pete said consolingly. "Desmond knows the score, he won't blame you." John Desmond was the district attorney for whom they both worked; she and Pete would be out of work in the fall if Desmond lost his bid to remain in his job.

"I know he won't blame me, but that doesn't make me feel any better," Sharon replied. "This one was a nightmare from the beginning. A dead body but no evidence, no witnesses, and a defendant with a distinguished service record in the navy. Why do I always get the stinkers?"

"Because you're good at your job," Pete answered. "Look, don't talk to me. The offer to go into real estate with my dad still stands. Just say the word."

"The temptation is growing," Sharon said dryly. Her outside line began to buzz. "Pete, I have to go. The other phone is ringing."

"Okay," Pete said. "I'll call you tonight."

Sharon switched lines and took the call, then hung up and grimaced at the pile of paperwork awaiting her. At this point her summation consisted of an assortment of scattered index cards with notes like "point out defendant's recent history of psychiatric treatment" and "remind jury of previous threats against victim's family."

Sharon made a face. This would never do. She instructed her secretary to hold all further calls and settled down to prepare for the court presentation.

But her mind kept wandering back to the subject of her father. Sharon's parents had divorced when she was twelve, and her father had moved to California and bought a horse ranch. Six years later he had remarried. When her stepmother died, her father had remained in California on his ranch with his stepson as the foreman. Her father visited Sharon in Philadelphia regularly, but she had not been back to California since the summer after she graduated from high school.

Ten years, she thought. During that time she had gone to college and law school, taken a job as an assistant district attorney in a major city and performed with notable success.

But somehow when she thought of California, she was always eighteen again.

At quarter to five Sharon gave up on the summation, deciding to keep her appointment with Crawford and then spend a couple of late nights getting the oral presentation ready. She packed her briefcase and walked the four blocks to Charles Crawford's office, enjoying the late-spring afternoon.

Mary, Crawford's secretary, waved her inside.

"Hi, Charlie," Sharon said, dropping wearily into the lawyer's conference chair and setting her briefcase on the floor.

Crawford looked at her over the tops of his glasses. "Bad day?" he said.

"Kind of."

He sighed. "I'm afraid I'm not going to improve it."

Sharon surveyed him. Charlie Crawford was one of her

father's oldest friends, and she'd known him since she was a child.

"What's the matter, Charlie?" she said easily. "Didn't the papers come through?"

"Oh, they came through, all right, but you're not going to like what they say."

"What do they say?"

"You'd better sit down."

"Charlie," Sharon said, staring at him, "I *am* sitting down."

"Get a grip, then."

Sharon leaned forward. "Tell me," she said tersely.

"Well, your father left you half the ranch in Glendora on one condition," Crawford said cautiously.

"Half?" Sharon asked, bewildered.

"Yes."

"What's the condition?" She had no idea what to do with a horse ranch, half or whole, in the first place, and couldn't think of any reason why her father would place a condition on her receipt of it, in the second.

"You must marry your father's stepson, Taylor Braddock," Crawford said, wincing.

Sharon's ivory skin became even paler, and her fingers closed around the leather-padded arms of her chair. Taylor Braddock. The name brought a flood of unwanted memories, and her mouth became a grim line.

"I will not marry that man under any circumstances," she announced flatly.

"Read it and weep," Crawford replied, shrugging, and tossed a file into Sharon's lap. "You get half the place and Braddock gets half. To keep it together and hold it as joint tenants, you have to get married."

Sharon flipped through the pages, reading intermittently, and then clipped the file together, replacing it on Crawford's desk carefully.

"Charlie, this is preposterous," she said. "Estates on

condition of marriage went out with the last century, you know that. The will would never hold up in court, the condition would be struck.''

Crawford pursed his lips. ''I told your father as much. I said that if you contested it the condition would fail, but he insisted.''

''So what am I supposed to do now?'' Sharon demanded, frustrated.

''Are you asking my advice?''

''I imagine I'd better hear it,'' Sharon answered wearily.

''Contesting this will take forever,'' Crawford said. ''The probate docket is backed up into next year. I know what your situation is at work. You're up against a tough thing there, and you don't need to be suing your father's estate at the same time. My advice is to take a leave of absence when your current case closes, go out to California and marry this Braddock. The fall election will take place in your absence and things will settle down one way or another. If you allow this will to go through, the estate will be probated in a few months and you can divorce the guy.''

''Charlie, you can't be serious,'' Sharon said, dumbfounded.

''Why not? Take a vacation in California. Your leave will be approved, I'll speak to John Desmond about it. God knows you haven't had a day off in four years. Go through a civil ceremony with the stepson and cut him loose when you get clear title. You and he can sell the place and split the money, or he can buy out your half.''

''You will not say a word to Desmond, because I'm not going to do it,'' Sharon replied, outraged.

''Is it something about this man, Braddock, that's bothering you?'' Crawford asked mildly, watching her face.

''Why do you say that?'' Sharon asked sharply.

''Your father gave me the impression that you knew him.''

''I knew him once,'' Sharon answered distantly, avoiding

the lawyer's gaze. "I spent the summer out there ten years ago when my father married his mother."

"Can you think of any reason why your father would force you to do this?"

Sharon was silent. Then, "He was old-fashioned, as you know. He thought I needed a husband. He was always after me to get married, and over the years he grew very fond of Tay." Sharon shifted in her chair, choosing her words carefully. "In the beginning, when Dad first married Tay's mother, Tay had some...problems. A lot of people wrote him off, I think, but Dad always seemed to understand him. After Tay's mother died five years ago, Dad sort of lost interest in the place and Tay really ran the ranch himself. Dad came to rely on Tay more and more, like a son. He had a great deal of respect and affection for him."

"But you don't have any affection for him."

"I haven't seen him in a long time," Sharon replied shortly, aware that she wasn't exactly answering the question.

Crawford let it slide. "What kind of problems did Tay have when you knew him?" he asked.

"My father told me that Tay was a sergeant in Vietnam, then a prisoner of war when the Americans pulled out. He'd only been home for a couple of years when I met him. He was still pretty disturbed, I guess—fighting, disappearing for days at a stretch, drinking."

"Really?" Crawford said, getting worried. "Was Braddock dangerous?"

"Not to me," Sharon replied softly, her expression changing.

Crawford nodded slowly.

"I guess my father thought he would be taking care of both of us, tying things up all neat and tidy this way," Sharon offered resignedly.

"He tied you up all right. You've got two parcels on the ranch, sitting side by side. Yours has the water rights and stream, Braddock's has the road access, neither one much good without the other. They have to go together, and in order to get them together you have to marry Braddock.''

''What happens if I don't marry him, if I don't contest the will but just refuse to comply with it?''

Crawford looked pained. ''I guess you didn't read that part. The whole place reverts to charity, becomes a wildlife refuge.''

Sharon stared at the floor morosely. The ranch was Tay's life, as it had been her father's before her stepmother's death. She hated to be pushed into this, but to deprive Tay of his home and livelihood was cruel, when all she had to do to prevent that was follow Crawford's advice.

She had to admit that her father had known exactly what he was doing.

''Marry him,'' Crawford said again. ''Why is that such an awful prospect? You can handle it in friendly fashion, can't you?''

Friendly fashion. Sharon didn't know whether she wanted to laugh or cry.

''Charlie, I have to think about this,'' she finally said. ''Let me have my copy of the will, and I'll study it. I'll call you in a few days.''

Sharon left Crawford's office with the estate papers in her briefcase. She got her car from the lot behind the district attorney's office and drove home slowly, her mind whirling, the past intruding on the present like old photographs superimposed upon more recent ones.

Tay Braddock. She had managed not to think about him for a long time, even when her father mentioned him in connection with the ranch. She would listen to the story about how Tay had gotten a good price on feed for the horses or purchased an Appaloosa at a bargain in Texas, and she would smoothly change the subject without comment. She had never thought her father picked up on her reaction, but maybe he had noticed something.

Sharon parked her car in the underground lot of her Society Hill apartment building and took the elevator to the eighth floor. She had chosen her apartment for its view of the Penn's Landing waterfront, a view she'd rarely had time to appreciate. She took off her suit and shoes and made herself a cup of tea, then sat in her slip by the bay window in the living room, looking out at the craft in the boat basin.

Dear old Dad, she thought grimly. Her grief at his loss was submerged in a welter of fury at this high-handed maneuvering, so typical of the arrangements he liked to make for his only child. He was still trying to control her life, even after his death.

As usual Sharon tried not to think about Tay. Over the years, she had perfected that art to such a degree that the very whisper of him in her mind triggered an avoidance response. But this time she let the image remain, remembering the man who had changed her life and spoiled her for anyone else.

She recalled him as he'd looked that August when she was eighteen; it was how she always pictured him, since she had never seen him again after that summer. He'd been slim, almost lanky, with wide shoulders and the sort of hipless, long-legged physique best served by jeans, which he wore constantly. He had the blackest hair she'd ever seen, shaggy but luminously clean and radiant with bluish highlights, shining in the pitiless California sun like polished coal. He'd been tanned from hours of working outdoors, his skin golden brown with a sharp border at his hips when his Levi's rode low. When he hoisted bales of hay or lifted her down from a horse, the long ropy muscles stood out in his brown arms like cords of steel.

Sharon recalled his face with a painful clarity that all the years of sublimation had not managed to dim: the deep-set brown eyes, the heavy black brows, the long, straight Barrymore nose. But most of all she remembered his mouth, its surprising softness and...

Her eyes filled with tears now as the bittersweet recollection washed over her. How could she have resisted him? Had an incubus been summoned by a spell to break her young girl's heart, it would have taken the form of Taylor Braddock.

He was the reason she could never make a commitment to another man; he was the reason she had broken her engagement to a fellow law student just before graduation. For all her refusal to think about him, talk about him, acknowledge that he still existed on the earth, he had dominated her life all these years.

Had her father sensed that?

Sharon stood abruptly, sloshing cold tea over the rim of her cup and dousing her slip. She had promised herself long ago that she would never do this, and here she was, wallowing in painful memories like a despondent schoolgirl.

She changed into slacks and a sweater and opened her briefcase, scanning her father's will again. She had to smile when she came to the wording about inheriting the ranch.

That sly old fox. He thought he had come up with the perfect solution for the two people he cared about most, his daughter and his stepson.

Sharon sat again with the document in her lap, thinking that the affection he had developed for Tay said a lot about her father's tolerance for difficult personalities. Overbearing and dictatorial he may have been, but he certainly gave Tay a chance when a lot of other men would have given him the boot.

She felt the sting of tears behind her eyes again. She couldn't believe that her father was dead or that she was now in this ridiculous predicament. Why did all of this have to dredge up an experience she preferred to forget?

But she knew now that she would not be able to forget it. Thanks to the will, her life was once again linked with Tay's, so she might as well deal with a past she'd been running from for the last decade.

The papers slid from her lap to the floor as she looked out the window again, seeing herself at almost eighteen, arriving in California.

Chapter 2

Sharon looked at the clouds floating past the airplane window, listening to the pilot announcing the descent to Los Angeles. Her stomach was knotted with excitement. This was her first time away from home without her mother (thank God), her first time on a cross-country flight and her first visit to her father's new house. She had just graduated from high school in Philadelphia the week before, and she was on her way to her father's wedding.

She'd never met her future stepmother, a widow with a grown son. Sharon's father knew his fiancée from the local rancher's association. She'd sold her own place when she decided to remarry; the couple planned to run the Philips ranch together. Sharon had seen a picture of her—a tall dark woman standing next to her father, who looked very happy.

Which was more than anyone could say about him during the thirteen years he'd spent with Sharon's mother.

The ground was rising up to the plane. Sharon could make out houses and cars below, miniaturized like Monopoly pieces. She sat back in her seat and closed her eyes, thinking about the ten weeks of freedom that awaited her. Her father was dictatorial about long-range plans and given to scattered outbursts of parental concern, but on a day-to-day basis he was much less exacting than her mother, who practically required an hourly check-in from her only child.

Sharon planned to make the most of her parole.

The jet's engines reversed and Sharon felt their backward thrust, then the jolt as the landing gear touched ground. She lifted her overnight case onto her lap and shouldered her purse, intending to be the first person into the aisle when the seat belt light went off. She had brought three suitcases, every stitch of summer clothing she owned, and she felt outfitted for anything.

Her father was waiting for her in the deplaning lounge alone. He enveloped her in a bear hug. Sharon closed her eyes and let him hold her as he'd done when she was little. She'd missed him.

"Honey, it's great to have you here," her father finally said, misty-eyed as he released her.

"Where's Rae?" Sharon asked after they had looked each other over in smiling silence.

"Oh, she thought it would be better if she just waited at home. She wanted to give us a chance to get reacquainted on the drive out to the ranch."

As they took the escalator down to reclaim her baggage, Sharon glanced around at the passersby. Everyone, including her father, had a tan.

"You look great, honey. I can't wait for you to see the ranch. I was telling Rae this morning, I just know you're going to love it," her father said.

"I still don't believe that Mom agreed to let me come out here," Sharon said to him, noticing his linen shorts and loose print shirt. He had never dressed that way in Philadelphia even in high summer.

"Well, let's say that since she canceled our last two

Christmas visits and wouldn't allow me to attend your graduation, she knew Charlie Crawford had a lot of ammunition if I chose to take it to court.''

They made small talk as they waited for her luggage to come up on the carousel, and when it did, Sharon's father stared in disbelief.

''Honey, you didn't tell me you were packing for the whole city of Philly,'' he said dryly, staggering as he lifted one of the overloaded suitcases to the floor.

''Did I bring too much?'' Sharon asked nervously.

''Nah, whatever gave you that idea.''

''I didn't want to have to buy anything, since I won't have a job.''

''Never you mind, if you want anything you just let me know.'' Dan Philips suffered from the overcompensation syndrome common to divorced parents and was as free with his checkbook as he was with advice.

They managed to get the luggage into the trunk of the car with the help of a porter. Sharon rummaged in her purse for her sunglasses as she settled into the passenger seat. It had been raining when she left Philadelphia, and here the sun was blinding.

Her father chatted about the ranch and his fiancée as they exited the airport and crisscrossed the network of freeways on the way out to Glendora. It was midafternoon, so the commuter traffic Sharon had heard so much about had not yet materialized, but even without it the highways were thronged and intimidating. Sharon had a Pennsylvania driver's license, but she thought it might be a while before she ventured forth on this terrain.

As they took the Glendora exit her father cleared his throat and said, ''Honey, there's something I want to discuss with you before we get there. I didn't mention it in my letters. We just found out yesterday that Rae's son will be coming in for the wedding tomorrow and might be staying on for a while.''

"Oh?" Sharon said, trying to remember what she knew about Rae's son. She had a vague impression that he was older than she was, in his twenties. She knew he'd been in the Army.

"Yeah, he had a job in Arizona, working in construction for some old service buddy of his, but he got laid off last week. Business isn't so good, and they had to let some of the laborers go. I think he had plans to leave when the wedding was over, but Rae talked him into working on the ranch for a bit. I could use the help." Dan glanced over at her. "Truthfully I think his mother would like to keep an eye on him."

"Why?"

Her father sighed. "He's had a little trouble readjusting after the Army," he said shortly in a tone that indicated the subject was now closed.

Sharon filed that away for future reference, turning her attention to the scenery as they drove through the town and upward into the foothills. The houses were landscaped with cactus plants and citrus trees rather than the evergreens that abounded in the eastern suburbs, and this, coupled with the sandy soil and sculptured rock gardens, gave the whole area the aspect of a blooming desert.

They ascended until the town lay below them and they reached a plateau with a double wrought-iron gate. Dan opened it and they drove up a dirt road with corrals on either side. He pointed out the various breeds of the horses to Sharon as they passed. She, who'd never even been on a horse, marveled at how much his life had changed from the one he'd left behind in Philadelphia.

The stables and bunkhouses were at the back, against the mountain rim and behind a one-story house that was shaped like an L, with long shuttered windows and redwood siding. They left the luggage in the car and went up a brick walk that was bordered on either side with pachysandra beds.

Sharon shifted her feet nervously while her father opened the front door.

"Rae, we're here," her father called as they entered.

A rawboned woman with streaked dark hair entered the cool, air-conditioned front hall. She was wearing jeans and a flowered blouse with sandals. She embraced Sharon.

"Welcome, dear. You're just as pretty as all of your photos. We're so happy to have you with us."

Sharon smiled and returned the hug, mentally comparing this woman to her mother, who would never have worn such a casual outfit to greet a guest. Rae gave the initial impression of being pleasant and relaxed, which would certainly be a change from the ex-Mrs. Philips, who ran her home and office like a military barracks and dressed in hose and high heels to go to the supermarket.

"Come inside," Rae said. "You must be hot and tired from your trip. I made some iced tea."

Sharon followed her father from the hall, past the living room, which was furnished with low sofas and chairs in beige linen and raw cotton, into a kitchen-den combination floored with Mexican tiles and dominated by a fieldstone fireplace. They sat in the breakfast nook and sipped iced tea flavored with lemon and lime slices.

"Your room is all ready for you," Rae said brightly. "Rosa just changed the linens this morning."

"Rosa?" Sharon asked, looking at her father.

"Our housekeeper. She lives in town with her little girl. She just went home for the day, you'll meet her tomorrow," Rae replied.

Housekeeper? Sharon thought. Horse ranching must pay better than she'd realized. When her father worked in a Philadelphia office, her mother had done the housework.

"Well," Rae said, standing when they had finished their drinks, "I imagine you'd like a tour, and we'll get your luggage into your room so you can unpack. We want you to feel at home."

Sharon rose dutifully to follow, noticing Rae's frequent use of the word *we*. She certainly wanted Sharon to perceive the residents of the house as a team.

"You can lie down for a while before dinner," Rae continued as they walked down the hall, "so you can be all rested for the evening."

Sharon felt too keyed up to sleep but was glad for some time alone to sort out her thoughts.

She followed Rae through the back door to have her first look at the ranch.

They went to a local restaurant for a welcome celebration that evening, then came home and stayed up talking until almost midnight.

Sharon decided that she liked her father's future wife, and she could see why Rae got along with Dan Philips. If Dan wanted to go out for dinner, Rae thought that was a great idea. If he fancied Italian food, Rae did, too. And if Dan got the urge to stop off on the way home for milk shakes, Rae applauded the impulse.

Sharon's parents would have had three fights during the course of the evening and ended it by not speaking to each other. By contrast, this harmony was wonderful. She looked across the den at the two of them side by side on the tweed couch and realized she was glad her father was getting married.

"I think you'd better get to bed, miss," Dan said to Sharon. "Your eyelids are slipping to half-mast."

"I'm wide awake," Sharon replied, stifling a yawn.

Her father was about to reply when the kitchen door opened abruptly. A duffel bag was tossed through the doorway, and then its owner appeared, clad in jeans and a pea-green Army T-shirt, his hair unruly, his skin as brown as a nut. He was wearing two days' growth of stubble and a Peck's bad-boy expression.

"Hi, Rae," the new arrival said, smiling the crooked

smile Sharon would come to know. "Am I still in time for the ceremony?"

"Tay!" Rae jumped up with a glad cry, embraced him and shot Sharon's father a worried look over her son's shoulder. Sharon, observing the scene, got the message this was expected to be a problem.

She studied Tay, wondering why. Her father's vague reference to adjustment difficulties after the Army didn't tell her much.

He was about eight or ten years older than she was, in his middle to late twenties, with the slow, graceful carriage of a roaming panther. When he walked over to shake her father's hand, his step was controlled and quiet, even though he stood a head taller than the older man and must have weighed nearly as much. Sharon knew the type from her observation of athletes at school. She suspected that he could explode into motion that would dazzle the eye in an instant. His dark gaze moved across the room to her and remained there. He examined her until she became uncomfortable and his mother intervened to say, "Tay, this is Dan's daughter, Sharon. She's staying with us this summer."

Sharon stood as if called upon in class to give an answer, and Tay walked over to her, looking down into her face. His eyelashes were very long, almost girlish, and he had a tiny mole at the corner of his mouth.

"Hi," he said briefly and offered his hand as he had to her father.

Sharon took it, feeling foolish. She had never shaken hands with a man before, and he seemed almost to be mocking her with the gesture, as it only served to emphasize her youth.

His hand was large and callused. He held her fingers trapped in his while he studied her for a moment, then let her go, turning away as if she were of no consequence.

"We expected you earlier," his mother said to him.

"Well, Rae, I got a late start," Tay replied, sitting as his mother gestured to a chair and stretching his long legs before him. He was almost too thin, but not quite. His upper arms were well developed, and the section of his abdomen exposed as his shirt rode up was ribbed with muscle.

"You must be hungry," Rae said. "Would you like something to eat?"

"Wouldn't mind," Tay replied.

Rae was getting up when the door opened and one of the ranch hands burst into the room.

"Fair Season is about to foal. You folks told me to let you know."

Dan and Rae both bolted for the door. "That's our prize mare," Dan called as he ran into the night.

"We've been waiting a week for this," Rae added, hot on his heels. "Help yourself to anything you like, the refrigerator's full," she advised her son before disappearing after her fiancé.

Tay and Sharon were left to share uncomfortable silence.

"Did you ever see so much fuss about a horse?" Tay finally said, shooting her a sidelong glance. "You'd think that mare was giving birth to the Prince of Wales."

Sharon watched as he sauntered over to the refrigerator and yanked the door open. His shirt was stuck to his back with perspiration, and she could make out the column of his spine through the thin cotton. He lifted his hair off his nape with a casual hand, and Sharon saw a ring of sunburn there. She looked away.

He withdrew an apple and turned to face her, leaning against the kitchen counter and crossing his legs at the ankle.

"So," he said, taking a large bite, "how old are you?"

"Eighteen," she replied. "In two weeks."

"As much as that?" he said, raising his brows. "I would never have guessed."

She knew that he was baiting her but wasn't sure how to reply.

"I suppose they warned you about me," he added.

Sharon looked down, nonplussed.

He nodded, pursing his lips. "I thought so. Well, don't worry. I haven't taken to carving up little teenyboppers yet, so you're safe."

"I'm not a teenybopper," she said, annoyed.

"Oh, no? What are you?" he asked as if genuinely interested, turning the apple and taking another huge bite of it.

"I guess I'm a...young adult," she replied, using a term from her high school, uncomfortably aware that she sounded juvenile.

He grinned. "What does that make me? An old adult?"

"Doesn't your mother mind you calling her 'Rae'?" Sharon asked, trying to change the subject.

"That's her name," Tay replied, looking away.

"Why don't you call her 'Mom', or 'Mother'?" she inquired.

"Who are you, Emily Post?" he countered archly.

"'Rae' just doesn't seem very respectful," Sharon said inadequately, flushing.

"And I can tell that's the type of thing that would concern a proper young lady—excuse me—young adult, like yourself," he said dryly. "Well, don't you worry about it," he continued, tossing the apple core into the garbage. "Rae doesn't need you to look out for her, she can take care of herself." He yanked open a cabinet and pulled out a cellophane packet of cookies. "So tomorrow's the big day, huh?" he said, sticking his thumb through the wrapper and pulling out two creme sandwiches. "Your old man and R— my mother—are going to tie the knot."

Sharon nodded.

He popped a cookie into his mouth. "How do you feel about that?"

"I'm happy for my father. He and my mother never got along, and he seems like a changed man now."

"My parents got along great," Tay offered, eyeing her steadily. "When my father died, Rae was devastated. I didn't think she'd ever marry again."

"Oh," Sharon said quietly as Tay bit into the other cookie. "If you'd stop inhaling that junk for a minute, I'll make you something to eat," she added shyly, attempting to gain control of the conversation once more.

"She cooks," Tay said wonderingly, dusting cookie crumbs from his fingers. "What does she cook?"

"Anything you like. Are there eggs in the refrigerator?" she asked, walking past him to look inside.

"Think so."

"How about an omelet?" Sharon asked, pushing items aside to find what she wanted.

"Sounds great," Tay replied, watching as she assembled ingredients and went looking for a skillet. It took her a little longer than usual, since she was unfamiliar with the kitchen, but she soon had an omelet simmering in the pan, filling the air with an appetizing aroma.

"I'm impressed," Tay said, kicking a chair loose from the table legs with his foot and dropping into it.

"Don't be. My mother works full-time. She goes in on weekends sometimes and stays late a lot. It was either learn to cook or starve."

"I've chosen the starvation option," Tay said. "Nutritionally, anyway. I'm a constant patron of convenience stores and vending machines."

"It sounds like you need someone to take care of you," Sharon said lightly, dishing up the omelet and putting it on the table before him.

"You volunteering for the job?" Tay asked casually, not looking up at her.

Sharon jumped as the outside door opened again and Rae entered.

"The foal's a beauty," Rae announced, beaming. She stopped short when she saw Tay shoveling in the food.

"I made him an omelet, I hope you don't mind," Sharon said hastily. "He was hungry. I'll wash the dishes."

"Don't be silly, sweetie, thanks for pitching in," Rae replied. "And leave the dishes, we'll do them in the morning."

Sharon said nothing. If she left a spoon in the sink overnight, her mother had a fit.

"So when's the christening?" Tay asked brightly, glancing at his mother.

Rae threw him a dirty look. "Make fun if you like. That mare cost us a fortune, and the stud fee was almost as much. We had a big investment riding on this foal."

"No birth announcements, no knitted booties?" Tay asked dryly, finishing the last of his omelet. "Rae, you're falling down on the job."

"You're talking nonsense," his mother said. "Go to bed."

"Be happy to, if you'd show me where the bed is," Tay replied, shoving his empty plate away from him and standing up.

"You're sleeping in the bunkhouse out back," Rae said. "The young lady gets the extra bedroom."

"Fine with me," Tay said equably, shouldering his duffel bag.

"Where's my father?" Sharon asked.

"He's helping the men clean up. I just came in to call the vet." Rae walked into the living room, patting her son's cheek as she passed. "Sleep tight, sweetheart. See you in the morning."

Tay nodded, turning to look at Sharon when his mother left.

"Thanks for the grub," he said.

"You're welcome."

He doubled his fist and tapped her lightly on the chin. "Good night, kid," he said softly.

"Good night," Sharon replied, watching him walk out of the room. She heard the back door close behind him.

Well, so that was Rae's son, the object of so much concern. Sharon could understand it better now. Although he hadn't done anything particularly unusual that evening, there was an aura of power about him, of danger. It was subtle, but unmistakable.

She wasn't sure what to think of him.

Sharon woke to the sounds of bustle and preparation outside her door. When she emerged, belting her bathrobe, she could hear the florists and caterers taking over the living room. Rae's voice dominated. Sharon bypassed the scene and entered the kitchen, where her father was nursing a cup of coffee morosely.

"I told Rae we should have gone to the justice of the peace," he greeted Sharon. "Did you see that chaos in there?"

"I'm sure it will be lovely," Sharon said soothingly.

Dan looked as though he wasn't so sure.

Sharon went to get a glass of orange juice, and from the window over the sink she saw Tay stacking a pile of bricks on the terrace next to the pool.

"What's Tay doing?" she said to her father.

"He's clearing off the patio for this afternoon," her father replied distractedly, wincing at a crash in the next room. He got up to investigate, and Sharon moved closer to the window.

Tay had removed his shirt, and the morning sun shone fully on his tanned torso as he shifted the stones. A thin stream of perspiration trickled down the middle of his back. Sharon watched for a long moment, then glanced over her shoulder to make sure her father was still occupied before she wandered outside.

"Good morning," she said to Tay, who looked up from his labors.

"Hi, kid," he said, unsmiling, wiping his forehead with the back of his arm.

"How long have you been out here?" Sharon asked.

"Oh, an hour or so. I thought I'd make myself useful, kill some time before the big event. How are things inside?"

"Loud."

He nodded. "When's the wedding?"

"Two o'clock."

"Who's coming?"

Sharon shrugged. "I really don't know. Some local people, friends of theirs, I guess."

He didn't look pleased at the prospect. In fact, neither of the men in the house seemed particularly delighted by the proceedings.

"Sharon, are you coming in for breakfast?" her father called from the doorway.

Sharon looked at Tay. "What about you?" she said.

"Not hungry," he answered, which, based on his behavior the previous night, she would have bet was a lie. Sharon turned and went back into the house.

Rosa had arrived while Sharon was outside. She was a beautiful dark-skinned woman in her late thirties, with waist-length hair. She nodded at Sharon when they were introduced and went back to cooking breakfast.

Sharon joined Rae and her father at the table. They discussed the upcoming nuptials with varying degrees of enthusiasm throughout the meal, and by the time Sharon got up to put her plate in the sink, Tay was gone.

He did not reappear for the rest of the morning, and around noon his mother started looking worried. Sharon went to her room to get ready. The tradespeople had all left and the house was curiously quiet, the calm before the storm. Sharon removed her dress from the closet and hung it on the back of the door. She examined herself in the cheval mirror, studying her shoulder-length dark blond hair, wide blue eyes and the slim legs revealed by her short robe. What did people see when they looked at her? A kid, Tay said, but was that really true? She sensed that this summer would forge a bridge between childhood and womanhood, and she felt poised on the brink of a new life.

She made up carefully and donned the expensive dress her mother never would have approved—a strapless pale blue sheath with a cap sleeved bolero jacket. With the jacket, it was quite proper, without—the possibilities for impropriety seemed endless. She'd managed to keep the dress a secret because her mother had been pretending that the wedding wasn't happening, so inquiries about her daughter's attire for the event were inappropriate. Sharon added a pair of white sandals, and pearls at her ears and throat, and she was ready.

Some of the guests were arriving, and Sharon's father introduced her to a few of them. When there was a lull in the conversation, he took her aside and whispered, "Honey, see if you can locate Tay. We're almost ready to do this thing and Rae can't find him."

Sharon nodded, slipping out the back door as soon as she had a chance. Rosa, standing at the kitchen counter, glanced after her as she left.

Cars were lining up on the driveway and the bustle of activity was increasing. Sharon bypassed it, going straight to the bunkhouse, which was empty. Tay's duffel bag was dumped on the floor, its contents spilling out, and the cot was rumpled. A razor in a mug was perched on one edge of the white porcelain sink in the tiny bathroom, and a damp towel was draped over the other. An empty hanger dangled from the doorknob, and the split paper bands from a dress shirt were scattered in the trash can. He must have dressed in his suit and vanished.

Sharon strolled around the grounds a bit more, but Tay

was nowhere to be found. Time was passing, and she went back to the house, signaling her father by shaking her head.

He closed his eyes briefly, disengaged himself from a conversation, took Sharon's arm and ushered her out the door again.

"I knew he would do something like this," Dan muttered. "We have to find him. Rae will be devastated if he doesn't stand up for us."

They widened the circle of exploration, proceeding down the back path to the staff houses and the horse stalls. They encountered nothing but empty space until Dan unbarred the door of the last stable.

Tay was sprawled in the hay, fully dressed in a dark blue suit, white shirt and maroon figured tie. His eyes were closed.

"Is he asleep?" Sharon asked anxiously, lifting her dress carefully out of the way and kneeling next to the inert man on the straw.

"He's drunk," Sharon's father replied, pushing Tay to a sitting position and slapping his cheeks. A half-empty bottle of bourbon rolled out from under him, dribbling dark liquid into the straw.

"Why?" Sharon asked.

Her father sighed. "I'm not sure, honey, but I can guess. He loved his dad a lot. He joined the Army to get away when his father finally died after a long illness. Now, I don't think he can face his mother marrying someone else." He shook the younger man briskly, and Tay mumbled, his eyelids fluttering.

"But he came here for the wedding," Sharon protested. "And he likes you, I can tell."

"He's trying, Sharon," Dan replied. "I know he wants his mother to be happy, but he's been through such a lot. I guess this was just a little too much for him." Dan propped Tay against the wall of the stall, and his head lolled.

"What has he been through?" Sharon asked, awed by the compassionate tone in her usually gruff father's voice.

Dan glanced at her as if to determine whether she could handle the information he was about to impart.

"He was in a prisoner-of-war camp in North Vietnam," Dan said flatly. "He was only a kid, a little older than you. I'm telling you this to help you understand, but I don't want you to mention it to him or anyone else, have you got that?"

"Yes," Sharon murmured, swallowing. "But how could he think that doing this would help?" she inquired after a thoughtful pause.

"He isn't thinking, baby, he's in a lot of pain. And not just about this wedding. Don't be fooled by that smart-aleck exterior." He shook Tay again, and this time Tay came around, coughing and blinking.

In the next instant Tay was on his feet and Dan was flung to the floor. Sharon jumped back, shocked, as Tay grabbed her, his eyes wild. She would never forget the strength of his grip, the expression on his face, as he struggled back to full consciousness.

He released her the instant he realized what he was doing.

"I'm sorry," he gasped in confusion. "I didn't mean to do that. Did I hurt you?"

His hair was disheveled, littered with bits of hay, and his eyes were bloodshot. He had whiskey stains on his shirt and tie.

Sharon shook her head, rubbing her bare arms where Tay's fingers had bruised the flesh.

Her father struggled to his feet. He took Tay by the shoulders and said, "Take it easy, son. You're safe, among friends. We've got to get you straightened out before your mother sees you, okay?"

Tay passed a shaking hand over his forehead and nodded dumbly. His eyes returned to Sharon and dropped. He walked unsteadily to the rough-hewn wall a short distance away and stood with one hand flat against it, his head bent, silent.

"Is he all right?" Sharon asked in an undertone.

Her father nodded. "I think so. But if he's like that drunk, I'd hate to see the damage he could do when he's sober." He pushed back the sleeve of his jacket and glanced at his watch.

"You go back, Dad," Sharon said quickly, making a decision. "They'll be looking for you, the minister will be here any minute. I'll take care of Tay. I'll get him together and we'll both be there on time."

Dan looked relieved for a split second before his expression changed to concern. "Are you sure you can handle him?" he asked, looking worriedly from one young person to the other.

"We'll be fine," Sharon said, kissing his cheek hurriedly. "Just help me get him to the bunkhouse and you can go ahead."

They got on either side of Tay and walked him back to his cabin. Dan shoved Tay into the bathroom, and Sharon heard some thumping noises while her father got him undressed and into the shower. After a minute Dan emerged, looking slightly rumpled but pleased.

"He's coming out of it, the cold water's doing the trick," Dan reported. "There's a hot plate in the corner and some instant coffee in the cabinet. Make him a strong cup and help him get ready when he comes out. His suit is all right, but I'll have to send over a shirt and tie with Rosa. The shirt won't fit right, but I don't think he has another one."

"I'll look," Sharon said.

"Good. Honey, thanks a lot. I'll see you back at the house." Her father fled, and Sharon emptied Tay's duffel bag on the floor. As predicted, it contained nothing but jeans and T-shirts. She was heating water for coffee when the bathroom door opened and Tay emerged, surrounded by a cloud of steam.

"How are you feeling?" Sharon asked.

He thumbed his damp hair back from his face. "Foolish," he said shortly. He had a white towel wrapped around his hips. The thatch of dark hair on his chest narrowed into a line that disappeared beneath the terry cloth. His bare feet left wet footprints on the wooden floor.

"I'm making you some coffee," Sharon said.

"Thanks." He sat on the edge of the cot and put his head in his hands. He looked so defeated and alone that her heart went out to him.

Sharon walked over and sat next to him. After a moment she put a tentative hand on his shoulder. His flesh was cool on the surface from the water, but warm underneath.

He looked up, his dark lashes still tangled and wet from the shower.

"I don't think I can face this," he whispered. The naked vulnerability in his expression took her by surprise; he seemed like a person who would keep such feelings to himself. But she had seen too much in the past hour to be fooled by false bravado, and perhaps he knew that.

"Yes, you can," she said quietly.

"You really know your father's gone when you see your mother marrying somebody else," he muttered.

"You miss him a lot, don't you?"

He didn't answer.

"I think I know how you're feeling," she said.

He studied her intently. "You do?"

She nodded. "It's hard for me to see my father marrying again, too. My parents never got along, but their divorce was still painful for me. Kids always have this fantasy of happy parents, happy family, you know? I guess I always hoped, in the back of my mind, that they would get back together and things would be different." She stopped and concluded, "It's hard for me to face this, too."

He sighed brokenly, his gaze focused on the floor.

"Let me bring you that coffee," Sharon said quickly, rising to get it. She handed him the cup and he downed half of it in one swallow.

"You're pretty grown-up for a little girl," he observed, looking at her.

Sharon didn't reply.

"I'm sorry you had to see this," he went on, shaking his head. "Sometimes I just can't seem to..." His voice trailed off into silence.

"It's all right," Sharon said reassuringly. "Nobody knows but my father and me."

"I'm such a jerk," he said, closing his eyes. "I really didn't want to ruin this for my mother."

"You won't," Sharon said firmly. "There's still time. Now get dressed and we'll go."

He nodded, swallowing the rest of the coffee, and rose, grabbing underwear and socks from the pile of clothes on the floor. He went back into the bathroom and emerged seconds later wearing his suit pants, with the jacket over his arm.

"No shirt," he announced grimly.

As if in answer, a knock came at the door. Sharon opened it to admit Rosa, who took in the scene at a glance and raised her eyes heavenward.

"Mr. Philips said to give you this," she declaimed, handing Sharon a folded shirt and tie.

"Thank you," Sharon said, taking the bundle. She looked back at Tay. "Rosa, this is just...I mean, we're..."

"I don't want to hear," Rosa said, holding up her hand and turning to pull the door closed behind her.

"Smart woman," Tay said dryly. He took the shirt and slipped into it, buttoning it hastily. It hung on his slim frame and the collar was too big. He stuffed the loose folds into his pants and knotted the tie tightly under the collar.

"How do I look?" he asked, putting on his jacket and turning to face her.

"Very handsome," Sharon said truthfully.

He came to her and took her face between his hands, kissing the tip of her nose briefly.

"You're a sweet girl," he said. "A liar, but a sweet girl."

She smiled at him.

"Now let's get a move on before Rae sends out the National Guard," he said briskly.

They ran back to the main house and entered just as the minister was arriving.

"There you are!" Rae said as they walked into the living room. Her forced smile became genuine when she saw her son. She took his boutonniere from a box on the coffee table and fastened it to his lapel.

"Look at you, your hair's still wet," she said, brushing back a lock of it as she stepped away from him.

"Everything looks great," Tay said. The whole room was banked with flowers, the dining table ablaze with candles and loaded with food. The well-dressed guests were milling about, drinks in hand.

"It sure does," Sharon seconded. "And so do you." Rae was wearing a pale pink drop-waist shift with a chiffon skirt. She had several clusters of tiny tea roses in her hair.

"Would you like a drink?" Rae said to her son.

Tay looked at Sharon, who glanced away.

"No, thanks," Tay said.

"And you are so lovely in that dress," Rae said, turning to Sharon. "Let me see, where's your bouquet?" She located it and handed Sharon an arrangement of irises and carnations. "Blue and white, as requested."

"Thank you."

"Doesn't she look like a picture in that outfit?" Rae asked Tay.

"She sure does," he said and walked away.

The two women looked at each other.

"Don't mind him," Rae said brightly. "He's just nervous. You'd think he was getting married."

Sharon's father appeared, looking stressed, and said, "Come on, Rae, let's get this show on the road. Dr. Henley is getting antsy."

Everyone assembled in the living room. The ceremony was mercifully short, and Tay said the right things at the right time. Afterward, during the flurry of congratulations, Tay sidled up to Sharon in the dining room and said, "We made it."

"Yes, we did," she agreed, smiling.

"Thanks to you," he added. "That's twice you took care of me in two days. Are you a ministering angel in disguise?"

"Maybe," Sharon said mysteriously.

"Then it's a bad disguise," Tay said, popping a Swedish meatball into his mouth. "You look too much like an angel in it."

Charmed into silence, Sharon didn't know what to say. Before she could reply, he was talking to somebody else.

"How'd I do?" Sharon's father asked behind her.

"You're a star," she said, kissing him.

A friend of Dan's came over to be introduced, and by the time Sharon looked around for Tay, all that was visible was his back disappearing through the front door.

He was following a young woman in a red dress.

"Daddy?" Sharon said.

Her father turned. "What, honey?"

"Who was that girl in the red dress? She was standing next to the fireplace during the ceremony."

"Oh, that was Josh Randall's daughter. He runs the local feed supply house. She works in the office."

Sharon watched for the rest of the afternoon, but Tay did not return. Her father and Rae went to bed around midnight, after everyone had gone home, and Sharon did the same a few minutes later.

She slept fitfully and awoke just before dawn.

Tay's truck was still gone.

For the next couple of weeks, Sharon saw Tay around the ranch but rarely spoke to him. He would wink or gesture to her when he saw her, but his days were occupied with working under her father's supervision, and he took his meals elsewhere.

At night he would vanish. Rae said to her friends on the phone that she'd had reports he was patronizing the local bars and honky-tonks, an expression that Sharon had previously heard only in the movies. And on weekends, he would disappear from Friday evening until Monday morning.

Sharon heard her father telling Rae to leave Tay alone, not to interfere, and her stepmother seemed to be taking that advice.

Sharon's birthday came at the end of the month. Dan and Rae had a horse show in the afternoon, but they were planning to return to take Sharon out to dinner in the evening. They had made a reservation in a fancy Los Angeles restaurant, and Sharon was planning to wear her blue dress.

Sans jacket.

She had been working on her tan, spending her afternoons by the pool. Her hair had lightened a shade and her skin had a healthy glow. Her father had remarked jokingly that it was a shame there were no suitable young men around to appreciate her California transformation.

Sharon agreed.

She was polishing her nails when the phone rang on the afternoon of her birthday.

"Hello," Sharon said, picking up the receiver. It was Rosa's day off and, anyway, she couldn't get used to having a housekeeper answer the phone.

"Hi, sweetie, it's Rae. Listen, this auction is running much later than we thought it would, and the horse your father is waiting for is scheduled last. We're not going to make it back to take you out for dinner."

"That's okay," Sharon said, trying to keep the disappointment out of her voice.

"But I called Tay at the bunkhouse, and he's going to take you. I hope you don't mind."

Sharon hesitated. That was certainly a switch.

"God knows how I managed to find him, he's never there," Rae went on. "I already called the restaurant and changed the reservation from three to two people. It's for eight o'clock, so I told Tay you'd better leave by seven-thirty."

"Fine," Sharon answered. What else could she say?

"Thanks for being so understanding, sweetie, we'll make it up to you. Your father has something for you when we get home. Happy birthday and have a good time."

"I will," Sharon said, hanging up. The prospect of spending an evening with Tay was a little unnerving. She tried to picture him in the ambience of the continental restaurant Rae had selected and couldn't do it.

She went into the bathroom, turned on the taps in the tub and turned them off again when she remembered that she was supposed to call her mother. That esteemed lady would not phone her daughter, since she had no desire to converse with either her ex-husband or his new wife, and either one might answer the phone. So Sharon had the standing duty of calling her mother twice a week (on Dan's tab) to report in to the provost marshal.

Her mother answered on the first ring. "I've been waiting for your call," her mother announced.

"I said Tuesday in the afternoon. It's Tuesday. It's the afternoon."

"Don't get smart with me, young lady. I'm having a bad day at work and I don't need you to add to it."

"Why don't you have your last bad day at work and quit that job?" Sharon said. Her mother was an office manager for an insurance company and hated it.

"And what would we live on, I'd like to know?" her mother asked.

"We've had this conversation before, Mother. We'd be fine," Sharon replied. Her mother's father had died a couple of years before and left her a considerable legacy. There was no reason for her to continue in the job except that if she left it she wouldn't be able to complain about it any more.

"What are you doing for your birthday?" her mother asked, mercifully changing the subject.

"I'm going out to dinner," Sharon said shortly. The fewer details, the better.

"With whom?"

"Mom, I know you don't like to discuss the situation out here. Do you really want me to go into it?"

There was a silence at the other end of the line, and her mother veered off in another direction while Sharon offered silent paeons of thanksgiving. They talked for another few minutes and Sharon hung up gratefully and went back to the bathroom.

She was ready at seven-fifteen. She was wearing mascara and eyeliner, which her mother did not allow, and had put her hair up in a chignon. She was feeling very nervous but wanted to put on a brave face.

Tay walked through the door at seven twenty-seven. He was wearing gray cotton slacks with a navy linen blazer, white shirt and navy-and-gray striped tie.

He must have bought some new clothes.

He stopped short when he saw Sharon. His eyes raked over her from head to foot and returned to her face.

"Where did you get that dress?" he said.

"This is the dress I was wearing at the wedding," she said, bewildered.

"It didn't look like that before," he said.

"I had the jacket on then."

"Put it on now."

"Why?" she asked, disappointed that he didn't like her outfit. She could understand why his mother worried about him. He was certainly mercurial.

He shrugged. "Have it your way. Well, I guess we'd better get going. I promised Rae I'd have you there by eight." His manner was less than enthusiastic.

"Don't do me any favors," Sharon mumbled under her breath.

"What?" he said, watching her.

"Never mind." He probably had to break a hot date to take the brat stepsister to dinner, she thought unhappily.

"Then let's just go, okay?" he said.

Sharon followed him out to Dan's car. Her father had taken his van to the auction, and Tay's pickup truck wasn't exactly suitable to be left with valet parking.

It was a strained ride in to Los Angeles. Despite his apology, Tay was still jumpy, and after a few faltering attempts at conversation Sharon gave up, sitting in silence until the attendant had taken the car and they were inside the restaurant.

It was decorated in Mediterranean style, with deep reds and dark woods and low lighting, little shaded lamps at each table. They were on time and were seated immediately. The wine list was propped on a silver stand, and when the sommelier arrived he asked, "Will there be anything to drink?"

"I'll have a bourbon, straight up, and you can bring the young lady a Coke," Tay said to the man.

"Yes, sir," he answered, smiling, and left.

"Do you think you should be drinking?" Sharon asked, concerned.

"Yes," he replied shortly.

Swell, Sharon thought. This duty is so onerous he has to fortify himself to get through it.

Their order arrived, and Sharon sipped her soda, examining the menu the waiter brought.

Everything was in Italian.

"Need a little help?" Tay asked, noting her expression.

"I suppose so," she admitted.

"Rae told me you like Italian food," he said.

"I do." I just didn't know I had to *be* Italian to get some, Sharon added silently.

"I speak Italian. I learned in the service. Do you want me to order for you?"

"Okay."

"What would you like?"

"A shrimp cocktail and veal parmigiana," she said.

When the waiter returned, Tay ordered for both of them.

"Were you stationed in Italy?" Sharon asked.

He shook his head, nursing his bourbon.

"Then how did you learn to speak Italian?" she asked, feeling as if she were extracting every word from him with pliers.

"I was locked up with a guy from Little Italy in New York," he said briefly. "We had to pass the time somehow so he gave me lessons."

"How long were you locked up with him?" Sharon asked.

"A year and a half, before he died," he answered.

Their appetizers arrived, and Sharon watched Tay push his salad around on his plate before she said, "Tay, what's wrong?"

He looked up as if remembering that she was there.

"Are you unhappy because your mother forced you to bring me here?" she asked miserably.

His face went blank, and then he looked concerned. "Oh, no, honey, it has nothing to do with you."

"Then what is it? Can't you tell me?"

He sighed. "I found out this afternoon that I'm not going to be rehired at my job in Arizona. I thought I could spend the summer here and go back in September, but my boss lost the road contract we were working on and another firm's picking up the assignment."

"Oh," she said softly.

"So it's take your father's charity or be out on the street," he added bitterly.

"It isn't charity, Tay!" Sharon said, outraged. "He needs the help, he told me so, and you're working very hard."

"I wouldn't have the work if I weren't Rae's son," he said stubbornly, finishing his drink.

"So what? You're not goldbricking, you're earning every penny. You got your construction job through an Army buddy. Is that so different?"

"You don't understand," he said. "I wanted to go back to Arizona, show Rae and your dad that I was independent. This way, everybody still thinks of me as..."

"What?" Sharon asked.

"A burden, a concern, a problem," he answered, and she couldn't disagree.

A dance band was assembling in the room behind them. Sharon was listening to them tuning up when two attendants opened a folding divider to their left, putting the band into the room with them. A pegged wood dance floor spread out in front of the dais.

"Isn't there some field you could go into? Didn't you learn to do something in the Army?" she asked, trying to be helpful.

"I learned to kill people," he said.

Sharon fell silent, chastened.

He signaled for another drink.

The band began to play, a cheerful counterpoint to their strained conversation.

Sharon stood abruptly.

"Where are you going?" he asked.

"To the ladies' room," she said quietly and fled.

He watched her leave and decided to buy himself some cigarettes in the lobby while she was gone.

When Sharon returned, the table was empty. For a brief wild moment she thought he had left, but she realized that Rae's son would never do such a thing, no matter how upset he was. She was standing uncertainly next to her chair when she felt a tap on her shoulder.

"Dance?" the young man said.

He was about twenty, dining with his parents a couple of tables away. They had come in while Tay was away from the table, and he obviously didn't realize that Sharon had an escort.

"No, I can't, I'm sorry," she said, flustered.

"Why not? Got a date?"

"Well, not a date actually, but…"

"Then dance with me," he said, taking her hand and guiding her onto the floor.

"Wait," Sharon said, but it was too late.

Tay appeared behind the boy and grabbed his shoulder, spinning him around with stunning force. Before the boy could say a word, Tay's fist crashed into his jaw and he fell.

Sharon clamped her hands over her mouth, horrified. Then she darted forward as she realized that Tay was bending down to grab the boy and hit him again.

"Tay," she screamed, throwing both arms around his neck and holding him back, placing herself between him and his victim. "What are you doing?"

He tried to put her aside, but she hung on with all her might, and he couldn't continue the fight unless he handled her roughly. As he paused to disentangle her, the boy's parents ran from their table and helped their son to his feet. At the same time, the maître d' and several waiters rushed to intervene.

"What is the meaning of this?" the boy's father demanded, sputtering. "You'll be hearing from my lawyers!"

"Forget it, Dad," the kid said, wiping his bloody mouth with his hand. "Let's just get out of here."

The family left in a huff, the father still muttering threats of litigation against both Tay and the restaurant as Tay pried Sharon's arms from his neck and reached for his wallet.

The enraged maître d' started to say something about unacceptable conduct and disturbing the guests and calling the police. Tay removed several greenbacks from his billfold and flung them onto the nearest table.

"Save it," he said to the man. "That's enough to cover their meal and ours and to pay for any damage. We're leaving."

He grabbed Sharon's wrist and hauled her after him through the dining room, where everyone stared as if they were a sideshow, and into the lobby. He paused long enough to look down at her and say, "Are you all right?"

"I'm fine," she responded shakily. "But I'm not the one you were beating up."

He didn't reply to that but merely said, "Wait here. I'll get the car."

Sharon spent several uncomfortable minutes as the object of sotto voce commentary from the late diners before he returned to get her. She slipped into the passenger seat beside him and he gunned the motor, leaving the restaurant behind as quickly as possible. He drove for a while with unrelieved concentration, not looking at her, until he surprised her by pulling into a rest area. It was paved for parking and had picnic benches by the side of the road. He shut off the motor and sat staring straight ahead until he said expressionlessly, "I'm sorry."

"Why did you do it, Tay?" she asked. "That boy wasn't really bothering me."

He sighed, rubbing the back of his neck. "I know," he said quietly.

"Then why?"

He shrugged, shook his head and looked out the side window at nothing.

"Come on," Sharon said impulsively. "Let's go sit under the trees."

He obeyed without protest, getting out on his side and following her to one of the benches. She sat, and he leaned against a tree trunk, lighting a cigarette.

"So, I guess I ruined your birthday, huh?" he said, inhaling.

"No, of course not. But I wish I could understand what happened."

"I screwed up, is what happened," he said flatly. "Nothing new."

"I think you were disappointed and unhappy, and you wanted to take it out on someone. That kid just gave you an excuse to do it."

He exhaled luxuriously before saying, "How did somebody your age get to be so smart?" He tapped ashes on the ground, smiling thinly.

"I'm a child prodigy," Sharon replied, and his smile widened. "That's better," she said.

"Better than what?"

"Fistfights in restaurants?" she suggested.

He nodded slowly. "You got a boyfriend back home?" he said.

Sharon shook her head.

"Why not?"

"My mother's kind of strict. She doesn't allow me to date much."

"But you'll be going to college in the fall. That'll change."

"I hope so," Sharon said fervently, and he grinned.

"What about you?" she asked boldly.

"Me?"

"Uh-huh. Rosa says you have lots of girlfriends."

"Rosa talks too much," he muttered.

"I saw you leave the wedding with Eloise Randall."

"You don't miss much, do you?" he said archly, dropping his cigarette and crushing it under his heel.

"Do you like her?"

"She's all right," he said dismissively.

"Do girls like that make you feel better?" she asked ingenuously.

He eyed her closely, wondering if he should be annoyed, but she seemed innocent. He looked at the ground. "No," he said remotely. "They're a quick fix for one night, maybe, but nothing changes."

"Then why do you go with them?" she asked.

"You're just chock-full of questions, aren't you, miss?" he said, taking her hand and pulling her off the bench.

"I'm sorry if I was nosy," she said quickly, realizing that she had been grilling him. "I'm just...interested."

"I'll say. Is there anything else you'd like to know?"

"Yes. Where I can get a hamburger. I'm starving."

"That's right, you missed your birthday dinner on account of me, didn't you? Well, the least I can do to make up for it is feed you. I know a good Mexican burger place in El Monte. Want to go?"

"You bet."

They were on the road again shortly, Tay humming along with the radio as he drove.

"Your mood has improved," Sharon said.

"Must be the company," he said, glancing at her.

"I was with you in the restaurant, too," she said impishly.

"Prolonged exposure may be required to have an effect," he said.

"Then you'll have to see more of me," Sharon suggested.

He glanced over at her but didn't reply.

Tay took her to a railroad-style diner with vinyl booths and a mini-jukebox affixed to each Formica table. They ordered burgers, and while they waited for them to arrive, Tay said, "So what do you want for your birthday?"

"Riding lessons," she said fervently.

"Yeah?"

"Yes. I'm the only one on the whole ranch who can't ride a horse, and I feel ridiculous. My father said Miguel Quintero could teach me, but he never seems to have any free time and…"

"I'll teach you," Tay offered casually.

"Are you serious?" Sharon asked, wide-eyed.

"Sure. If you're not scared of me after tonight, that is," he added, watching her face.

"I'm not scared of you," Sharon said softly.

"Brave girl," he said wryly, seeming relieved. "Okay, I'll work the time out with your father. We can start tomorrow."

"You sure you don't mind?" Sharon asked, delighted.

"Nah, it'll give me something constructive to do."

Their food came, and Tay asked Sharon about her life in Philadelphia as they ate.

"Boredom," was Sharon's description. "I couldn't wait to get out here for the summer."

"Are we that much more exciting?" he asked, raising his brows. He seemed so relaxed now, his coffee-colored eyes smiling, that it was difficult to recall the violent stranger who had erupted in the restaurant.

"Anything is more exciting than living with my mother," Sharon said around a mouthful of hamburger. "As a jailer, she's about on a level with Ernest Borgnine in *From Here to Eternity*."

"Fatso Judson, sergeant of the stockade," Tay said, grinning. "You remember that old flick?"

"I love old movies. My mother doesn't let me go out

much, and when I get tired of books the television's about the only thing left."

"So what's your mother's problem?" Tay asked, popping a French fry into his mouth.

"She's a single parent with an only child, that's her problem. She thinks every guy under the age of sixty is after me."

"I'm sure some of them are," Tay said evenly.

"I wish as many were as she thinks," Sharon said glumly, and he smiled.

"How was the burger?" he asked as she enthusiastically finished the last bite.

"Great. This is more my kind of place anyway. It was your mother's idea to go to that other restaurant. I mentioned that I liked Italian food and she thought it would be a treat. I didn't want to disappoint her."

"Some treat it turned out to be," Tay observed dourly.

"I'm having a good time now," Sharon said brightly.

"Really?" he asked, as if he doubted it.

"Sure. Why not?"

He shrugged. "I guess I don't consider myself very entertaining outside of..." He stopped.

He didn't say "bed," but the implication was clear. Sharon could feel herself blushing. So that's why he pursued women like Eloise Randall. They made him feel successful when he felt like a failure everywhere else.

"I think you're very entertaining," Sharon said gently.

"I think you're just easily amused," he responded, smiling, and she had to smile, too.

The waitress arrived to clear their plates, and Tay ordered dessert in a low tone while Sharon selected a number on the jukebox. The waitress returned with coffee for Tay and a chocolate cupcake with a candle in it for Sharon.

"Surprise," Tay said.

Sharon was touched. He lit the candle with his cigarette lighter and insisted on singing an off-key rendition of

"Happy Birthday" with the waitress, who thought the whole thing very cute.

Sharon was embarrassed by the performance but pleased by his attempt to repair the wreckage of the evening. As far as she was concerned, he had succeeded.

They divided the cupcake in half, Tay wolfing his portion in one bite. He glanced at his watch and said, "I'd better get you home. Your dad will have my tail if I keep you out too late."

Sharon didn't want to go, but agreed reluctantly. The drive back to the ranch was quiet yet companionable. When they arrived home, the house was dark.

"Cinderella's back from the ball before midnight," Tay said as he unlocked the door. He walked into the kitchen with Sharon and turned on the lights.

"Thank you," Sharon said. "I had a wonderful time."

"I'm glad. And I'm sorry about what happened earlier. I didn't want to ruin anything for you."

"You didn't." She stood on tiptoe to kiss his cheek, and for just a moment his arm came around her, pressing her close. She felt his hard, muscular body along the length of hers, inhaled his masculine scent, and then he released her.

"I'll come by for your first lesson at one," he said softly. "Good night."

"Good night," she whispered.

And he was gone.

Sharon wandered back to her bedroom, thinking about the evening she had just spent. What a contradiction Tay was; she could certainly see why he was considered a troublemaker, but he had been so nice to her later on. It was as if two natures were at war within him, and it was a toss-up as to which one would win.

Sharon heard the back door open, and the sound of her father's voice drifted down the hall. She changed quickly into her bathrobe, washed her face and stepped into the hall.

Rae looked up as she entered the kitchen.

"There's the birthday girl," she said, smiling. "Did you have a good time?"

"Wonderful." No lie.

"How was the dinner?"

"Great." The hamburger was pretty good.

"Oh, that's nice. Where is Tay?"

"He went out to the bunkhouse," Sharon replied. "Did you get the horse?"

"Sure did," her father said from the depths of the refrigerator. "She's a beauty, too. Anybody want a sandwich?"

"Dan, how can you be hungry again?" Rae asked, shaking her head at Sharon.

"That measly take-out dinner we had wouldn't fill a cavity," Dan muttered, depositing a plate of cold cuts on the counter. He turned to kiss Sharon and added, "Happy birthday, honey. Your present is on the table."

There was a large box sitting next to her place mat. Sharon unwrapped it and discovered an outfit she had admired with Rae in a downtown Glendora store. She thanked them both and joined them at the table as they had their snack.

"Daddy, Tay is going to give me riding lessons, if that's all right with you," she said, nibbling a ham slice as her father piled meat on a kaiser roll. "We're starting tomorrow afternoon."

"Wonderful," said her father, who approved of his daughter's interest in anything horsey.

"He said he'd have to work out the time with you."

"No problem," Dan said. "I'll talk to him in the morning." He glanced at Rae and said to Sharon, "Did you call your mother today?"

"Yes, I did."

"Good."

"So how does it feel to be eighteen?" Rae asked, eager to change the subject.

"I feel the mantle of maturity settling over my shoulders," Sharon said solemnly.

"I see," Rae said, nodding. "Well, before the mantle settles too far, how about some ice cream?"

"I'll never be too mature for some things," Sharon replied, and they all agreed that was true.

Chapter 3

Tay gasped aloud and sat up, coming wide awake immediately. He was bathed in sweat, his hair plastered to his head. That was a bad one. Ever since he'd regained his freedom, his bad dreams consisted of thinking himself once more trapped in a bamboo cage. The nightmares had been tapering off, but they had a tendency to return when he was nervous or tense.

Both of which he was tonight.

He slid off the cot and padded to the bathroom, splashing cold water on his face and neck. He emerged seconds later, rubbing his torso with a towel.

The atmosphere in the cabin was stifling. Dan had suggested a window air conditioner, but Tay was used to the heat and tolerated it very well. After Saigon and Bangkok, California seemed temperate to him.

He returned to his bed and collapsed on his back, staring at the ceiling. It was doubtful he'd get back to sleep easily.

He found himself thinking about Sharon. He was touched that she'd understood his outburst the way she had. She was intelligent and kind and courageous. She'd looked scared and rattled at the restaurant, but she had rebounded quickly, and they wound up having a pretty good time.

That surprised him. He was planning a late evening with a girl from town when Rae called, and he hadn't wanted to go with Sharon. He tried to talk Rae out of it, but she had insisted. He'd canceled the date to substitute for his mother, intending to remind her of the favor when the time was right.

Now he didn't feel as though Rae owed him anything.

He'd also found himself volunteering to give Sharon riding lessons.

He didn't quite understand it.

Certainly Sharon's freshness, her innocence, were attractive to a man like him, who'd already seen and experienced too much that he wanted to forget. And he remembered her gentleness the day of her father's wedding to his mother. He didn't know too many other women who would have helped him without feeling the need to follow it up with a lecture. He knew quite a few who wouldn't have helped him at all. In that uncomfortable situation she had acted with a graciousness that was remarkably consistent with her behavior in the restaurant that evening.

He smiled now as he thought of the expression on her face when she saw the Italian menu. Poor kid. She was still young enough to regard lack of experience as a terrible flaw.

He stood abruptly, listening to the crickets and cicadas racketing in the bushes. Insects battled against the window screens and swirled around the yellow outside light. The air was heavy and breathless, seeming to press on him with a tangible weight. Nights like this reminded him of his time in the Asian jungle, when silent danger lurked behind every tree. And after he was captured, the nights were endless, punctuated only by the screaming of nocturnal birds in the underbrush and the muttering of the guards as they gambled to pass their shift.

They tortured him only during the day, when the officers could supervise. He remained sane during those sessions by thinking about home and his normal, happy childhood.

Maybe that's why Sharon appealed to him so strongly. She reminded him of his former life, when his father was alive, before everything bad had happened to him. He was her equal then, in youth and optimism, and perhaps he thought he could reclaim that period in her company.

He wandered back to the cot and dropped onto it, praying for sleep. He had to work in the morning, and Dan Philips was a tough, albeit fair, taskmaster.

He would give Sharon her first lesson after lunch.

Sharon was waiting for Tay at the riding stable when he arrived the next day. He stopped short when he saw her, taking in her outfit.

"You can't wear those sneakers," he said in greeting.

Sharon looked down at her feet. "Why not?"

"You need hard-soled shoes for the stirrups. And change those pants, too, they're too thin. Jeans would be better."

Sharon trudged back to the house to change, thinking that he was certainly taking all of this very seriously. When she returned he was sitting on the corral fence, smoking.

"Ready?" he said, tossing his cigarette onto the ground.

"I hope so," she replied.

They went into the stable, and Tay showed her to a back stall where an obviously elderly horse was munching hay contentedly.

"This is Lightning," Tay said to her, stroking the animal's nose.

"Obviously not a generic name," Sharon commented dryly.

"I thought we'd better start off slow. I don't think you're ready for a derby winner just yet."

"Come on, Tay, this looks like Rocinante. He's one step away from the glue factory."

"Fortunately, we'll never know what he thinks of us," Tay replied. "Today we're going to practice mounting."

"You mean we're not going to ride yet?" she asked, disappointed.

"First you have to get up there, okay?" Tay said patiently. "I'll show you how to saddle him later, but I thought for now you'd like to get the feel of it."

"Thank you so much."

"I'm going to give you a leg up this time, but you'll have to learn how to do this alone eventually."

"Okay."

"Now when I bend and make a cup of my hands, step into it with one foot, lift up and throw your far leg over the horse's back."

"Gotcha."

He bent and Sharon obeyed his instruction. She was trying so hard that she overshot her mark, however; she slipped off the saddle on the other side and landed loudly on the ground.

Lightning continued to chew his hay, oblivious to her humiliation.

Tay came around and crouched next to her in the dirt.

"Lesson number one," he said. "Try to remain on the horse."

"Very funny," Sharon said, standing and dusting off the seat of her pants with her hands.

"Ready to try again?" he asked archly.

"You bet," she said grimly.

After a couple more attempts she was able to find and maintain her seat. Tay explained how to grip the horse's flanks with her knees and control his head with the reins. They ended the session with Tay leading Lightning around the corral, Sharon seated on his back. She was bouncing too high and pulling back too much on the bit, but she was riding, and she felt triumphant.

Lightning maintained an attitude of polite disinterest throughout.

"So, what do you think?" Tay asked as he led Lightning back to his stall and gave him a drink.

"I guess I did all right," Sharon replied. "I've been picturing myself galloping through long grass like that actress in the perfume commercial, but I guess that will have to wait."

"We can gallop, if you like," he said. "I'll take you out on Moonrise, she's a good galloper."

"We?"

"Sure. You just sit behind me and hang on tight. I'll do all the work. Come on."

Tay got Moonrise, who was obviously ready to roll, dancing in a circle as he led her out of the stall. Tay mounted easily and reached down for Sharon, hoisting her onto the horse behind him as if she were weightless.

"Put your arms around my waist," he said.

Sharon obeyed. His midsection was lean and firm, and he smelled wonderful, of soap and sun and the musky base note of his skin.

"Don't let go," he said, turning his head.

Sharon had no intention of letting go. Tay trotted out of the corral area and onto the road, heading for the open field behind the stable.

"Ready?" he called.

"Ready," she said into his ear.

Tay bent his head and said something to the horse, then kicked her sides sharply.

Moonrise took off like an arrow released from a bow. Obviously delighted to be given her head, she ran full out, her flashing feet throwing up tufts of grass.

Sharon was jolted forward with the initial thrust and clung to Tay in terror for a minute or so before she began to believe they would survive this excursion. It was another minute before she could relax enough to enjoy herself, but when she did, it was heavenly.

Tay was an expert horseman. He leaned forward in the saddle, controlling the horse just enough to keep her on track, and Sharon tightened her grip, watching trees and bushes fly by like scenery glimpsed from a speeding train. Tay's hair blew back into her face, surprisingly fine and silky against her skin, and after a while she let her head fall forward, pressing her cheek into the hollow between his shoulder blades. She felt at one with the man and the animal and wished, just for those fleeting moments, that she could stay where she was forever.

But of course she couldn't, and the ride ended too soon. Tay slowed the horse to a canter and headed back to the barn. When they got there, he vaulted to the ground and reached up to help Sharon dismount. He gripped her waist, his fingers slipping upward as she moved down. For an instant his hands brushed over her breasts, but before she could react, he released her and stepped back, avoiding her gaze as her feet touched the dirt floor.

"That was wonderful," Sharon said breathlessly.

"Glad you liked it. You can take off now, I have to rub Moonrise down before I put her up."

"Can't I watch? I have to learn that, too."

"Another time," he said distractedly. He seemed bothered by something, as if he wanted to be alone.

"When's my next lesson?"

"I'll let you know," he said distantly, rummaging in a tack box for rags.

Sharon left, glancing over her shoulder once to see him rubbing the horse's neck with long, even strokes.

He didn't look at her.

She went back to the house.

Sharon thought a lot about the wild ride with Tay after that; she had an idea that it told her more about his char-

acter than any amount of talking ever could. He continued
with the lessons but never rode double with her again. It
was as if he had revealed too much of himself that day and
didn't wish to again.

Sharon, for her part, was fascinated with him. She ad-
justed to his changeable nature pretty well, enjoying the
good days and enduring the bad ones. And he seemed to
take comfort in her nonjudgmental presence, spending more
time with her than with anyone else, though he still preferred his own company most of all.

About three weeks after she began her lessons, at the end
of July, Sharon had trouble sleeping one night and went
down to the kitchen to get a glass of milk. She was turning
away from the refrigerator when she heard Tay's truck
drive past the house and turn down the lane toward his
cabin. She glanced at the clock on the wall. It was almost
two in the morning.

Curious, she put the milk container on the counter and
went to the back door, peering through the sheer curtain on
its upper half. She saw the brake lights go out on the truck
and seconds later the driver's door opened. Tay put one
booted foot on the ground, and in the next instant he tum-
bled out of the cab and sprawled headlong into the dirt.

Sharon watched, alarmed, and when he didn't move
again, she bolted through the door, holding her ankle-length
nightgown up her calves and scampering across the wet
grass in her bedroom slippers. She left the lawn and scram-
bled down the dusty lane, dropping to her knees next to the
prone man.

There was a half-moon, and by its light she could see a
dark sticky fluid matting Tay's hair and running down the
side of his face. She touched his shoulder and he stirred,
groaning and turning toward her. She saw his face and
gasped aloud.

He had a deep gash on his forehead and another one just

at the hairline, along with a black eye and a swollen lip.
He had either lost a fight or won a Pyrrhic victory, paying
too high a price for the crown.

"Tay?" she called, shaking him. "Are you okay? Can
you sit up?"

He blinked up at her. "Sharon?"

"That's right, it's me. I want to get you inside and take
care of these cuts. Can you help me?"

"S'awright, I'm fine," he mumbled, struggling to a sitting position and putting his head in his hands.

"Yeah, you look fine," Sharon muttered, putting her
arms around him and hauling upward. She landed on her
fanny for her efforts; it was like trying to dislodge an obe-
lisk.

"Tay, you have to help me," she panted. How could
someone who looked so slim be so difficult to move?

He nodded groggily, and on the next try he cooperated,
lurching to his feet and leaning against her with his arm
across her shoulders.

"It's not far to the bunkhouse," she said breathlessly.
"Can you make it?"

He nodded again, and step by step they made clumsy
progress to the cabin. Tay tripped on the stairs and for a
moment Sharon thought she would drop him, but he recovered and they stumbled inside to the cot. She let him go,
and he slumped gracelessly across it like a felled ox.

Sharon leaned against the wall to catch her breath. The
night was warm, and she could feel a trickle of perspiration
running down her sides from the exertion.

After a few moments she wiped her forehead with the
back of her arm and went to the bathroom, where she filled
Tay's shaving basin with water. He didn't have any disin-
fectant and she didn't want to go back to the main house,
so she settled for soap and a clean washcloth. When she
got back to the cot, he was lying on his back with his eyes
closed. She was standing uncertainly, wondering whether

she should disturb him, when his lashes lifted and he looked at her.

"How are you doing?" she asked, pulling a chair next to the bed.

"I'll live," he murmured, closing his eyes again.

"Tay, how did this happen?" she asked, dipping the cloth into the water.

"Fight," he said.

"No kidding." She dabbed at the cut on his forehead. "What were you fighting about?"

He winced. "Woman," he replied.

Of course, Sharon thought, what else? "How did it happen?"

"We were talking...in a bar. Some guy...started...up with me."

"Some guy?"

"Husband."

Sharon stopped her ministrations and stared down at him. "You were picking up a married woman in a bar and her husband did this to you?"

"She...picking me up," he corrected.

"Oh, excuse me," Sharon said. "That made a world of difference to her husband, I'm sure."

"Didn't know...she was married."

"Thank heaven for small favors," Sharon muttered under her breath. She resumed cleaning his cuts with rather more vigor than necessary, and finally he sat up, pushing her hand away.

"That's enough," he said. Obviously some of his customary starch was returning.

"You should put iodine on those cuts. How did you get them?"

"Broken bottle."

Sharon sucked in her breath. "Tay, they could get infected!"

"I never get infections."

"You could have scars."

He examined her, his gaze lopsided. "Sharon, do you think this is the first time this has happened to me?"

She stood, shoving the basin onto the bed. "Is that supposed to make me feel better? Do you realize you could have been killed driving all the way out here from town in this condition?"

"I got here, didn't I?"

Sharon answered this question by bursting into tears.

He stared up at her, his damaged face incredulous. "What is it? Why are you crying?"

"Because you're hurt, and I care about you," she sobbed. "I only wish you cared about yourself."

Tay didn't know what to say. He sat watching her cry in silence until he couldn't stand it anymore.

"All right, come on, stop that," he said, standing unsteadily and putting his arm around her.

She sniffled loudly.

"I'm okay, you can see that," he said. "There's nothing to cry about."

"You'll do it again," she said, her voice muffled by his shoulder.

"Don't worry about me," he soothed her, pulling her closer, his hands moving over her back.

"I can't help it." She hiccuped. "I don't understand how you can be so good and patient when you give me lessons, and then do things like this."

That gave him pause. "Good and patient?" he said, unable to relate those attributes to himself.

She nodded, rubbing her face against his shirt. "You never yell at me, and I know I make a lot of mistakes. You just help me do it over until I get it right, and you don't make me feel stupid about it."

Sharon couldn't see his expression, but she felt his grip tighten. He was listening intently. "Why would I make you feel stupid?" he asked, stroking her hair.

She shook her head as if disagreeing with something he had said. "You don't know. I'm not good at physical things. I was hopeless in gym, I almost failed last semester and it would have kept me from graduating. I had to make up extra credits doing routines on the gymnastics equipment. I fell off the sawhorse and hurt my foot, and then I couldn't do the balance beam, so I had to learn the parallel bars, and Miss Masters was so mean about it. She can do everything. She climbs the rope like a snake, and I couldn't make it to the top. She said I had no strength in my arms." She started to cry again, remembering it.

"You have strength where it counts," he said quietly, putting his cheek against her hair. It smelled sweet and clean. He closed his eyes.

Sharon sensed the change in him, felt the tension growing in his body. His lips moved in her hair and she sighed, pressing closer.

She was wearing only a thin summer nightgown and seemed almost naked in his arms. Tay felt a surge of longing so intense he was nearly dizzy with it. He wanted to comfort her and protect her and keep her with him. He wanted this clean, sweet girl to change his life and make it right, and for that moment he believed she could do it.

Then he remembered who she was and how old she was, and he stiffened, pulling back. He gripped her upper arms and set her firmly away from him.

Sharon looked up, examining his face, but it was unreadable.

"Go back to the house," he said, not meeting her gaze. "I'm all right now."

Sharon stood flat-footed, bewildered. What had happened?

"Go on," he urged, turning away. "I just have to sleep this off, I'll be fine in the morning."

Her expression registered her confusion.

He lay back down on the cot, sighing deeply and closing his eyes.

"Good night, and thanks a lot," he murmured, feigning exhaustion.

Sharon remained a moment longer, and then, aware that Tay certainly needed to rest, put the basin back in the bathroom and slipped quietly from the cabin.

Tay's eyes opened as the door closed behind her. He sat up again, putting his feet on the floor and clasping his hands between his knees. He was shaking.

Thank God, she had listened to him and left. He was no model of control under most circumstances, and where women were concerned his self-restraint was especially slim.

Well, now he would have to deal with it. He had been telling himself that it wasn't happening, that she was a kid and his fondness for her was merely brotherly. After this evening, that pretense was ludicrous.

He was in a hell of a mess, which was certainly nothing new, but this particular mess was far worse than usual. He was falling for Sharon in a big way. It had crept up on him gradually during the long summer hours he had spent with her, getting to know her and like her. It had happened when he wasn't looking or when he'd been pretending not to look, because he'd been subliminally aware of his feelings for some time. They had driven him to more and more nights in bars, not even admitting to himself that he was trying to forget about her with other women.

He stared at the worn wooden floor, his cuts throbbing, his fat lip stinging, and wondered despairingly what to do. He couldn't betray her father's trust. Dan Philips had let him stay at the ranch when Tay needed a home and had given him a job when he needed a salary. Dan let him spend so much time with Sharon because he obviously thought his daughter was too young to interest Tay in that way, but he was wrong. Dan was a parent, and he saw his child, a girl not out of her teens. Tay, in recent days and especially tonight, had seen a woman.

Tay thought about it and resolved to do two things.

First, he would clean up his act for Sharon's sake. He hadn't realized how much his carousing was upsetting her. Second, he would limit his time with her to insure that what had happened tonight would not happen again.

He lay back down, feeling a little better.

But not much.

Things changed after that night. Tay's drinking and fighting tailed off to nothing, so much so that Dan remarked on it, but Sharon couldn't enjoy his new pattern. Tay had told her that she was riding well enough now to go out on her own, and he restricted the lessons to once a week in the area of the ranch where they were always observed.

Sharon, of course, was in love. Tay had unwittingly done the one thing that was guaranteed to intensify her feeling for him—expose her to his personality, which in nonthreatening circumstances was his old, winning one, without any physical involvement, for which she was not ready. Her life became their rides together, the intervals between them a time of waiting.

Sharon was amazed at Tay's tenacity. He had made up his mind about their relationship, and he stuck to his resolution. Before she met Tay, honor had been an abstract concept, but his behavior with her gave new meaning to the word. She knew intuitively underneath his distant exterior he wanted to carry things further between them, but it was clear that he never would.

Which gave her the idea that she might have to take matters into her own hands.

One evening at the end of August, Sharon talked Tay into a ride up into the foothills just as the sun was setting. She knew that he gave in because she was leaving in just a few days, but she planned to make the most of their time together.

Tay had been grooming horses all day, and he was tired. He led the way up the scrubby path they had followed before to a small mesa where they stopped to rest. They tethered the horses to a locust tree and sat admiring the view. The whole valley was spread out like a carpet at their feet, the crimson sky fading as stars appeared and lights blinked on below them.

"I never get tired of this sight," Tay said with satisfaction, lying back with his arms folded beneath his head.

"I know what you mean. There's nothing like it back in Philadelphia, that I can tell you." Sharon glanced over at him. "Have you always lived in California?"

He nodded. "Except for the time in the Army."

That was a subject he never seemed disposed to discuss. He skirted it deftly, like a field runner avoiding a tackle, which only whetted Sharon's curiosity all the more.

"How long were you in?" she asked casually.

"I was in the Army for three years, a prisoner for two," he replied shortly.

"How did you get away?" she asked.

"I escaped." He looked over at her. "Killed a guard."

"Oh," she said, swallowing.

"I wasn't discharged right away after that," he went on. "They had me in a hospital for a while. In Thailand."

"What's it like there?" she asked, seeking to shift the subject to somewhat safer territory.

"Thailand?" He rolled over, propping himself up on his elbow with his palm cupping his ear. "Hot. Very hot. Strange people, strange food. They have all these gods and goddesses like the Chinese, and they eat dogs, cats, everything. They're so poor, they see all forms of life as food, I guess."

"Dogs, uh," Sharon said.

He nodded. "I had this Thai doctor, little guy about five

feet tall, couldn't understand a word he said. He thought he was speaking English, by the way, but his accent was so thick it could have been Farsi. He invited me home for dinner when I was discharged, and they were having roasted dog. It's a delicacy.''

"What did you do?" Sharon asked, horrified.

"Oh, I pretended to eat it, threw it away when they weren't looking. His wife's name was Lar Park Sing. She had never cut her hair all her life. It hung to the back of her knees."

He was half smiling at the recollection, and Sharon was emboldened to say, "How did you get captured?"

The smile faded. "Six of us were on patrol and we were ambushed. There were about fifteen VC, and they were just waiting for us. It was as if they knew we were coming. Four guys were killed. Wilson and I were captured." He shrugged. "Lots of times later I thought it would have been better off if we had been killed, too."

"Oh, don't say that," Sharon whispered.

"Do you know that the whole country is communist now, anyway?" he asked Sharon, his tone amazed. "What I went through, my friends who died, all for nothing. The Khmer Rouge took over when we pulled out, killed all the American sympathizers, anybody who helped us, and accomplished in a few months what we were over there for years trying to prevent."

"I know it's hard," Sharon said inadequately, restricting her comments to keep him talking. He had never been so voluble on the subject, and she drank in every word. It might be her last opportunity to learn about him.

"Hard," he said, snorting. "It's more than hard. It makes you wonder what anything is for, why we should try for a future, make any plans. Everything can be taken away, just like that, the way the South Vietnamese lost their country and their lives when the Red Army swept down from the north."

"That's always been true of life, Tay. You can be killed in an accident or stricken with a fatal disease at any moment, but knowing that can't make us give up hope."

"Is that the way you really feel?" he asked, staring at her.

"Yes, it is."

"I wonder if I could ever get that back again," he said, half to himself.

"Will you miss me when I go back East?" she asked softly.

"We all will," he replied noncommittally.

"I wish I didn't have to go," she said.

"You shouldn't bypass college."

"There are plenty of colleges in California."

"Your parents agreed that you would live with your mother for the first couple of years."

"You seem to know a lot about it," Sharon commented.

"Your father told me."

"Have you two been discussing me?" Sharon asked suspiciously.

"A bit."

"What does that mean?"

"It means that we're both concerned about you."

"Well, don't be concerned about me," Sharon said huffily. He sounded like a guidance counselor.

"You should be glad that people are interested in you."

"I don't want people interested in me, I want you interested in me," she replied. There, she had said it.

"I am."

"You know what I mean."

"It's getting late," he said, standing up. "We'd better head back."

"Tay, I'm going to be gone next week. Can't you sit here for once and listen to me?"

He sat. "I'm listening," he said.

"Will you write to me when I leave?" she asked.

"I don't think that's such a good idea, Sharon," he replied.

"Why?"

"The purpose behind going to college is to meet new people, guys your own age, and I think you should concentrate on that."

"I thought the purpose behind going to college was to get an education."

"That, too," he said, stretching out.

"Are you telling me that I won't hear from you after I go?" she asked, disbelieving.

"That's probably best."

"Best for who? For you, because you want to get rid of the kid and go back to chasing people like Eloise Randall?"

He looked at her, then away. "You don't know what you're talking about," he said flatly.

"You like her better than you like me. I'm sure she's mature and grown-up and responsible, right? You won't be packing her off to college."

"Shut up."

Sharon stared at him, amazed. He was furious, and she felt like crying.

"Why won't you write to me when I leave?" she said desperately.

"Drop it."

"Why are you always in charge?" she demanded. "Why do you make all the decisions?"

He wouldn't answer, just sat looking out over the valley. The moon had risen, and his clean profile was etched in silver as she watched him.

"You were the last thing I expected to happen to me this summer," he finally said thoughtfully. "When I came here I was running away."

"From that construction job in Arizona?" she asked, puzzled by the turn of the conversation.

"From life, from the past. From the pictures in my head."

"Pictures?"

"Memories." He looked back at the view. "When I was locked up over there," he said softly, "there was a guy in the cage next to me, the one who taught me Italian. He had a daughter. He was older than I was, divorced, and he lived for that kid. We could talk sometimes at night when the guards were drunk or just busy. I figured it out, and his kid would have been about your age now. All that kept him going was the idea that he would get home and see that girl again."

"Did he?" she asked.

He shook his head. "He died there. They tortured him, well, they tortured all of us, but I guess he wasn't as young or as healthy, and his heart just gave out. Maybe the heat was too much, I don't know." He bent his head.

"Oh, Tay," she murmured.

"I used to encourage him, try to buck him up when I could," he said, "but it wasn't enough."

Sharon nestled against him, and to her surprise he allowed her to remain. They sat still for a long time, and she inched closer, pressing into him. Finally, he stirred, sighing, and nuzzled her neck. She leaned back and he bent his head, opening his mouth against her breasts, wet heat burning through the cloth that covered them in a gesture that was frankly sexual.

Sharon gasped aloud and he pulled away.

"Scared?" he said hoarsely.

She couldn't answer.

"Isn't that what you wanted?" he demanded. "Don't play with me, or you might get what you're asking for." He stood up.

"Tay…"

"No more," he said huskily. "Let's go."

"Tay, wait…"

"Sharon, I mean it. I'll leave you here if you don't get on that horse."

She obeyed meekly, still stunned by the impact of those few seconds when he had responded to her.

They rode back to the house in silence, and Tay went immediately to the stables, leading the horses on foot.

Sharon knew that Tay would never lower his guard again, and she saw herself going back to Philadelphia and being cut off from him forever.

She had to do something about it, but the opportunity didn't present itself until the night before she was to depart.

Her bags were packed and sitting on the floor in her room. Her father was planning to drive her to the airport in the morning, and they all had a family dinner at the house to say farewell.

Tay was very quiet during the meal, and anyone could see that he wasn't happy. Sharon allowed this to encourage her in her plans, and when he took her aside after dinner she played along.

"Well, I guess this is it," he said. "You'll be leaving tomorrow."

She nodded.

"I'll see you in the morning."

"Okay," she agreed.

He looked at her closely, as if surprised by her acquiescence. He was wearing a yellow shirt that set off his dark good looks, and a recent haircut had left him looking less rakish than usual.

"See ya," he said and left by the kitchen door.

"Where's Tay?" his mother asked as she entered from the living room with Dan.

"He just went back to the bunkhouse," Sharon said.

"He doesn't look too good," Rosa offered as she cleared the plates.

Rae and Dan exchanged glances.

"Well, we're all going to miss Sharon around here," Rae said.

Rosa looked at Sharon, then away.

"Sharon, we're going down to the convenience store in Glendora," her father said. "Is there anything you need for your trip?"

"No, thanks, Dad."

"We'll be back in an hour or so," Rae said. "Sure you don't want to come?"

"No, I'll stay and help Rosa clean up," Sharon said.

They left, and Rosa inquired, "What are you going to do?" She didn't have to elaborate; Rosa was Sharon's confidante and had closely followed her developing relationship with Tay.

"I don't know," Sharon said, rinsing cups in the sink.

"You've got a plan?"

"I'm thinking about trying something," Sharon replied.

Rosa wiped her soapy hands on a dishcloth and took Sharon's chin in her fingers.

"You listen to me, *niña*, be careful. I know how you feel, it wasn't so long ago for me. But you could make a mistake now that could ruin your whole future."

"But, Rosa," Sharon said, "you saw how he was tonight. He's just going to let me go."

"And maybe that's for the best," Rosa said, nodding. "Sometimes in life the timing is just not right."

Sharon didn't answer, and when her father returned she went to her room, saying she had some last-minute packing to do.

By midnight, the house was quiet. Rosa had gone home without further conversation, and Dan and Rae had retired early to prepare for the drive in the morning.

Sharon took a shower and washed her hair, then dressed in her best nightgown and applied perfume to her wrists and throat. When she felt that she was ready, she slipped out of her bedroom, pausing to listen in the hall, her heart pounding, before she hurried out of the house and down the lane to the cabin for the last time.

The night was cool and breezy, with a full moon that illuminated Sharon's path as she walked. The fresh scent of the citrus trees hung in the air, and the dew on the grass soaked her ankles, dampening the hem of her gossamer gown. She ran lightly up the steps to the cabin and pushed in the door.

Tay was asleep on his side in a shaft of moonlight, his bare torso visible above the muslin sheet drawn down below his waist. Sharon stood next to the cot and studied him, aware that this might be her only chance to do so.

His skin was tanned so deeply that the sheet looked snowy by comparison. She could see the tracery of thick veins, developed from long hours of manual labor, running down his arms and across the backs of his hands. There was a dimple at the base of his spine, almost obscured by a patch of down, black and silky like the hair on his chest.

Sharon moved closer, her fingers itching with the urge to touch. She could see only one side of his face, the luxurious lashes, the strong nose, the full lower lip that still bore a faint mark from his last fight. His hair, slightly wavy and curling inward at the tips, lay against the base of his neck in a series of elongated commas. She touched one of them gingerly. He didn't move.

Emboldened but trembling, Sharon raised the sheet and crawled in beside him. His body heat, trapped by the cotton cover, radiated around her, and she could see beads of perspiration dappling his shoulder blades. He must have been asleep for some time.

Sharon put her arms around his neck and kissed his cheek. He stirred, murmuring in his sleep, and turned toward her, slipping his arm under her. He was naked.

She had never felt a nude man all along the length of her, and she shuddered with the sensation as he took charge of the situation, pulling her on top of him. He ran his hands down her body, his eyes still closed, and searched in the dark for her mouth with his.

She had dreamed of kissing him for so long that the reality was like a dream, too—the surprising softness of his lips, the vise of his arms binding her to him, his sigh of gratification as her mouth opened to admit his probing tongue. It was more wonderful than she had ever imagined. Before this, she had kissed only high school boys, who didn't know what they were doing.

Tay knew what he was doing.

His mouth moved to her neck and he plucked at the folds of her gown, obviously searching for the way to remove it. Sharon shifted to accommodate him, and he moaned, clutching her tightly as he felt her slip into the cradle of his hips. He turned and rolled her under him, kissing her breasts through the thin batiste nightdress, raising her nipples with his tongue. Sharon whimpered, throwing her head back as he pressed into her, and she felt him ready against her thigh.

"Tay," she whispered feverishly. "Oh, Tay, I love you."

Her voice seemed to trigger some sort of recognition within him, and he sat up abruptly, pushing her away from him.

"My God, Sharon, what are you doing?" he gasped, struggling out of the half sleep in which she had caught him.

"Making love to you," she replied, trying to wind her arms around his neck again.

He held her off, trapping both of her wrists in one of his hands. "Go back to the house," he said harshly. His breath was coming in short bursts, and she could see his pulse pumping madly in his throat.

"Let me stay," she pleaded, kissing the only part of him she could reach, which was his left bicep. "You want me, I know you do. You can't deny it now."

Tay looked at her, so soft and pliant and scented in his bed, wearing two ounces of nothing, her pale hair aglow in the moonlight streaming through his window. He wanted her more than she could ever guess. He wanted her unstained soul as much as he wanted her body, but he was about to do the most unselfish thing he had ever done, though he knew she wouldn't see it that way.

"Get out of here now," he said, turning his head. "I don't want you and never have. You're a baby, and I need a real woman. Go back home to school and play with your pencil box."

Sharon stared at him, stunned. "But just now..." she began.

"Just now you could have been anyone. I was asleep, you became part of my dream. You were a female body in bed with me, like one of the whores I used to patronize in Saigon. I'm a man, what do you expect?"

"Then, you don't...care about me?" Sharon asked, the threat of tears trembling in her voice.

Tay steeled himself. He had to be convincing or she would never make a clean break.

"You were all right to pass the time," he replied neutrally. "I had nothing better to do this summer."

Sharon tore away from him and bolted from the bed, her bare feet slapping the floor, her nightgown flying. Tay didn't look after her, but remained staring at her abandoned slippers upside down on the dusty floorboards, waiting for his heartbeat to return to normal.

He would always remember the look on her face as she reacted to his cruel words. He felt his own throat tighten with unshed tears. God, he had hurt her. But he had no choice. Or did he?

He stood abruptly, thrusting his hands through his damp hair. She had really worked him up; he was still charged, jittery. He went to the window and gulped the night air.

If she only knew his real feelings. The truth was that he

was desperate to keep her from leaving and had spent long hours that evening by himself in the bunkhouse, wondering what to do. He had gone to sleep exhausted when he couldn't think about it anymore, and had awakened to find her in his bed.

He could ask her to marry him, he thought wildly. Eighteen-year-old girls got married all the time. Hell, in New Guinea they got married at thirteen. He could go up to the house right now and talk to Dan, tell him that he was in love with Sharon and wanted to take care of her.

That, of course, was the problem. He had unfortunately spent most of the summer demonstrating to anyone within earshot that he was hardly capable of taking care of himself. He wouldn't be surprised if Dan punched him. What father would want his daughter to marry Tay Braddock? Especially when the daughter was a young and innocent girl like Sharon. Tay knew better than anyone else how damaged he was, how unable to offer a future or even the hope of one.

He sat down again, dispiritedly. He shouldn't deprive Sharon of her chance to get an education, see the world, perhaps meet another man far more suitable than himself; Tay had so little going for him to counterbalance that possibility that thinking about it drove him to distraction.

He was her first love, and he wanted to be her only one, but he knew that she couldn't make an informed choice until she was older and more experienced. It wasn't fair of him to pick her off the tree before anyone else got into the orchard.

All of these things he knew, but what he wanted was to run after her and keep her for himself. Instead he got his cigarettes and sat up smoking until daybreak, feeling more lonely and bereft than he ever had in his life.

Sharon spent a sleepless night also, crying intermittently. She wound up putting ice packs on her eyes at six in the morning to reduce the redness and swelling before Rae and Dan saw her. She dressed desultorily as the sun rose, glancing at her packed luggage and thinking that by nightfall she would be back in Philadelphia with her mother.

She couldn't believe it.

She forced down some breakfast, said her goodbyes to Rae and Rosa and the other people on the ranch and climbed into the car with her father. Her eyes filmed over again as they drove down the road that ran between the corrals, and she turned her head so her father wouldn't see.

She didn't notice Tay standing just inside the stable door, watching her leave, his expression bleak.

She never saw him again.

Chapter 4

The doorbell rang and Sharon snapped back to the present, glancing at the clock as she got up to answer it.

She had spent over an hour thinking about the past, remembering her relationship with Tay Braddock.

And now, God help her, she was expected to *marry* him.

She opened the door to admit her neighbor, who had accepted a package for Sharon that day while she was at work. Sharon chatted with her for a few minutes and, when the woman left, tossed the box onto her coffee table. She'd lost interest in the sweater she'd ordered two weeks earlier. She had more important things to consider now.

The burning humiliation of that last night with Tay had stayed fresh in her mind all through the years. She'd experienced other painful and embarrassing situations since then, of course, but her age at that time, combined with the depth of her feeling for Tay, always made her remember it with special chagrin.

Sharon picked up the papers she'd been reading when

her reverie began and stacked them on her chair. She would get back to them later.

She made a tuna fish sandwich for dinner and spent the rest of the evening reexamining her father's will. Crawford was right. There was no way around it, she had to marry Tay in order to solve this problem. By the time she got to work the next morning, she had made up her mind, however reluctantly, to do it.

She spoke to Desmond about a leave and then called Pete Symonds to arrange to meet him for lunch. She had to persuade him to take over her files once she completed her current case so that she could go to California.

The restaurant was a little café that catered to the legal crowd, with glass-topped tables and lots of hanging plants. Pete was already seated, and he stood when the hostess showed Sharon to their table.

"Hi," he said as she slipped into a chair across from him. "What's up?"

"I need to ask you a big favor," Sharon said.

"Shoot."

"I have to go to California, and I'd like you to cover my cases while I'm gone," Sharon said quickly, wincing.

He stared at her. "California? Now?"

"To settle my father's estate."

"I didn't think you'd have to go out there to do that. When did this happen?"

"Just yesterday. The will is a mess, and I really should be there in person to straighten it out. I've already spoken to John and told him I would ask you to help."

"How long will you be gone?"

"A couple of months."

His mouth fell open. "A couple of months! Honey, Henry Ford's will wasn't that complicated. What's going on?"

For some reason Sharon didn't want to tell Pete the whole truth about the situation. Probably because it might lead to a discussion of Tay and the past, a subject she heartily wished to avoid.

"It's actually kind of a combination leave and vacation," Sharon said weakly. "John already okayed it."

"Well, if John okayed it, I guess there's nothing I can do," Pete replied unhappily. "When are you leaving?"

"As soon as the Hammond thing wraps up. John said you could hire a law student to help with the work load. I'll put ads in the school newspapers this afternoon, and I've already sent a messenger over to Penn and Temple with notices for the intern employment bulletin boards."

"Not wasting any time, are you?" Pete said.

"Well, there is a certain urgency because my stepbrother is involved, too," Sharon replied uncomfortably.

"Oh, right."

"He runs the ranch, and he has to know how this is going to be handled."

"I see." Pete brushed back a lock of medium brown hair and gazed at her with his medium brown eyes. Everything about him was medium. Maybe that was the problem, Sharon thought. Her response to him was medium, too.

"I sure am going to miss you," he added.

"I'll be back before you know it." Sharon privately thought that some time away from Pete might be a good idea. He had been dropping hints about marriage lately, and she was far from ready to take such a step.

"I guess you'd better brief me on what you're carrying," Pete said, referring to her caseload.

Sharon nodded and picked up the menu as he signaled for the waitress.

Her leave came through a week later. She packed and closed up her apartment, booking a direct flight to Los Angeles. On the way to the airport she sent a telegram to the ranch, announcing her arrival. She deliberately avoided calling long-distance, preferring to deal with Tay in person rather than a disembodied voice on the phone. Tay was aware of the will and would know that Sharon's arrival meant that she accepted its terms.

The flight to Los Angeles was a long one and Sharon had plenty of time to think. She was dreading the reunion but at the same time felt a sort of resignation about it. In a very real sense she had been heading toward this for a long time.

Sunlight streamed into the glass-fronted arrival lounge as she left the covered walkway that connected the plane to the terminal building. She was fishing in her purse for her baggage tickets when she realized that someone was standing off to one side, watching her. She turned her head and looked at Tay Braddock.

Any hope that he might have become unattractive were dashed immediately. She had been wishing for fat or bald, but neither was true. If anything, he was more compelling than she remembered. Her heart sank.

He walked toward her with the measured stride she recalled so well. He had filled out a little and looked, not heavier, but broader. There were silvery threads of gray in his thick dark hair, which was shorter now and layered in a current style. He was wearing a light blue shirt that flattered his dusky coloring, with faded jeans and worn moccasins. His brown eyes met hers as he stopped in front of her.

"Hello, Sharon," he said quietly.

They examined each other for several seconds in silence. His gaze was riveting. "Eyes of gold and bramble dew," she thought; it was a romantic description, but accurate.

"How did you know which plane to meet?" she finally asked.

"Is that all you can say to me after ten years?" he countered, his expression sober.

"Well, this is hardly a conventional reunion," Sharon said stiffly.

"Hardly," he murmured, watching her face. There were lines around his eyes and mouth, etched by time and exposure to the sun, but the rest of his face was remarkably the same.

"How did you know which flight?" she repeated.

"I checked around," he said vaguely.

"What?"

"I knew the day you were arriving, so I checked the flights coming in from Philadelphia," he explained inadequately.

She saw that he wasn't going to elaborate, so she didn't pursue it. She didn't need any further evidence of a determination she remembered vividly.

"It would have been easier if you had just told me," he suggested, falling into step beside her and taking her overnight bag.

"Did it ever occur to you that I might not want to be met?" Sharon inquired.

"It occurred to me," he said mildly, shooting her a sidelong glance that Sharon ignored. She marched beside him in silence until he added, "You cut your hair."

"I cut my hair eight years ago," she replied crisply.

"I know. I saw the pictures."

"My father showed them to you?"

"I asked to see them," he answered.

She let that pass. "How are things at the ranch?"

"All right. The place isn't the same without your dad."

His voice was tinged with sadness, and Sharon realized that he was grieving, too, perhaps more than she, because he had seen her father every day.

"So you're a lawyer now," he said, still trying to make conversation.

"That's right."

"Do you like it?"

"I like it well enough."

"I just can't picture you doing that," he said, shaking his head.

"Why not?"

"You were so...delicate," he said as if that explained his attitude.

"I'm no longer the impulsive child you remember," Sharon said crisply, not looking at him.

"What a shame," he said softly. "I liked her quite a lot."

Sharon stopped short and faced him. "Is that right?" she said tightly. "Funny, that's not the way I recall it."

He dropped his eyes. "Sharon, let's not do this. I get the message. You resent being here and you clearly don't want to see me. Okay. But there's no point in denying reality."

"Which is?"

"You're here because we're getting married. Do you think we can pretend that isn't true?"

"I'd like to pretend it isn't true," she muttered.

He sighed as they got on an escalator to descend to the baggage area. "You don't have to be so defensive."

Sharon looked at him, and he met her gaze squarely.

"Oh, this whole thing is so bizarre," Sharon mumbled irritably, looking away. "I feel like giving the ranch to a tuna cannery."

"Gotta marry me first."

Sharon refused to smile.

He waited a moment, then touched her arm. She stared up into his face.

"Sharon, look. I know I'm the last man on earth you would marry if it were your choice, but all we have to do is tolerate each other long enough to get through the formalities. That lawyer, Crawford, called me, and if we don't do this, we're going to spend a long time in court untangling the mess. You understand that better than I do. Let's take the easy route, okay? I'll stay out of your way, I promise, and in a couple of months it will all be over."

The easy route? Sharon thought. Easy for him, maybe.

"Why did my father set his will up this way?" she asked as they walked to the baggage carousel. "Do you know?"

"He wanted you to be settled, and…" He stopped.

"And?"

"He always remembered the good influence you were on me that summer our parents got married," he concluded quietly.

"So he was thinking of you?" Sharon said.

"He was thinking of both of us." He pulled her bags from the carousel as they passed. Sharon handed him her stubs as he shouldered her carryall and grabbed a bag with each hand. He showed her tickets to the attendant, and they passed into the throng of milling travelers.

"Wait here," he said abruptly. "I'll come back for you."

Sharon had no choice but to obey, since he strode away immediately, blending into the crowd.

When he returned, her bags were gone and he had a bunch of keys in his hand.

"The truck is at the curb," he said, and she followed him outside to a more recent version of the pickup he'd been driving ten years earlier. Apparently he still didn't approve of cars.

Sharon climbed into the cab when he held the door for her and sat staring straight ahead as he got in beside her, shifted gears and pulled out into the airport traffic.

The freeways sped by as he drove efficiently, glancing over at her several times during the ride. As they were approaching the entrance to the ranch he said dryly, "Your spine will snap if you don't relax."

"It's my spine," Sharon replied evenly.

But she did change position as he drove up the road that wound between the corrals. She leaned forward, looking closely at everything. The redwood fencing she remembered had been replaced by expensive locust wood, and several of the ramshackle outbuildings were gone. New frame structures stood in their place, and the ranch house had been recently sided with vinyl, the trim freshly painted. The number of horses had doubled, and there was a new paddock, cut from the woods that stood to the east of the house. The whole place looked extremely prosperous. Her father had always made a comfortable living, but this was something else, and Sharon knew it was Tay's doing. He had, indeed, "taken hold," as her father said.

He was watching her, observing her reaction to the changes. She thought he was waiting for her to comment, so she said nothing.

They pulled up to the house, and some of the hands paused to stare as Sharon got out and Tay brought her bags into the house.

"I had Rosa prepare your old room," he said as they entered. The living room had been redecorated in a breezy patio style, with painted wrought iron tables and white wicker furniture.

"Is Rosa still with you?" Sharon asked, delighted at the prospect of seeing an old friend. They walked down the hall to her old room.

He nodded. "She'll be in later." He set her bags on the floor. "I should tell you," he went on, "we tore down the old bunkhouse last year. I'm sleeping across the hall."

Wonderful, Sharon thought sourly. Well, at least the bunkhouse was gone. She had no desire to revisit that scene.

She looked around. The decor in the bedroom, unlike that in the rest of the house, was as she remembered it. She felt a wave of nostalgia for the four-poster with the lumpy mattress and the maple rocking chair and the priscilla curtains at the window.

"I've set the civil ceremony for tomorrow morning," Tay said.

Sharon whirled to face him. "Not wasting any time, are we?" she said sarcastically.

"I thought you would want to get it over with," he said, obviously startled. "We can put the will into probate as soon as the marriage license is certified to the court."

Sharon put her hand to her forehead wearily. "Yes, of course, you're right. I'm sorry. I'm afraid this has all been a bit much for me."

"Maybe you'd like to be alone for a while, get settled in," he said.

"That's a good idea," she replied quickly.

"Well, I have some work to do. I'll ask Rosa to stop in and see you when she comes, okay?"

"Thank you." Sharon listened to his footsteps recede down the hall.

She sat down in the rocker and took off her shoes, easing her weary feet, preoccupied with her host.

It was obvious that Tay wasn't going to make reference to the last time they'd seen each other, when she'd crept into his bed and thrown herself at him. Maybe he didn't remember it as vividly as she did. Maybe he didn't remember it at all.

There must have been a lot of beds and a lot of women since.

Sharon got up and opened her large suitcase, taking out garments and hanging them in the closet. She had finished and was assembling toilet articles in the adjoining bathroom when there was a tap on the bedroom door.

"Sharon? It's Rosa."

Sharon ran to the door and pulled it wide, embracing the older woman as she stepped in from the hall.

"Rosa, oh, it's so good to see you," she said, standing back and taking a long look. "As beautiful as ever," she pronounced.

"And you're too thin," Rosa replied. "Chili con carne tonight. And my special *enchiladas encantadas*."

Sharon laughed. She had kept in touch with Rosa through cards and letters over the years, but had missed her practical no-nonsense presence.

"How is Pilar?" she asked.

"Raising cain. She starts high school in the fall."

"High school," Sharon said wonderingly. When she last saw Rosa's daughter she was about to enter kindergarten. "I'll bet she's gorgeous."

"Hmmph," Rosa said, but her pride shone through. "She is. And she knows it." Rosa glanced over her shoulder. "Did you see Tay?"

Sharon nodded. "He picked me up at the airport."

"How did that go?" Rosa asked in a low tone.

Sharon shrugged and sat on the bed, gesturing for Rosa to join her. "I don't know. It's impossible to tell what he's thinking. At least we didn't come to blows in the arrival lounge."

"I'm relieved to hear it."

"I suppose you know about the will," Sharon said.

Rosa nodded.

"Can you believe my father did that?"

"What I can't believe is that you're going along with it," Rosa said frankly.

Sharon threw up her hands. "What can I do? Challenging it would be worse. Do you think I'd be here if there were any other way out of this?"

Rosa fingered the design on the bedspread. "There was a time when marrying Tay Braddock would have been your heart's desire," she said slowly.

"That time has passed," Sharon said dryly. "Rosa, can you imagine how I feel? The last time I saw Tay I made a complete fool of myself. Now Dad's will is compelling me to marry him, a prospect no more pleasing to him than it is to me, I'm sure. It's just awful."

"Are you sure?"

"That it's awful?"

"To him, I mean," Rosa said carefully.

Sharon stood and began to pace the room. "Rosa, he doesn't want me. He made that clear the night I left here ten years ago."

"What happened?" Rosa said. "I knew something did."

"How?"

"From the way Tay was acting after you were gone. You never mentioned it in your letters, and I didn't think it was my place to ask."

"I was trying to forget it," Sharon replied darkly.

"Tell me."

"Well, I got it into my head that he was really madly in love with me and just needed a little encouragement. I decided to provide that encouragement by slipping into the bunkhouse when he was asleep and climbing into bed with him."

"Oh, dear," Rosa said.

"Yeah. It was the least successful seduction in history. It lasted about ninety seconds. Once he realized who was inside the nightie he was trying to remove he gave me the bum's rush."

"Well, *niña*, you were so young. He was trying to protect you."

"I don't think so, Rosa. He said something about my being no different from the whores he used to patronize in Saigon. I believe that's an exact quote."

Even Rosa didn't know how to respond to that.

"So," Sharon went on, "I had that fond memory to go on when I made my triumphant return."

"Sharon, he's changed," Rosa said.

"Really?" Sharon said in a tone signifying that she doubted it.

"Look at this place," Rosa said, making a sweeping gesture to indicate the whole ranch. "Tay did this. After Rae died, your father didn't care what happened. The bills wouldn't even have been paid if it weren't for Tay. He took over and did everything. Gradually your father regained interest, and when he saw how well Tay was doing, Dan just let him keep on running things.''

"I knew Dad took Rae's death hard,'' Sharon said thoughtfully. "I always felt bad that I missed the funeral. I was having final exams when she went into the hospital, so Dad didn't tell me. He didn't want to disturb my concentration. By the time exam week was over, she was dead and buried.''

"There was nothing you could have done. Dan and Tay went around this place for weeks like a couple of wounded animals in a cave. The difference was that Dan couldn't work and Tay did nothing else but. He drove himself to exhaustion every night.''

"I would have thought he'd drink himself into bed,'' Sharon said.

Rosa shook her head. "No more.''

Sharon unzipped her dress and stepped out of it. "Is Eloise Randall still around?'' she asked casually.

"Josh Randall's daughter?''

"Yep.''

Rosa's brow furrowed. "I think she took up with some guy about five years ago and moved to Nevada. Why do you ask?''

"No reason.''

Rosa's eyes narrowed. "Wait a minute. The last time you were here Tay was seeing her, wasn't he?''

Sharon shrugged.

"Are you trying to find out if he has a girlfriend?''

"Well,'' Sharon said, "this little plan of ours to get married might run into a snag if he did and she objected.''

"As far as I know he isn't seeing anybody special.''

Sharon snorted. "I suppose now you're going to tell me he's become a monk.''

"Not him,'' Rosa said flatly. "No way. Opportunity knocks constantly. Women are always after him.''

"I know. I was one of them."

Rosa got up and put her hand on Sharon's shoulder. "Don't be too hard on yourself. You were just a kid."

"Yeah, well," Sharon said as she changed into a blouse and slacks, "I'm not a kid anymore, and this time our relationship is going to be strictly business."

"Good luck," Rosa said dryly.

Sharon turned to look at her. "Don't you think I can do it?"

"No," Rosa said.

"Thanks a lot."

"Sharon, your relationship with him ten years ago was special, and for Tay, very unusual. Even I could see that. You affected him, he listened to you when no one, not even his mother, could get his attention. Maybe it ended badly for whatever reason, but I don't think you can go from that to the emotional indifference of a business relationship just because you're both a little older."

"Well," Sharon said in a subdued tone, "I guess you told me."

"You asked."

"So you think this is a doomed enterprise?"

"I think you'd better be careful."

"I intend to be. Starting tomorrow morning when we get married."

"Tomorrow?"

"First thing. It's all arranged. And here I thought all along that when I got married it would be in a white gown in a church with bridesmaids in organdy dresses." She tossed her shoes onto the floor of the closet. "What a gyp."

"You don't have to go through with it."

"Yes, I do. I came here to marry Tay Braddock and I'm going to do just that. I didn't fly thousands of miles to back out now."

Rosa turned for the door. "I'll start dinner."

"Will Tay be joining us?" Sharon asked warily.

"I don't think so. He usually tells me if he'll be in for dinner, and he didn't say anything."

"I guess he plans to hide out until his presence is required," Sharon said nastily.

"What are you going to wear?" Rosa asked.

"I brought a blue suit."

"A blue suit? Are you planning to take a deposition from the justice of the peace?"

"Rosa, what difference does it make what I wear? It's not a real wedding anyway."

"That beige dress would be better," Rosa said, pointing at an outfit visible through the open door of the closet.

It was an eggshell silk sheath. "I don't know why I brought that with me," Sharon said uncomfortably.

"Let me press it for you."

Rosa departed with the dress over her arm and Sharon felt silly, aware that she wasn't deceiving Rosa for a minute.

Regardless of whether it was a real wedding or not, Tay would be there, and Sharon wanted to look nice.

She spent the dinner hour with Rosa, and, as expected, Tay did not appear. After Rosa left, Sharon felt as though she was rattling around in the house with the ghosts of her father and Rae whispering in the shadows, so she went outside and sat on the patio.

The last time she was on the terrace it had been strung with lights for a night barbecue over the Labor Day weekend. Her father had cooked burgers with long-handled tools, wearing an apron that said Too Many Broths Spoil the Cook. Rae had made her lemon-lime iced tea, and Sharon had worn her sky-blue maillot bathing suit with the navy trim.

It was so hard to accept that they were both dead now and that she was here on this fool's errand. Her eyes filled with tears and she wiped at them awkwardly, ashamed of her weakness.

Sharon sat outside for a long time. After darkness fell it grew chilly, and she went into the empty house. She tried to watch television, but the images blurred and the laugh tracks sounded more annoying than usual, so she went to bed around eleven.

Sleep would not come. She dozed fitfully for short intervals and finally gave up after a couple of hours. She rose and put on a bathrobe to go to the kitchen for a cup of tea.

She stopped on the threshold. Tay was sitting at the table, his shirt off and draped on the chair back, a half-empty glass cradled in his hands. Sharon hadn't heard him come in and had assumed that he was out somewhere enjoying his last night of "freedom."

He looked up as she entered and then stood, kicking the chair out of his way.

"I'll go," he said shortly.

"That's not necessary," Sharon replied, determined not to let him see how much he still got to her. "This is your house, too. If we can't learn to coexist in it, this arrangement we've planned will never work."

He didn't reply but sat down again, leaning back and taking another sip of his drink. Sharon went to the stove and got the kettle, filling it with water and putting it on to boil. When she turned to look at him, he was sitting with his head bent, staring into the portion of amber liquid that remained in his glass. She was facing his back, which was as golden brown as a hazelnut, freckled lightly across the shoulders. His hair, which she remembered as curling against his neck, was cropped shorter now, revealing sunburned creases in his nape. She was seized with the sudden urge to touch one, and she shoved her hands into the pockets of her robe.

"Couldn't sleep?" he said without looking at her.

"No, I couldn't."

"Is that because you were worried about me?" he asked flatly.

"Worried?" Sharon said uncomprehendingly.

He turned. "Worried about having me in this house, that I might bother you," he said.

It was the last thing she had expected him to say, and she was so startled that she replied frankly, "Tay, I'm not worried. I remember all too well that where I'm concerned, your self-control is second to none."

She saw in his face the impact of her careless statement. If she'd thought he might not remember that night in the bunkhouse ten years earlier, she saw now that she was wrong. He flushed a dull red under his tan, and he stood again, his half-naked body looming large and formidable in the small kitchen.

"Good," he said huskily. "Because I want to make something clear before we go ahead with this. I was going to tell you in the morning, but I might as well say it now."

Sharon waited, her fingers clenching inside her pockets.

"I'm not going to take advantage of this situation," he said. "You'll stay in your own room, and I'll keep away from you. I realize that a beautiful, successful woman like you has her own life, and I won't interfere. The only thing between us is the piece of paper we'll get tomorrow, and when all this is over you can go right back to what you left."

"Fine," Sharon said softly.

He finished his drink in one gulp, as if glad to have that speech behind him. He walked past her to the sink and set the glass on the drain board.

"I'll see you in the morning," he said. "The appointment at city hall is at nine o'clock." He left the room, and a second later she heard his door shut down the hall.

The kettle began to whistle, and Sharon removed it from the heat, turning off the burner automatically.

So he wasn't as cool about all of this as he'd seemed at the airport, she thought. It gave her some satisfaction that he was losing sleep over the situation, too, that it wasn't some minor annoyance he could dismiss in the company of a doxy in a Glendora bar.

Rosa had said he'd changed, and maybe he had.

Sharon no longer wanted the tea, and she went back to bed, passing Tay's door quickly.

She didn't lie awake this time, but fell into a dreamless slumber.

Tay listened to the faint sounds Sharon made as she settled into her room and tried not to picture what she was wearing or not wearing under her robe when she removed it for bed.

This was going to be even more difficult than he'd thought.

When he had first heard about Dan's will, he wasn't exactly surprised. He always suspected that Dan knew he'd fallen in love with Sharon all those years ago and respected him for letting her go. Maybe this was Dan's way of paying him back, giving him another shot at the prize.

Except the prize wasn't entirely in the mood to cooperate.

Tay couldn't blame Sharon for being angry. The terms of the will were antediluvian, and on top of that she had the memory of his behavior toward her on the night before she left for home. She didn't know how much he'd wanted her to stay; all she recalled was the bitterness of rejection.

But did she have to be so damn beautiful, he thought, in agony at the prospect of trying to keep his hands off her for the next couple of months. The puppy prettiness of her teen years had matured into a fine-boned porcelain loveliness that took his breath away. He'd recognized her immediately at the airport; she was the Sharon he remembered, and then some.

And now, of course, she was old enough to love.

Had he spoiled that chance forever? he wondered. Did she have someone back in Philadelphia, some sophisticated, educated city type who would make him look like a dirty fence mender?

Probably. He couldn't picture her spending her nights with frozen dinners and the metromedia movie.

That thought did not comfort him, and he punched the pillow behind his head, abandoning the idea of sleep.

Sharon had showered and was brushing her hair in the bedroom the next morning when Rosa knocked on her door.

"Come in," Sharon called.

Rosa entered, carrying a cup of coffee.

"Thanks," Sharon said, accepting it. "I didn't know you were coming in this morning."

"I thought I'd better stop by and see how things were going," Rosa said nervously.

"Have you seen Tay?" Sharon asked, her eyes meeting Rosa's over the rim of the cup.

Rosa nodded.

"Where is he?"

"Waiting in the living room. He's all dressed."

"Already? How does he seem?"

"He seems tense. He looks gorgeous."

Sharon shook her head and smiled. Rosa had an enthusiast's frank appreciation of the opposite sex, which she expressed freely.

"Where's your dress?" Rosa asked.

"On the back of the door, where you left it."

Rosa got it and helped Sharon get into it, zipping the back and adjusting the hem.

"You look beautiful," she said to Sharon, who stared at herself in the mirror.

"Too bad this is such a farce," Sharon said, applying her lipstick.

"You'll get through it," Rosa said firmly. "Just think, it could have been worse. Your mother could have been here."

Sharon had to smile. Her mother, to everyone's eternal amazement, had met a widower and remarried, moving to Chicago when her husband was transferred to another office of his company. Since she now had a life of her own, she was far less fixated on Sharon, who had told her mother she was taking a California vacation to settle her father's will. Period.

Sharon added a necklace and a pair of earrings to her ensemble, and she was ready.

"What time is it?" she asked.

Rosa glanced at her watch. "Eight-forty. Is that all you're going to have for breakfast?"

"I don't have time for anything else. We have to go." She picked up her purse and opened the door. "Wish me luck."

Rosa nodded, following her out of the bedroom and down the hall.

Tay rose as Sharon entered the living room. His eyes moved down, taking in her outfit, and up again to her face.

"You look nice," he said briefly.

So did he. He was wearing a dark gray-and-blue pin-striped suit with an off-white shirt and a navy-and-gray-striped tie. His hair was wet with recent combing and his shoes were polished to a high gloss.

"Be right back," he said and went to the kitchen. When he returned he was carrying a florist's box.

"Here," he said, handing it to Sharon.

She took it, surprised.

"I thought you should have that," he said, obviously uncomfortable.

Inside was a small arrangement of irises and carnations.

"This is the same bouquet I had for my father's wedding," Sharon said in wonderment, lifting the spray out of the tissue paper and holding it to her nose.

He nodded. "You chose them before, so I knew you would like it."

Sharon glanced at Rosa, who raised her brows. He had remembered a detail like that all these years?

He cleared his throat. "We'd better get moving," he said.

"Rosa, why don't you come along?" Sharon asked. "You can stand up for us."

"No, I can't. I have to pick Pilar up from dance class in an hour," she said. "I'll see you later."

Tay and Sharon went out to Dan's car, and Rosa looked after them, shaking her head.

She couldn't bear to witness the sham ceremony. If ever two people belonged together, she thought sadly, they did. Ten years ago they couldn't work it out, but they had a second chance now.

She wished with all her heart that they would transform this paper marriage into the real thing.

Dan Philips had been wiser than they knew.

The drive to the Glendora municipal building was brief, and Tay and Sharon signed the necessary papers in minutes. She had brought her blood test results with her, and the license was issued. Two clerks were the witnesses, and afterward their congratulations rang hollowly in Sharon's ears.

Her expression must have shown what she was thinking, because Tay said as they left, "Not exactly what you had in mind for your wedding, was it?"

Sharon didn't answer.

"I'm sorry," he said.

"It's all right," Sharon replied. "I understood what was going to happen when I came out here. It's just that it all seemed so…"

"Cold?" he suggested.

"Yes."

"How about some breakfast? You didn't have any at the house, and I'd like to talk to you about a few things."

"All right."

He pulled the car into the lot of a pancake house and parked. Sharon left her flowers on the passenger seat and followed him into the restaurant.

When they were seated and had ordered, Tay said, "There's a problem you should be aware of in connection with the ranch."

"What is it?" Sharon asked.

"A couple of developers, Citrus Farms and Sun City Homes, have been competing to buy it for a while."

"And you don't want to sell?"

"Do you?" he countered.

"How should I know? I just got here, I don't know what's going on. Why do they want it?"

"The property around here has become very valuable in the last few years. The town is within commuting distance of Los Angeles and the scenery is pretty. The schools are good. The developers have been moving in like a wolf pack circling a lame dog. They want to put subdivisions of tract houses on the ranch land."

"Tract houses, you mean a bunch of cookie-cutter bungalows, all alike?"

"That's right."

"My father would have hated that," Sharon said softly.

"He always refused to sell. The developers started in on me as soon as he died. When they find out about this wedding, they're going to be after you, too. They're offering a lot of money."

"And you still don't want to sell."

He lifted one shoulder. "This ranch is my life, but you may feel differently. You may want to take the money and go back to Philadelphia. In any case, once we inherit, they'll have to deal with us together. One parcel is no good without the other."

"So you want us to stick together, is that it?"

"Do you want to see a bunch of stucco bread boxes sitting on your dad's place?" he countered.

"Crawford didn't say anything about this to me," Sharon said as the waitress brought their coffee.

"He doesn't know."

"But you said you had spoken to him."

"I didn't tell him," Tay replied, taking a sip of his drink.

"Why didn't you tell *me* before the wedding?"

"I didn't want you to change your mind," he said evenly.

"In other words, you tricked me."

"How did I trick you?" he replied equably. "The terms of the will would have been the same. I just didn't inform you that there were buyers out there waiting in case you wanted to sell."

"You should have gone to law school," Sharon muttered, and the trace of a smile flickered across his lips.

The waitress brought their food, but Sharon had no appetite. She cut her pancakes into little sections and rearranged them on her plate until Tay said, "You really should eat some of that."

"Now you sound like Rosa."

"Rosa's right. You've gotten skinny."

Sharon stared at him, annoyed. "Haven't you heard that it's chic to be thin?" she demanded, somewhat misleadingly. A desire to be stylish was not the reason for her slenderness. Since learning about the will, she hadn't been able to eat much in anticipation of this reunion.

"Where? In Philadelphia?" He said the word as though it were a disease.

"Everywhere."

"You weren't always such a rail," he said, biting into a piece of toast.

"I was chubby ten years ago."

"I didn't think so."

"Really?" she said, holding his gaze, and he looked away.

"How did you get the time to come out here?" he asked after she had returned her attention to the decorative placement of her food.

"I took a leave of absence."

"On such short notice?"

"They owed me several vacations."

"You work for the D.A.'s office?"

"Yes."

"Prosecuting murder cases."

"They're not all murders, but the one I just finished was. How did you know?"

"Crawford told me."

Charlie Crawford seems to have developed a sudden case of bigmouthitis, Sharon thought. He had babbled quite a few details to Tay, who in return had apparently told him nothing.

"Did you win?" Tay asked.

"No."

"Why not?"

She looked up at him. That sounded like a challenge.

"It's complicated," she said.

"Try me," he said tightly. "I may surprise you by being able to comprehend more than you think."

Sharon hesitated. She hadn't meant to insult his intelligence. He was certainly prickly.

"Well, we wanted a conviction on murder one, premeditation. That carries the maximum penalty," she explained. "Frankly, I thought the guy deserved it, he seemed to have planned it all and taken his time setting it up. But his lawyer was able to get the charge knocked down to third degree, with a sentence of fifteen to twenty, eligible for parole after five. The defense hit heavily on the defendant's service record and his work history. The guy had an honorable discharge from the navy and had held the same job for ten years, but that didn't convince me he couldn't have killed his girlfriend.''

''He must have convinced the jury.''

Sharon shook her head. ''No. He was a poor witness.''

''Then what happened?''

''The evidence made his girlfriend, the victim, sound like a tramp, and the jurors didn't like what they heard about her. They decided that a tart like that deserved to die, so they weren't going to sentence her boyfriend to death for finally getting fed up with her.''

Tay stared at her, shocked.

''It's the truth,'' Sharon said, shrugging. ''I tried to control the jury during voir dire....''

''What's that?''

''The questioning of prospective jurors, the selection process. The people I liked kept coming up with reasons to be excused from duty, and I was discounting too many possibles. The judge censured me for wasting time, so I wound up with an unbalanced jury. It was bad from the start.''

''Does that happen often?''

''Too often.''

Tay shook his head. ''I'm glad that all I have to worry about is the price of feed and the due date of the next foal.''

''It isn't always like that,'' Sharon amended quickly. ''There are good moments, too.''

''Such as?''

''When you're able to help someone who really needs it. A couple of months ago I prosecuted a man for attempted murder. He had been abusing his wife and kids, and once he was in the court system all of that came to light. We were able to get his wife into a counseling program and the kids into day-care. The wife is taking classes at night now to become a practical nurse. Once she's able to support herself, she won't have to endure mistreatment in order to keep a roof over her head.''

Tay nodded.

"I wish we could do more, but we do what we can."

"My mother always wanted to be a nurse," Tay said softly.

"I didn't know that. She seemed so happy with her horses."

"She was, but she always regretted the chance she missed when she was a kid. She'd had a scholarship to nursing school, but my grandmother died a few weeks before she was to go, and Rae stayed at home to help with her sister. Her father had to work."

"I miss her around the place," Sharon said quietly. "It's like a ghost town, with her and my father both gone."

"Tell me about it. I would have moved back to the bunkhouse already if it still existed. As it is, there's no place to go. Every available bed is occupied with the increased staff."

"You've done wonders with the place," Sharon said grudgingly. "I can tell just by looking around that it's very successful."

"We're doing all right," he said shortly.

"I saw the new paddock."

"We needed it. We're stabling more than twice the number of horses we had when you were here. Miguel runs a riding school in the old paddock now."

Sharon smiled, making a pancake dam to contain a burgeoning river of maple syrup. "Remember when you taught me to ride?"

He grinned, the first genuine smile she'd seen since she arrived.

"How could I forget?" he said. "The first time you sat on the horse you fell off into the dirt."

"Lightning. He was so old and slow."

"Lightning was slow when he was a year old. He lived to be twenty and ate us into hock. Miguel was always talking about putting him down, but we both knew we'd never

do it. He died in his sleep. After a huge meal, of course.''
He drained his coffee cup. ''Did you keep up with the
riding?'' he asked.

Sharon sighed. ''I'm ashamed to tell you this, but I
haven't been on a horse since I was last in California.''

''I can't believe it,'' he said. ''I never saw anybody who
wanted to learn so much.''

''It did mean a lot to me, and I always appreciated your
help. But when I got to school other things became more
important. You know how it is.''

He nodded slowly. ''Want to do something about it?''

''What do you mean?''

''We can go for a ride when we get back. I'll take you
around the place, show you the changes.''

''Tay, I'd fall off the horse again, I know it.''

''Nah. Just like riding a bike.''

''I didn't bring riding clothes.''

''I've got some in the house.''

''To fit me?''

''Sure.''

Sharon tried to think of another objection and couldn't.
''You'd better call the paramedics and tell them to be on
the alert,'' she said as he called for the check.

''You'll be fine.''

''Only if you can resurrect Lightning.''

''I've got another one just as slow.''

''Impossible. What's its name?''

''Thunderbolt.''

Sharon laughed. ''Are you kidding me?''

''I am not.''

''Who does the baptizing?''

''Miguel. He thinks that's funny.''

They went back to the car, and on the drive home Tay
outlined the changes he'd made in the ranch operation, how
he'd streamlined the purchasing and hired new vets to supervise the breeding of the horses. It was clearly a subject

he loved, and Sharon just let him talk, wondering how any developer in the world thought he was going to get this man to sell to him.

When they got back to the house, Tay took her to the storage closet next to the garage and said, "There's a box of riding clothes on the floor. See if you can find something to fit you."

He went to change. Curious, Sharon took the container he had indicated to her room and sifted through it, amazed to discover an assortment of pants and shirts in various sizes, even a couple of leather belts. Where on earth had he got this stuff?

She selected a loose shirt and a pair of pants that were a little too big and cinched them with one of the belts. Tay was waiting for her in the living room when she emerged.

"Whose clothes are these?" Sharon asked.

He shrugged. "Beats me."

"Tay, is the stuff in that box your bimbo bin?"

He stared at her. "My what?"

"Castoffs from your old girlfriends, things they left around that you just didn't bother to return."

He shook his head. "Sharon, I told you that Miguel runs a riding school now. Sometimes the students leave things behind and don't come back for them. We save everything in there in case they come looking for what they left. That's all."

Sharon could feel herself flushing. "Oh," she said in a small voice. Why on earth had she made such a big deal about it?

"There are boys' clothes in there, too," he said gently.

Sharon looked down at the shirt she was wearing. It had seemed odd when she was dressing; the buttons were on the wrong side.

"Ready?" he said, looking at her.

Sharon followed him to the stable, where he led her to a horse that looked almost as phlegmatic as Lightning. He was methodically swatting flies with his tail and surveyed her with exquisite boredom.

"I take it this is Thunderbolt," she said.

"Yep."

"Maybe I could handle something a little more lively," she ventured bravely.

"You could?" Tay said, looking down at her.

"I'd like to try."

"Fine with me." He readied another horse, named Melody, and helped Sharon into the saddle. His hands lingered at her waist no longer than necessary, and she felt perversely disappointed.

He followed Sharon out on his own horse and took her on a tour of the ranch, ending at the old paddock where Miguel gave lessons. Sharon had done pretty well riding up until then, but Miguel had neglected to tell Tay that he'd been teaching Melody how to jump. When the horse saw the stanchions, she charged forward through the open gate and ran for the jump. Sharon hung on, but she had never jumped an obstacle in her life. When the horse went over, she went down, landing in an undignified heap on the ground.

Tay pulled up and leaped off his horse while it was still moving. He ran to Sharon's side and took her face in his hands.

"Are you all right?" he demanded, his expression anxious.

She nodded. The wind was knocked out of her and she couldn't talk, but otherwise she felt okay.

"Just stay here," he said. "I have to get the horses."

She nodded again, and he took off. She watched as he tethered his horse to a tree and then coaxed Melody into the paddock. He locked the gate and left her there, returning to kneel next to Sharon in the grass.

"How are you doing?"

"All right," she said breathlessly.

"I want to get you into the shade," he said. "Can you walk?"

"Think so."

He helped her to her feet, but when she tried to put weight on her left foot she cried out in pain.

"Guess not," she gasped.

He scooped her up in one smooth movement and carried her to a huge elm that bordered the ranch property. He held her for only a few seconds, but it was enough for all the sense memories of the last time she was in his arms to come rushing back. The sensation was the same, but intensified. Even his smell was familiar. She closed her eyes. Oh, Tay, she thought.

He knelt and set her on the ground. "Better?" he said. "That sun is awfully hot."

"This is fine." She looked around her. "I used to picnic under this tree."

"Let me see that ankle," Tay said.

He removed her shoe and sock and manipulated the joint. "Hurt?" he said.

"A little. Not bad."

"I don't think it's broken," he pronounced, "just sprained. It may bruise, we'd better put some ice on it when we get back."

She nodded.

"So," he said, sitting next to her with his back against the tree, "I guess Melody wasn't such a great idea, huh?" His expression was teasing.

Sharon smiled ruefully. "I didn't know she was trying out for the Olympic equestrian team."

"Miguel must have been using her in his classes. I'll have to talk to him. Apparently she's too undisciplined for that."

"Now you tell me."

"I thought she was all right for you," he said, turning his head to look at her. "She always seemed pretty docile."

"I guess she just likes to jump."

"Horses can be like women that way," he said softly. "They seem laid-back and restrained, but when they see what they want, they go for it."

He was very near, close enough for her to see the gold flecks in his amber-brown eyes. The tiny mole at the corner of his mouth was so well placed that on a woman it would have been called a beauty mark.

"I tried that once," Sharon said. "It doesn't always work."

He dropped his eyes and stood. "We should go back to the house. Dr. Jensen can take a look at that ankle."

"Dr. Jensen is a vet."

"So? A doctor is a doctor, he can tell if the bone is broken."

"You said it wasn't."

"I said I *thought* it wasn't. I'm not a doctor. I'll get my horse, we can ride back double. I'm not taking any more chances with Melody, I'll send somebody out for her later."

I guess I brought that conversation to an abrupt end, Sharon thought morosely as she watched him walk away. Obviously any reference, no matter how oblique, to that last night ten years earlier was going to be met with silence.

He returned with the horse and mounted, pulling her up behind him. Sharon remembered the last time she had traveled this way, but this trip was a lot more sedate. He kept the horse at an even canter all the way back and carried her into the house.

"Just stay there, don't try to walk," he said as he deposited her on the living room couch.

"Yes, sir," Sharon replied and saluted.

"I'll see if Jensen is still in the stables. He was supposed to give the horses their shots today," he said and left.

Sharon's ankle was beginning to throb, and she was contemplating disobeying orders and hobbling to the bathroom for aspirin, when she heard voices. Tay entered through the back door, followed by Dr. Jensen.

"She's in here," Tay said, leading the way.

Dr. Jenson, a handsome man in his fifties, surveyed the patient with a critical eye.

"George," Tay said, "this is my wife, Sharon."

Sharon almost fainted. She glared at Tay while Jensen bent over her foot, saying, "Congratulations, Mrs. Braddock. What a terrible thing to happen on your wedding day."

Tay, who was pretending not to notice Sharon's reaction, said, "It isn't broken, is it?"

"No, no. But it's a pretty bad sprain, and once the shock wears off it'll be painful," the doctor said. "Are you feeling it yet?"

"A little," Sharon said.

"Do you have any painkillers here?" Jensen asked.

"I have something I took for an abscessed tooth in my bag." She took out the bottle and showed it to him.

"They're an opiate," the doctor said. "People take them all the time. You won't be able to sleep without them."

Sharon swallowed two of the pills.

"Make sure she takes two every four hours," Jensen said. "And put some ice on that foot."

"I will," Tay assured him.

"It's a sorry way to spend your wedding night," the doctor said sympathetically.

"There'll be other nights," Tay said, and Sharon wanted to hit him.

After the doctor left, Sharon hissed, "Why did you tell him that we were married?"

"We are married."

"You know what I mean. I thought we agreed that we were going to handle this discreetly."

"What was I supposed to do?" Tay asked. "He knows you're staying here with me."

"Tay, I remember my father talking about that man. Dad said he's a nice enough guy, but he spreads more information than Reuters. Everybody for miles around will know we're married now."

"Maybe that's better. How could you live in this house without an explanation? What would people think?"

"What would people think?" Sharon repeated, staring at him. "Tay Braddock, you're talking to me, the person who put you back together after more drunks and fights than I care to remember. You were the scandal of the San Gabriel Valley for years. You expect me to believe that you suddenly care what people think?"

"Maybe I'm changing my image," he said mildly, propping her leg on a pillow.

Sharon eyed him narrowly as he fussed over her. There was a reason for what he had done, and she was certain it had nothing to do with his concern about their reputations.

"I'll get the ice," he said and rose to go to the kitchen.

She listened to him emptying ice trays and opening cabinets, and by the time he returned she was feeling spacey.

"Here you go," he said, putting her foot into a dishpan and packing it with ice bags. "This ought to do it. Now just lie back and try to take a nap."

Sharon found that advice easy to follow, and when Tay came back later on to give her more pills, she wasn't sure if she was awake or dreaming.

She swallowed dutifully and closed her eyes again.

He hesitated, then kissed her lightly on the mouth, certain that she wouldn't remember it.

Chapter 5

Sharon awoke the next morning in her own bed. She spent the next several days there, tended mostly by Rosa, who took over for Tay once she saw what had happened. Tay came and went, going out in the morning and returning in the evening, or sometimes not returning at all. Sharon felt that she was not entitled to any explanations, so she asked no questions.

On her first day up she was in the kitchen, helping Rosa with the breakfast dishes, when the phone rang. Sharon was passing it and picked up the receiver.

"Hello?"

"May I speak to Mrs. Braddock, please?" a man's voice said.

Sharon thought briefly of Rae, but her name hadn't been Braddock since she married Dan Philips.

"Uh," she said.

"Mrs. Taylor Braddock," the man said.

That's you, fool, Sharon said to herself. "Speaking," she replied.

"Congratulations on your wedding," the voice continued.

"Thank you," Sharon said briefly. "Who is calling, please?"

"Mrs. Braddock, this is David Morse. I represent Citrus Farms. We're a land development company licensed to operate in Los Angeles County. I assume you're heard of us."

"My...husband mentioned you," Sharon replied.

"Yes, I thought he might have done that. We approached your husband several weeks ago about selling your father's property to us. At that time he was not receptive to our plan, but I would like the opportunity to present our case to you, since I understand you have a half interest in the ranch."

"You understand quite a bit, Mr. Morse," Sharon said dryly, rolling her eyes at Rosa, who was listening.

"You're a lawyer, Mrs. Braddock, you know that things like titles and deeds are matters of public record," Morse replied smoothly.

"And I imagine you spend quite a bit of your time sifting through those records, looking for potential sellers to contact," Sharon said.

"That's the way to do business, Mr. Braddock," Morse said, unoffended. "I wonder if we might meet sometime soon and discuss what kind of a deal my associates and I have in mind."

"Well, Mr. Morse, I'd like to be frank with you. My father would not have approved of my selling to you or any other developer, and, as you know, my husband is also against it. But I'd like to keep an open mind, and so I think it only fair that I hear your proposal."

"Wonderful," said Morse, obviously surprised that she was willing to listen. "Would it be possible for you to see me this afternoon if I came out there?"

"I'll be here," Sharon said, amused. He wasn't wasting any time.

"Two o'clock?"

"Two is fine."

"I'll see you then, Mrs. Braddock."

"Goodbye."

Sharon hung up and shrugged at Rosa, who was shaking her head.

"You should have met him in town," Rosa said. "You'd better hope Tay doesn't see him."

"What's Tay going to do, run him off the place with a shotgun?"

"Maybe," Rosa said.

"Tay knew they would contact me."

"That doesn't mean he's going to like it."

"All right," Sharon said. "What's on your mind?"

Rosa folded her dish towel smartly. "You have no more intention of selling this place than I have of flying to the moon. You're just doing this to aggravate Tay and show him that he can't control you or make decisions for you."

"You think it's a bad idea for me to explore all the angles before making a decision?"

"I didn't say that. I said that your motivation for meeting Morse is not what you're telling yourself it is."

"Practicing psychiatry without a license, Rosa?"

"Humph," Rosa said. She put the last dish away and shut the cupboard door firmly. "You know I'm right." She marched out of the room.

Tay chose that day to come back to the house at lunchtime to change his clothes. He'd been breaking horses in the new paddock after a heavy rain, and he was caked with mud. Sharon was installed in the living room going over the ranch deeds when he returned, wearing fresh clothes, his hair damp. He stood behind her shoulder and asked, "Why are you reading that stuff?"

"I have a meeting with Citrus Farms at two," Sharon replied.

He walked around slowly and faced her. "Why didn't you tell me that?"

"I'm telling you now."

"You know what I mean," he said.

"Must I inform you in advance of my every move?" she inquired.

He swept the papers off the coffee table and onto the floor. Sharon leaped to her feet and flinched as her ankle protested.

"Are you okay?" he asked, stepping forward and taking her arm.

Sharon snatched it from his grasp. "Leave me alone. What do you think you're proving with that infantile display of temper? I have every right to talk to anybody I please concerning this ranch, and I will."

"Fine, Miss Know-it-all. I'm sure he'll be impressed with your vast knowledge of real estate and everything else, especially after talking to me." He stalked out of the house, slamming the door behind him.

Two for two, Sharon thought. I wonder who else I can infuriate before dark?

Morse arrived on the dot of two. He was a neatly dressed, well-spoken man with the understanding, ingratiating manner of a coffin salesman. He seemed to be strangely nervous, until Sharon realized that he was afraid Tay was going to appear suddenly and break his neck. She assured him that her husband was out working and would not be back until evening, and they got down to business.

"Did your husband discuss our financial terms with you?" Morse asked after they had gone over the preliminaries in some detail.

"No."

"I thought not," Morse said with satisfaction, clearly certain that he was about to play his trump card. "We are prepared to pay $80,000 an acre, half on signing and the rest on final transfer of the deed. I feel confident that you will not do better anywhere.''

Sharon was stunned. The ranch was over twenty acres. They were talking about a figure in excess of a million and a half dollars.

''And the money is only part of it,'' Morse said, pressing his assumed advantage. ''Think of all the jobs you'll be bringing to the area. We hire locals for construction and road work. And we pay for all the improvements like sewer and water systems, the hookups to existing homes, street lamps and underground utilities....''

Morse continued to extol the virtues of Citrus Farms while Sharon pondered Tay's behavior. He had told her everything except the amount of the offer. He must have thought that so much money would sway her; no wonder he was upset when he found out that Morse was coming later that day.

Sharon assured Morse that she would think about it and got rid of him as soon as she decently could. She was waiting for Tay when he returned to the house at six.

''Did you have a nice time this afternoon?'' he asked as he strolled through the door.

''Why didn't you tell me that Morse was offering eighty thousand an acre?'' Sharon countered.

''Not beating around the bush, are we?'' Tay said. ''Let's get right to the heart of the matter. Money.''

''Tay, that's over three-quarters of a million each,'' Sharon pointed out reasonably.

''I got an A in arithmetic in fourth grade,'' he replied. ''I figured that out already. And I'll tell you something else I determined with my superior mathematical ability. Morse will put four boxes on every one of those acres and charge two hundred grand for each of them. Can you multiply? That means his company makes ten times what he paid us for the land.''

"Most people wouldn't care how much Morse's company made, as long as they got their money."

"I'm not most people."

"Aren't you even tempted?"

"So you want to take the money and run, huh? Forget all the blood and sweat your father put into this place and go back to Philly with a little nest egg. You can play lady lawyer all you want, you won't have to make a dime at it with that kind of money."

"I'm not playing at it, I'm a good lawyer," Sharon said quietly.

"Well, at least we know you can count." He yanked open the refrigerator door and removed a can of beer, popping the top with his thumb.

"You won't even consider it," Sharon said, determined not to let his attitude deter her from a thoughtful discussion.

"I've never been long on consideration," he replied, taking a healthy swallow of his beer. He faced her directly. "Look, you can pocket the cash and go back to your job. If we sell this place what do I have?"

"Seven hundred and fifty thousand dollars," she replied, lifting her shoulders.

He shook her head. "I've got zip. I'm a bum, which is what I was before I got here."

"Nobody with that kind of money is a bum," Sharon said.

He stared at her. "You think money makes the difference? You've got a lot to learn. I've met more rich bums than I care to count. If you're not useful, productive, involved, you're a bum."

"You can buy another, smaller place, and keep the difference," Sharon said. "That amount is only for the value of the land. If you sell off your inventory—"

"My horses?" he said, outraged. "I'm not selling my horses!"

"Will you please listen to me and let me finish? I'm not

talking about the horses, you can transport them to wherever you're going. I'm talking about excess machinery and equipment; this ranch is too big for your operation anyway. Ten acres would be enough, and you'd have the rest of the money to invest. I'd help you find another place.''

"I don't want another place, I want this one." He sighed, obviously trying to control himself, and then said, "I can't believe you're talking this way, Sharon. You know what this ranch meant to our parents, and it means as much to me. I had nothing when I came here. I was...nothing. Your father took a chance on me, helped me to believe in myself because he believed in me. I turned my life around, right here, and I don't want to leave. Ever.''

Sharon nodded slowly, inwardly elated. She had been playing devil's advocate to eliminate any shadow of a doubt, but now she was convinced. She didn't want him to know that yet, however.

"So what are you going to tell Morse?" Tay asked, watching her.

"I don't know," she said. "I have to think about it."

"What's to think about?" he said impatiently.

"Unlike you, I *am* long on consideration," Sharon said. "I've learned not to make snap decisions."

"I suppose you'll be talking to Sun City, too," he said.

"I suppose so."

The telephone rang.

"Maybe they're on the phone right now," he said with false cheer. He picked up the receiver and barked, "Yeah?"

There was a pause and then he said, "Oh, George."

There was another, longer pause before Tay said, "I don't know, you can talk to her."

Sharon stared at him as he handed her the phone.

"What?" she said.

"I'll let him explain it to you," he said shortly and left the room.

"Dr. Jensen?" Sharon said.

"Hello," the doctor said. "How's the ankle?"

"Oh, much better, thank you. You were a big help."

"Good. Listen, I've been trying to persuade your husband to come to a little get-together the wife and I are having this Saturday night. It's an anniversary party, and we've invited some people from the area. Tay would never come to anything by himself, he always made an excuse, so we didn't bother to send him an invitation. But when I told my wife he was married, and to Dan Philips's daughter, she insisted that I call you. Some of your father's old friends will be there, they'd love to see you."

Emotional blackmail, Sharon thought. Wonderful. "Well, I don't know," Sharon said feebly. "My foot still isn't right and..."

"I thought you just said it was much better."

"It is, but Tay and I have been busy..." Busy fighting, that was true. The thought of spending an entire evening being congratulated on her marriage was more than she could bear.

"Well, if you're sure you can't make it..." Jensen said. He sounded so disappointed that she felt churlish and relented. He had been kind to her. Getting Tay to show up at anything was probably an accomplishment, and with Sharon in tow it would be a coup.

"All right," she said. "We'll make the time."

"Great," he replied. "We'll look forward to seeing you around eight. Black tie."

"We'll be there." Sharon hung up the phone, certain that Tay wouldn't mind going, or he would have refused the invitation without consulting her. For some reason, he wanted people to know they were married and see them as a couple. Maybe he thought she would find it harder to sell the ranch and take off if she felt a part of the community.

"What did you tell him?" Tay asked, coming back into the room.

"I told him we'd go. Isn't that what you wanted?"

"I don't care either way," he said with infuriating indifference.

"It's formal, you know."

That gave him pause. "You mean like a tux?"

"That's what I mean."

He looked pained.

Hoist with your own petard, my boy, Sharon thought with satisfaction.

"I'm going out," he announced. "Rosa will be in to make dinner in a few minutes."

"You don't have to keep bringing her here to cook," Sharon said. "If you're not going to eat, I can make something for myself."

"Not with a bad foot."

"The foot's all better." Sharon dropped her eyes. "You can eat with me if you want, you know. You don't have to shun this place during the day as if it were a plague house."

"I've got a lot to do," he replied, not meeting her gaze. "And Rosa doesn't mind stopping by, she told me so."

"I feel funny having her come over here to make an elaborate meal just for me."

"She wants to check up on you. Don't you know that?" Tay said. "She cares about you."

He didn't add, "I can't imagine why," but Sharon thought she heard it in his tone. She was sitting on the couch, depressed and staring into space, when Rosa arrived.

"You look about as happy as Tay did when I passed him on the way in," Rosa greeted her. "You two been torturing each other again?"

"He gave me his reaction to Morse's visit."

"Morse?"

"The guy from Citrus Farms."

"I see." Rosa put her bag of groceries on a chair.

"We were discussing some economic realities. Or rather, I was discussing them and Tay was arguing with me."

"You know my feelings on that subject," Rosa said briefly, folding her arms.

"I also accepted an invitation to a party at George Jensen's house Saturday night."

"I assume you're going by yourself. Tay can't be dragged to one of those things at gunpoint."

"With Tay."

Rosa's mouth fell open.

"Black tie."

Rosa started to laugh. "This I've got to see. It took his own wedding to get him into a suit, I can't wait for the tux."

"Yeah, well, I don't have anything to wear, either. I wasn't expecting to attend any formal parties. I brought that one beige dress and a suit, the rest of my stuff is shorts and slacks."

"You can wear the beige one again," Rosa said.

Sharon didn't reply.

"Of course, Tay has already seen it," Rosa added airily.

Sharon shot her a look. "I wish you would stop trying to turn this arrangement into something it's not," she said sternly.

"We'll see," Rosa said and drifted out of the room.

Sharon stared at the carpet for several seconds, thinking, and followed her into the kitchen.

Sharon went shopping for a dress the next day. She took her father's car, which technically belonged to the estate. Both she and Tay used it when his truck was unsuitable. For Sharon, this was all of the time. The Glendora shop she had patronized during her last visit was still there and still run by the same woman, who was happy to cater to an old customer. Sharon found a black satin cocktail dress with spaghetti straps studded with rhinestones, a fitted bodice and a bell skirt. At first she thought it was too much, both too dramatic and too expensive, but she allowed herself to be talked into it. She wanted to make an impression on Tay, and this was just the dress to do it.

She tried it on for Rosa when she got home. For the first time in Sharon's memory, that estimable lady had nothing to say.

"Don't you like it?" Sharon asked.

"Did it have any warnings about flammable material on the label?" Rosa asked dryly.

"Don't be silly. I got it on sale."

"I hope so. I can only imagine what it cost at full price."

"It's something, isn't it?" Sharon said, turning for inspection.

"It's something, all right."

"Should I wear my grandmother's necklace with it?" Sharon asked.

"*Niña*, I think that lily needs no gilding. The only thing you should wear with that is a flak suit."

"You don't think it's flattering," Sharon said, disappointed.

"Oh, of course it is. It's just that I don't think you have to do this to get his attention."

"Whose attention?" Sharon asked innocently.

"He already watches every move you make," Rosa said.

"Don't be ridiculous," Sharon replied, dropping the pretense. "He's never here. Since I arrived, he treats this house like a hotel. He comes and goes like a boarder."

"He's doing that deliberately."

"I didn't think it was an accident."

"He's afraid to be around you too much, don't you see that?"

Sharon turned for the other woman to unzip the dress. "Rosa, you're an incurable romantic, and I wish you were right, but you're not." She stepped out of the dress and hung it on the hanger. "I'll take this back and get something else."

"Don't do that. I didn't say you shouldn't wear it." She

grinned mischievously. "You might stir something up, at that."

The outside door slammed and they heard Tay moving in the kitchen. Sharon grabbed the hanger and the dress box and scurried down the hall.

On Saturday night Sharon stayed in her room until the last minute. Her palms were clammy and her heart was in her mouth. She felt as though she were going on her first date and told herself to grow up.

She examined herself in the mirror for the tenth time. She had put her hair up and taken Rosa's advice: her only jewelry was a pair of pearl-and-diamond studs her mother had given her when she graduated from college. She had accented the short hem of the dress with dark hose and a pair of plain black high-heeled pumps. Her makeup was understated, and her nails were done. There was no doubt about it, she was ready.

When her wristwatch told her she could delay no longer, she stepped into the hall and went to look for Tay. Rosa was packing some leftovers to take home and glanced up at her approach.

"Madre de Dios," she said.

"Nope, just me," Sharon said. "Where is he?"

Rosa nodded toward the rear of the house.

Sharon found Tay outside on the patio, his hands in his pockets, looking up at the stars. The floodlights were on, and they bathed him in a yellow radiance like moon glow. He turned at her step and stared at her. He didn't say a word, but his expression told her everything she needed to know.

The dress was a success.

He was wearing a black tuxedo with a boiled shirt and a black satin tie. The dark tailored clothes made him appear slimmer than he actually was, and his black hair shone like sable.

"You are the most beautiful man," Sharon whispered. She didn't even try to stop the words; she had to say them.

He looked away. "Men aren't beautiful," he said huskily.

"You are. I always thought so." She moved closer until she was standing in front of him and reached up to touch his hair. "So soft," she said. "I remembered how it felt all this time."

He closed his eyes.

Rosa opened the back door and said, "I called Miguel and he said he left the car..."

Sharon's hand fell away and the magic moment passed.

"At the main gate," Rosa finished weakly, aware that she had interrupted something.

"I'll get it," Tay said and walked around the corner of the house.

"I'm sorry," Rosa said to Sharon.

"Don't worry about it," Sharon said wearily. "Timing has always been a problem for Tay and me."

"Good luck tonight," Rosa added.

"Thanks."

They went back into the house, and when Tay pulled up to the front door, Sharon got into the car without a word.

George Jensen lived only three miles away, in a stucco hacienda surrounded by four acres of fruit and flowering trees. He had his own horses, and two of them raised their heads inquiringly as the car drove past the corral. Three dogs—two spaniels and a black Labrador—raced madly around the front yard as a valet hired for the occasion appeared to take the keys from Tay.

Tay and Sharon walked past a splashing fountain in the center of a circular driveway paved with crushed white stones and up a wide front staircase flanked by reclining lions.

"It looks like the New York Public Library," Sharon whispered.

"Vets do very well in horse country," Tay replied, smiling slightly.

The house was ablaze with light. The carved double doors were opened by a uniformed maid who showed them into a two-story entry hall inlaid with ceramic tiles in a Toltec design. Scattered rugs picked up the black-and-white accents from the floor and walls, and a gleaming brass chandelier suspended from a medallion in the ceiling dominated the visual space. Two huge aquariums filled with exotic tropical fish hummed and bubbled on either side of them, and a mynah bird screamed in a glass cage.

"I can understand why George became a vet," Sharon said.

"You haven't seen the monkeys yet," Tay replied, glancing at her.

"Monkeys?" Sharon said, looking around nervously.

"They're in a separate building out back. He also has several cats and a couple of ferrets."

"Ferrets? You mean like rats?"

"No, these are domesticated little furry things that crawl all over George. They wind themselves around his neck and take naps in his pockets."

"I hope they're also in the building out back," Sharon said fervently.

They entered a large dining room where they were greeted by their hostess, a youthful-looking woman in her forties, who obviously had a high tolerance for lower forms of life. An elaborate buffet was laid out on the dining table of Spanish cedar, and Tay had just gone to get drinks from a bar set up in the adjoining living room when Sharon felt a hand on her shoulder.

"Who are you?" a man's voice said.

Sharon turned to see an attractive blond in his thirties, smiling down at her.

"Hello," he said. "I've never seen you before, I certainly would have remembered."

"No, we've never met," Sharon replied.

"Let me remedy that immediately. I'm Jim Sanders, George's accountant."

Sharon shook his hand, saying, "Sharon Phil... Braddock. How do you do?"

"Braddock? Any relation to Tay Braddock?"

"His wife," Sharon said, thinking here it comes.

"His wife! When the hell did he get married?"

"About ten days ago."

"That so-and-so, he never said a word to anybody. He goes around here for years like he's in love with those horses of his, and all of a sudden he turns up with *you*. How do you like that?"

Sharon smiled inanely, trying to think of a way to make a graceful exit.

Sanders was still gripping her shoulder. She was moving backward to elude his grasp as he said, "I love that dress."

"Take your hand off her or you'll be wearing it," Tay's voice said behind them.

Sharon closed her eyes. Please, she prayed silently, please let him behave.

"Sure thing, pal," Sanders said frostily, glancing at Sharon as if to ask *Who's your crazy friend?* He turned and melted into the crowd.

"Was that absolutely necessary?" Sharon said to Tay through clenched teeth.

"He was mauling you," Tay replied, handing her a glass of champagne.

"I was handling it."

"Didn't look like it," he observed, his gaze penetrating.

"Are you suggesting that I was enjoying his attentions?" Sharon demanded, her temperature rising.

"Why not? You're not committed to our...arrangement, as you constantly find ways of reminding me. Why don't you go after him? Maybe you can meet him later and have a great time."

Sharon walked away, too angry to reply. She was munching a canapé, silently fuming, when a woman in a blue dress with a deep décolletage walked up to her and said, "So you're Tay's wife."

Here we go again, Sharon thought. She definitely should have stayed home.

"That's right," Sharon said politely.

"I never expected him to get married," the blue lady said, sipping ruby claret from a delicate glass.

"Is that right?"

"Yeah. He always seemed like a free spirit to me. But then, some guys get married and still don't change, you know?"

Thank you so much for that piece of wisdom, Sharon thought. "Excuse me," she said aloud and fled.

Sharon didn't see a person she recognized, not even George. Apparently all the old friends of her father were arriving late or in the powder room. She stood next to a fieldstone fireplace in the living room, feeling like a wallflower, until a woman in her thirties with frosted blond hair came up to her and said, "Mrs. Braddock?"

"Yes?"

"I'm Claire Bryant. I used to date Tay a couple of years ago when I was a sales representative for Dover Dry Goods. He was one of my best accounts."

I'll bet, Sharon thought.

"How do you do?" Claire said.

Sharon shook hands with her. This isn't a party, she thought despairingly, this is a convention of Tay's old girlfriends. Apparently there wasn't anyone in the state of California he had missed. Was this why he wanted her to come tonight, because he knew that these people would be on hand to torment her?

"That's quite a man you caught there," Claire said, smiling. "I was madly in love with him, I'm sure you are, too."

Sharon smiled back but didn't reply.

"I never thought he would get married," Claire said.

Join the club, Sharon thought. "I guess the time comes for most people," Sharon replied, appalled at her own banality.

"Will you be living on the ranch?" Claire asked.

"Yes."

"That must be quite an adjustment for you. I heard you're from the East."

Word was certainly getting around fast. "Not really. The place was my father's, I spent time out here years ago. My dad left it to Tay and me."

She saw the information register with Claire and knew that she was thinking, so that's why Tay married her.

"I see," Claire said, satisfied that she had solved the mystery. "Well, I see my date over there, it was nice meeting you."

Sharon nodded miserably and watched the other woman walk away. She was seriously considering going out to sit by herself in the car when George Jensen popped out of the crowd at her elbow and said, "Look who I found."

Tay was with him, wearing his "I'm going along with this but I'm not happy about it" face.

"Thanks so much for coming," George said, kissing her cheek. "Is the ankle okay?"

"Good enough to wear heels," Sharon replied.

"I'm so glad." George reached past her and removed a small brass gong from the mantelpiece at her back. As she watched he began to strike it, making a sound sizable enough to attract the attention of the gathering. She waited, thinking that he was going to announce dinner. But when his guests quieted, George said, "Ladies and gentlemen, we have a pair of newlyweds in our midst. I'd like you to join me in congratulating Mr. and Mrs. Taylor Braddock, who just tied the knot last week."

Everyone applauded, and Sharon shot a quick glance at Tay, who looked as horrified as she felt.

Someone began to tap a glass with a spoon, and soon the crowd followed suit, making a chiming noise that set Sharon's nerves on edge.

"I think it's time you kissed the bride, Tay," George said, beaming.

Sharon knew he was a decent man who meant well, but at that moment she felt like kicking him.

The group picked up the refrain, and Sharon saw that they were not going to get out of it. Tay moved to her side and put his arm around her, kissing her lightly on the mouth.

Boos and catcalls followed.

"Is that the best you can do?" Jim Sanders yelled, getting some of his own back.

"You're slipping, Braddock," somebody else caroled, laughing.

"Let me at her, I'll show you how it's done," a third man shouted.

Sharon could see Tay's expression change, and she knew he had decided to give the audience what it wanted.

He turned to her and embraced her, bending his head to hers swiftly. He took her mouth with his, gently at first, and then with increasing intensity, pulling her against him fully and slipping his tongue between her lips. She felt the muscles of his thighs tighten against her legs and his hands move caressingly across her back.

Sharon couldn't restrain herself from cooperating. This might be her only chance to kiss him, and she forgot their cheering section and everything else in the pleasure of the moment. She sank her fingers into his hair and stood on tiptoe, letting him take her weight.

The approval of the onlookers was enthusiastic and vocal. The whistling and clapping escalated to such a point that it finally intruded on their daydream, and Sharon drew back, her mouth wet and her breath coming in short gasps.

Tay, who was also breathing harshly, looked down at

her, his expression more vulnerable than she had seen it since she came back to California. Then he bowed to his admirers and turned away, downing half a glass of wine in one swallow.

Sharon leaned against the mantelpiece, trembling, and was relieved when George clapped Tay on the back and laughingly started to tell him a story. She waited until she was steady enough to walk before she started toward the door.

A decade had been erased in an instant. During that kiss the sense memory of being with Tay in the bunkhouse came back with such power that she was lost in it.

Sharon plowed through the crowd, nodding and smiling automatically when people congratulated her or commented on Tay's performance. She didn't hear a thing they said. She finally found herself in the kitchen and bypassed the staff working there, ending up in a sort of pantry where the tableware was stored. She closed the door behind her and sat on the stepladder under the china cabinet, wondering how long she would be able to remain there before she was discovered.

I'm as much in love with him as ever, she thought. It was depressing to admit that nothing had changed in all the time they'd been apart, but lying to herself wasn't going to help.

She was sitting with her arms wrapped around her knees when the door opened suddenly and Mrs. Jensen walked into the room. She stopped short when she saw Sharon.

"My dear, what are you doing in here?" she asked, startled.

"I, uh…" Sharon said.

"Aren't you feeling well?"

"I guess not," Sharon said, seizing upon the excuse. "I didn't want to make a fuss, and I just needed to be alone for a few moments."

Mrs. Jensen picked up the silver set she'd come to get

and handed it through the door to one of the caterers. "Well, you must come upstairs and lie down in the guest room."

"Oh, don't go to any trouble...." Sharon began, feeling trapped by her lie.

"Nonsense. I'll show you to the room and bring you a cup of tea. Then I'll go and find that handsome husband of yours."

"No," Sharon said quickly. Too quickly. Mrs. Jensen stared at her.

"I mean," Sharon amended, "I want him to have a good time. He so rarely gets away from the ranch."

"But he'll be concerned about your absence, won't he?"

"Not for a while. He was talking to some of the men when I left him, and he was absorbed in the conversation."

"All right. Come along now, I want you to rest. Do you think something you ate disagreed with you?"

"No, I'm sure it was just the champagne. I really shouldn't drink the stuff, it's been disagreeing with me lately." Sharon smiled weakly.

"It's this way," the older woman said, leading her through the kitchen and up the back staircase to the second floor of the mansion. They passed an elaborate master bedroom suite and stopped at the end of the hall.

"Here we are," Mrs. Jensen said, pushing open a door to reveal a bedroom and bath decorated in neutral tones. She switched on a bedside lamp and said, "Just make yourself comfortable. I'll bring up the tea in a bit."

"Please, that's not necessary. I've kept you from your guests long enough."

"Don't be silly. You *are* one of my guests. Be back in a jiffy." Mrs. Jensen went out, closing the door. Sharon felt ashamed about lying to such a nice lady, but the alternative would have been to tell her the truth, that she was hiding in a china closet from her husband.

Straightforward people like Mrs. Jensen did not understand such things.

Sharon read a magazine she had found on a rack near the bed, until Mrs. Jensen returned with a flowered teapot on a little tray. Sharon made small talk until her hostess left and then dutifully drank some of the tea.

It wasn't long before there was a knock at the door. Thinking that one of the staff had arrived for the tray, Sharon said, "Come in."

Tay entered the room and surveyed her with folded arms.

"Faking?" he said, raising his brows.

"Not exactly," Sharon replied. "Mrs. Jensen found me and jumped to conclusions. I didn't dissuade her."

"Where did she find you?"

"In the pantry," Sharon mumbled.

"Where?"

"In the pantry," she said loudly.

He sat on the edge of the bed, like a parent reasoning with a child who refused to go to sleep.

"Why were you in the pantry?" he said patiently, as if it were a normal question.

"I wanted to get away."

"You wanted to get away from me."

"I didn't say that."

"Who, then?" he said sarcastically. "Santa Claus? I was the one who kissed you."

Sharon stared at him, annoyed by his tone. "Perhaps I wanted to get away from the hordes of your ex-girlfriends parading through the rooms downstairs."

"Are you on that kick again?" he demanded. "Remember the bimbo bin?"

"I am not imagining this one. Half of the women at this party are your ex-lovers, and I think you knew they would be here."

"Are you suggesting that I set you up?" he said, his eyes narrowing.

''What would you call it?''

''I would call it George Jensen inviting the entire San Gabriel Valley to one of his parties.''

''You weren't privy to the guest list?''

''Privy? What is that, lawyer talk?''

''Did you know who was coming tonight?'' Sharon rephrased the question.

''I am not George Jensen's social director. I can't help it if he invited some women I used to date.''

''Date? Date? Like in Frankie and Annette? Come on, Tay, you did more than *date* them.''

''So what if I did?'' he demanded, standing. ''I suppose you've been in a convent for the last ten years.''

''We're not talking about me,'' Sharon said.

''We are now. I know why you didn't want to come tonight.''

''Of course you know why. I don't like putting on a show, pretending to something that doesn't exist.''

''That's not the real reason.''

''Then what is?'' she said, playing along.

''You know that people think you married down, a lady lawyer hooking up with her father's hired hand to hang on to the family ranch.''

'`Tay, nobody thinks that,'' she said, surprised by how much this apparently bothered him.

''I think that,'' he said flatly. ''You wouldn't be in this if your father hadn't forced it on you, you certainly never would have married me. Have you even thought of me in all the time since you left?''

''I've thought of you,'' Sharon said quietly.

''I'll bet. You thought about a ridiculous teenage crush you were glad to leave behind the instant you entered college. I became an embarrassing memory.''

''How dare you say that to me?'' Sharon said, sitting up. ''You know that we agreed...''

''Can we stop talking about agreements and arrangements for one minute? How do you feel? Did you want to come here? Are you happy being here now?''

''That's not a fair question,'' Sharon began, and he held up his hand.

''I don't want to hear that,'' he said. ''Fair, unfair, all of your fancy talk boils down to one thing: you can't wait to dump both me and the ranch and run back to Philly with your pockets full of pesos.''

''Now wait a second. Just because I talked to that man from Citrus Farms doesn't mean I've made up my mind.''

''You can't wait to dump me, then. Let's leave the ranch a separate issue.''

''I can't wait to dump you? You're the one who avoids me.''

''You've made it clear you don't want me around you.''

They were staring at each other hostilely when Mrs. Jensen knocked on the door.

''Sharon, are you still in there?'' She opened the door and saw Tay. ''I thought I heard voices,'' she added, smiling. Her smile faded when she noticed their expressions.

''Is everything all right?'' she asked, looking at Tay.

''Everything is fine,'' Tay replied. ''I was just saying that since Sharon isn't feeling well, I'd better go down and get the car. I'd like to take her home.''

''I think that might be best,'' Mrs. Jensen said. ''You two will have to come back another time when Sharon can stay longer.''

Tay left, and Mrs. Jensen said, ''My dear, I hope you won't think I'm prying, but is it possible that you're pregnant?''

Sharon looked at her, nonplussed.

''Oh, I know you two haven't been married that long, but I'm aware that young people nowadays don't wait. And I must say it could be just the thing. I was telling my husband...'' Her voice trailed off and faltered into silence when Sharon did not respond.

"I don't think I'm pregnant," Sharon said quietly.

"Maybe you don't know. The symptoms are there. When I was carrying my first, I couldn't abide liquor in any form, it just turned my stomach on a dime."

Sharon looked away. "Other things can cause an upset stomach."

Mrs. Jensen nodded. "Well, you should check it out, just in case. Now let me clear these tea things away, and you take your time coming downstairs. If you'd like to rest a little more, that would be fine."

"I'm feeling much better, thank you. And I appreciate your kindness."

"Oh, anything for Tay's wife. George and I are very fond of that boy. I have an idea that you're just what he needs."

Mrs. Jensen left, and Sharon felt absurdly like crying. That sweet lady, dreaming of happy families and happy babies, when in reality nothing could be further from the truth.

How long can I take this, Sharon wondered? It was turning out to be more difficult than even she had anticipated.

She glanced in the mirror above the dresser and straightened her sparkling straps, then marched out of the room and down the stairs.

She was met at the bottom by one of the old friends George had promised, and he took her to meet some more. She was distracted for a few moments while she talked to them, but the problems came back in a rush when she looked up and saw Tay standing to one side, watching her.

She excused herself and went over to him.

"Waiting for me?" she asked.

"That's my job, isn't it?" he said.

Sharon ignored that one and said, "I have to say goodnight to George and his wife."

"I did that already. Let's go."

He was still acting distant as they went out to the car, and Sharon said, "What's wrong now?"

"Martha Jensen just told me she thinks you're pregnant."

Sharon glanced at him and then looked again. He was perfectly serious.

"Tay, she thought I wasn't feeling well and made an assumption," she said, amazed. "We're supposed to be married, how could I tell her that couldn't possibly be the case?"

"Are you?" he said. "Pregnant?"

Sharon stopped walking. "Of course not. What are you talking about?"

He turned and faced her. "You wouldn't be the first woman who found herself in that situation. Maybe you had a stronger motivation for marrying me than just your father's will."

Sharon slapped him as hard as she could, her eyes stinging with tears as if she were on the receiving end of the blow. "You are despicable. I'm not going anywhere with you. Drive home by yourself!" She turned and headed back for the house.

"Sharon," he called after her. "Sharon, wait."

She ignored him.

He stood uncertainly on the driveway, watching her walk back to the house, then jammed his hands into his pockets and headed toward the car.

Sharon climbed the stone steps again and, once inside, told the maid that she needed to use the phone. The woman took her to a back room on the first floor, which turned out to be the library, and Sharon used the extension there to call a cab.

"Shall I get Mrs. Jensen?" the maid asked, noticing Sharon's unhappy expression.

"No, no," Sharon said quickly, thinking of the new set of lies she would have to tell her hostess. "There's no need.

My husband took the car earlier, that's all.'' About sixty seconds earlier, she added silently.

The maid was satisfied and left, and after a few minutes Sharon got up and waited outside until the cab came.

The house was dark and silent when she got back. It was obvious that Tay had not returned, and Sharon assumed he was off comforting himself elsewhere.

She undressed and got into bed, but she couldn't sleep. The events of the evening kept replaying themselves in her mind. She saw Tay's face after he kissed her, and his expression when he accused her of being pregnant. She was falling into a doze when a loud thud from the vicinity of the kitchen snapped her awake.

She thought of prowlers but realized it was much more likely to be Tay, drunk from his nocturnal escapade. She got up and went down the hall, thinking that her presence was forcing him to return to old, bad habits.

He was slumped on the floor in a sitting position, his back propped against the legs of a chair. His tux was ruined, the jacket ripped and stained, the shirt filthy and practically in ribbons. His mouth was bloody and his knuckles scraped raw. He was cradling his left side with his arm and wincing.

This scenario has a certain familiarity about it, Sharon thought as she knelt next to him. But as she took a closer look she realized that he wasn't drunk, just hurt.

''Tay?'' she said, shaking his shoulder.

He blinked up at her, seemingly dazed.

''What happened to you?''

''Got jumped,'' he mumbled, trying to sit up straight.

''Where?''

''Town,'' he said, closing his eyes as she pushed his arm aside. She unbuttoned his shirt and found a large purpling bruise over his ribs. She touched it gingerly with a forefinger and he gasped.

"This looks bad, Tay. We should have it X-rayed. Something could be broken."

He shook his head. "No hospital."

She realized that it was more important for him to rest at the moment, so she helped him to stand and, supporting him with his arm across her shoulders, walked him down to his room. She switched on the light and eased him onto the bed, allowing him to sit before she lifted his legs onto the coverlet. She took off his shoes and worked the jacket off his shoulders and down his arms, then tossed it onto the floor.

He fell back against the pillows and propped himself on his elbows, watching her as she wiped his mouth with a towel from his bathroom.

"This doesn't look too bad," she said. "I'm more worried about those ribs. How did that happen?"

"Used me for a punching bag," he said.

"Who did?"

"Some townies."

"Why, Tay?"

"They know I don't want to sell the ranch," he said. "They're out of work, and they need the jobs the developers would bring." The speech exhausted him, and he fell back, drained.

And I guess it didn't help that they heard your wife was undecided, Sharon thought. She had probably brought this on by entertaining Mr. Morse. She finished cleaning Tay's face. When she couldn't get his shirt off the conventional way, she got Rosa's sewing scissors from the den and cut it off him. It was a loss anyway.

She brushed his side as she was pulling the scraps of material from his body, and he flinched visibly.

"Tay, I still have some pain pills," Sharon said. "Do you want some?"

He made a dismissive gesture. "No pills. Thirsty."

"I'll get you some water." She went to the kitchen, filled

a glass and then on impulse got the bottle of pain pills from her room. Her dosage had been two, so she guessed Tay would need two and a half. She crushed them up with a mortar and pestle that Rosa kept in the utility drawer and dissolved the powder in the water.

She returned to Tay's bedroom, and he drained the glass when she held it to his lips.

"Can I get you anything else?" she said.

He shook his head. But when she moved for the door, he grabbed her wrist.

"Stay," he said.

She hesitated.

He drew her to him with surprising strength, and she finally relented, stretching out next to him on the bed.

"Sorry," he muttered as she settled her head on the pillow.

"For what?" There were so many things for both of them to be sorry about.

"What I said...about...pregnant." His voice was growing fainter, slightly slurred.

"Forget it. Just take it easy."

"Jealous," he sighed, his arm tightening around her.

"Jealous?"

"Of the father," he mumbled.

"Tay, there is no father, because there is no baby," Sharon said, turning her head to look at him.

He was asleep.

She let her head fall to his shoulder, being careful not to jostle his injured side, and soon she was asleep also.

When Sharon woke she didn't realize where she was at first. It was the middle of the night, the room was not her own, and there was somebody in bed with her.

In seconds her memory returned and with it the awareness that Tay was also stirring, pulling her into the curve of his body.

"Baby," he said, locking his hands over her stomach.

He was still obsessed with that idea and now doped to the gills to boot.

"Sh," Sharon said, aware that he didn't know what he was saying.

He pushed her flat on the bed and bent, placing his cheek next to her belly. Sharon didn't move, afraid to struggle with him and injure his side.

"Not my baby," he murmured. "Wouldn't want my baby."

His voice was so forlorn that Sharon was touched. Her heart was pounding as he wrapped his arms around her hips. He won't remember this in the morning, she told herself reassuringly.

"Don't love me anymore," he said, shaking his head. "Missed my chance."

What was he talking about? Sharon wondered, trying to piece together his ramblings.

"Should have done it then," he said and dropped his hands to her ankles, then ran them up her legs, under the hem of her gown.

Done what? she thought, panicked as he reached her thighs. She twisted away, closing her eyes. He doesn't know what's happening; you can't allow this, she told herself. But part of her did not want him to stop.

Suddenly he pinned her and rolled on top of her, pressing her into the mattress. She could feel him hard against her thighs; he may have been medicated, but he was far from incapable.

Sharon bit her lip in frustration. Why was it her luck to be in bed with this man only when he was half-asleep or drugged out of his mind? It wasn't fair.

"Love me now," he said. "Love me again." He kissed her, and she responded long enough for him to relax his hold. Then she pushed him off her and vaulted from the bed.

He stared at her hazily in the dark and rolled onto his side, breathing heavily. After a few moments his respiration slowed and became even.

Sharon shrank against the wall, her hand to her mouth. She waited until she was sure he was asleep again before she crept from the room.

Please don't let him remember it, she thought as she went across the hall to her own bedroom.

And please let me forget it, too.

Chapter 6

When Tay woke up in the morning, he had a dull head-ache and his side felt like it was on fire. His memory of the night before was foggy, but he knew he hadn't been drinking. He'd taken a beating but was sure he gave better than he got. It was the dreams that bothered him.

They were not the nightmares that tormented him when he first got out of the Army. He hadn't dreamed of the war in years; hard work and a purpose in life had managed to exorcise those demons. These dreams were about Sharon, and they remained with him in daylight, erotic wisps and snatches that tantalized with their very brevity. Images assaulted his consciousness as he rose and went to the bath-room, splashing cold water on his face. He remembered soft thighs under his hand, yielding flesh that was as smooth as milk. At least the pictures seemed like a memory, but he knew they couldn't be. He felt cheated and deprived.

He glanced at himself in the mirror over the sink and cringed; what woman would want to get into bed with this? He had a terminal case of five-o'clock shadow, his blue-black beard casting a sinister shadow on his jaws and chin. His fleshy lower lip, always a target in a fight, was split and scabbed. He washed his face gingerly and tried to put on a shirt, but his ribs protested. The damn things probably *were* broken, or at least cracked. They'd been broken before and had felt the same.

He left his room and went to the kitchen, where Rosa and Sharon were making breakfast. He took a cup of coffee from the pot and was attempting to beat a hasty retreat when Sharon said, "I made an appointment at the clinic in Glendora for you at ten. I'll drive you in to see the doctor."

Tay stared at her. "I'm not going to see any doctor."

"Yes, you are, and we're not going to argue about it. You were in so much pain last night that I had to slip you a mickey."

"A mickey?" he said, smiling slightly. She sounded as though she had stepped out of a Humphrey Bogart movie.

"I put pain pills in the drink I gave you." She poured cream into a pitcher and handed it to him.

He thought that over, adding a dollop of cream to his coffee and rubbing his side with his other hand. That explained the headache. Maybe the vivid dreams, too.

"I don't have time to go into town today," he said, trying again.

Both women looked at him.

"You're acting like an *idiota*, Tay," Rosa said sternly. "A broken rib can puncture a lung."

Tay glanced from one face to the other and knew he was outgunned.

"All right," he said reluctantly. "But I can only spare an hour."

"You'll spare whatever it takes," Rosa replied flatly. "Maybe you'll remember this little inconvenience before you get into your next fight."

"I think I've already had my last fight," he said, sitting down carefully at the kitchen table. "I'm getting too old."

"Huh," Rosa said. "I did think you were over this kind of thing, but it looks like you had a big lapse last night."

"It wasn't my fault," Tay said.

"It never is," Rosa replied, scrambling eggs.

"Some townspeople jumped him because he doesn't want to sell the ranch," Sharon explained. "They need the work the developers would bring."

"That's clever on the part of the developer, isn't it?" Rosa said. "If they can't persuade you to sell, they can spread the word about your refusal and get the locals to 'persuade' you for them."

"Do you think Citrus Farms paid them?" Sharon asked, listening.

Tay shook his head. "I don't think Morse would be dumb enough to do anything that could be traced. If one of them talked, the company would be in a lot of trouble. I think paying people to beat up other people is still against the law, isn't it?"

"Illegal contract, aggravated assault, civil and possibly criminal charges," Sharon said.

"Really?" Rosa said.

"There you go," Tay observed, jabbing his thumb in Sharon's direction. "Ask the answer man. Excuse me, woman." He stood and drained his cup. "I'll go clean up. I don't want to scare the doctor."

"The eggs are ready," Rosa said, turning from the stove.

He shook his head. "My gut is still rocking and rolling." He looked at Sharon. "Give me ten minutes," he said.

"Fine with me," she replied.

There was a silence in the kitchen after Tay left, and Sharon finally broke it by saying, "I never should have spoken to that man Morse."

"It might have happened anyway. The other company, Sun City, could be behind it."

"I still feel that talking to Morse added fuel to the fire.

He got the impression I wasn't decided yet, and that didn't help.'' Sharon sat disconsolately.

Rosa put a plate in front of her. Sharon surveyed it as if it were a pit of snakes.

"If you don't start to eat, there isn't going to be enough of you left to ship home in a thimble,'' Rosa said. "Tay is off his feed, too.'' She sighed dramatically. "It must be love.''

"It's aggravation,'' Sharon said.

"Or frustration,'' Rosa noted wisely.

Sharon ignored that as she picked up a piece of toast and nibbled on it.

"How is Pilar?'' she asked.

"She says she needs fifty dollars for her dance outfit for the summer recital,'' Rosa said. "I should tell you that this outfit includes items like a silver lamé spandex top and black satin tights.''

"I didn't know tights came in satin,'' Sharon said, trying not to laugh.

"She's making them herself. I just bought her new tap shoes last month. I'm going to have to take another job to keep that kid in equipment.''

"You have to make sacrifices for an artist in the family.''

"Yeah, well, when she's dancing at Radio City Music Hall I'm submitting a bill.''

They chatted until Tay walked back into the room. He had showered and shaved and combed his hair, but he still looked a little shaky.

"Ready?'' Sharon asked.

He nodded. They walked out to Dan's car together, and Sharon got behind the wheel as Tay slipped in beside her.

"I can drive,'' he said.

"I didn't know who your regular doctor was, so I just called the clinic,'' Sharon replied, ignoring his protest as she drove down the access road.

"I don't have a regular doctor," Tay said. "I haven't been to one in years."

"Don't you ever get sick?"

"Not often. When I do, I wait it out until it goes away."

"If everyone had your attitude, the medical profession would be bankrupt," Sharon said dryly.

"Did I say anything after you gave me those pills last night?" Tay inquired suddenly, looking over at her.

"What makes you ask that?" Sharon replied, stalling.

"I don't know," he said, frowning. "I'm kind of confused. It all seems like dreams."

"It probably was," Sharon said quickly. "The medicine really knocked you out fast."

He seemed to accept that and looked out the window broodingly for the rest of the trip. When they reached the clinic, Sharon parked and they went inside, where Tay gave his information at the window and then sat waiting restlessly, looking as if he were about to bolt any minute. The room was crowded, and he got up to pace several times, looking longingly at the door. Sharon was beginning to think he would leave regardless of what she said, when his name was finally called by the nurse.

He seemed to be in the doctor's office for an inordinately long time, and when he finally emerged, Sharon was able to determine why. The white-coated physician was with him. She was about thirty, with thick chestnut hair and large green eyes. She was wearing nonregulation high heels, and a blue silk dress showed beneath her jacket.

They were deep in conversation, and Sharon felt sure it had nothing to do with cracked ribs. Tay finally tore himself away from his medical adviser and came through the door, a prescription slip in his hand.

"So?" Sharon said to him.

"She taped them for me. Hairline fractures, she said."

"Gee, she developed the X rays right there, huh?" Sharon said.

"Yeah, they can do that now," Tay said, staring at her.

"For special patients?" Sharon asked.

"For everybody. What's the matter with you?"

"I've been waiting almost an hour, that's what's the matter with me," Sharon replied irritably.

"I'm sorry it took so long. When I told her I hadn't seen a doctor in a while, she gave me a thorough exam."

"I'll bet," Sharon said under her breath.

"What?"

"That's good. Do you have to get that filled?"

He nodded.

"Did she say anything about curtailing your work schedule?" Sharon asked suspiciously.

He didn't answer.

"Tay. I'll call and ask her myself."

"She told me I can't lift or do heavy work for a week," Tay replied unhappily.

"I'll see that you follow that directive," Sharon said.

He looked at her as they left the office. "How do you propose to do that?" he asked.

"I have my ways."

"Gonna sit on me?"

"If I have to."

"I'm looking forward to it," he said, smiling, and she let that pass.

They stopped at a pharmacy in town to fill his prescription, and on the way out Tay said, "Do you want to have lunch? There's a good place around the corner."

"All right," Sharon said, wondering about the invitation. He had made a science of avoiding her since her arrival, and she suspected that there was an ulterior motive for his sudden chumminess.

The hostess in the restaurant knew Tay, and they bantered amiably as she seated them. They had ordered and were waiting for the waitress when Tay said, "There's a zoning meeting tonight."

This is it, Sharon thought. "And?" she said.

"I'd like you to come with me."

"Why?"

"I want you to see how many people are opposed to bringing the developers into our area. The streets would have to be rezoned residential for the houses, and they're going to debate the question in an open session."

"What's the zoning now?"

"Residential business. That means you live where you run the business, and both take place on the same lot."

"I know," Sharon said gently.

"But if it's rezoned strictly residential, then all the ranchers will be driven out. We won't be able to keep horses or livestock at all."

"I see."

He toyed with his napkin. "I'm afraid the developers are going to grease a few palms to get their plans through. They have a lot of money, and they stand to make a lot more."

"The developers won't be able to get anywhere if all the ranchers stand together."

"*If* they do," Tay said. "Money talks. You were listening."

"I was considering," Sharon corrected him.

"How do you feel now?" he asked, not looking at her, as if he were afraid to see her answer in her face.

"I think I would find it hard to do business with anyone who engaged in the kind of practices you're describing," Sharon said.

"I can't prove anything," Tay said, raising his eyes.

"I saw the condition you were in last night," Sharon said. "I didn't imagine that."

"You heard Rosa. The townies may have taken it upon themselves to rough me up."

"Do you believe that?" Sharon asked him.

"No," he said as the waitress delivered their orders.

"Neither do I," Sharon said, digging into her chicken salad. "Why do you think they picked on you?"

"I'm kind of perceived as the ringleader of the ranchers who are holding out," he answered, taking a bite of his sandwich.

"Perceived?" Sharon said, arching her brows.

"Okay. I am the ringleader."

"How many ranchers are we talking about?" Sharon asked.

"About fifteen in the county, but I'm the only one in Glendora. They're offering the most for our property, too."

"That doesn't surprise me, it's the closest to L.A.," Sharon observed.

"So you'll come tonight?"

Sharon nodded.

"Thanks."

The waitress returned and said, "Everything all right?"

"Fine," Tay said.

She winked at him and favored him with a sidelong smile.

"Another member of your fan club?" Sharon asked archly when she left.

"Never saw her before in my life," Tay replied, deadpan.

"We hardly had time to pick up our forks before she came back," Sharon said. "Usually you have to send out a search party to get your waitress once she's delivered the food."

"Maybe she's conscientious," Tay said, shrugging.

Sharon studied him a moment and said quietly, "My arrival has really cut into your social life, hasn't it?"

He didn't answer, taking a sip of his drink.

"It must be hard for you, pretending to be married."

"I am married," he replied. "I've got the paper to prove it."

"You know what I mean. Pretending to be in love with me."

"That's not such a stretch," he said.

"No?" Sharon murmured.

"People believe it," he went on. "I mean if you were sixty or ugly or something, it would be different, but this way, it's not difficult to pull off."

"Oh." She hesitated and then added, "But you can't see other women while I'm here."

"You won't be here forever," he answered flatly.

"Right," Sharon agreed. She sighed and said, "I guess you're anxious for this to be over."

"Aren't you?" he countered.

"Sure," Sharon said lifelessly.

Something in her tone must have alerted him, because he looked up at her. Their gazes met and held.

"Would you like anything else?" he said.

"Pardon?"

"Anything else to eat? Dessert?"

Sharon shook her head.

"Then let's go."

They rose together and Tay paid the bill.

As they left, Sharon saw the waitress looking after them.

As they drove to the Glendora municipal building that evening, a rainstorm was gathering. The sycamore and pepper trees bent in the wind, and dead palm fronds rattled to the pavement with every gust. By the time they pulled into a parking space, droplets the size of dimes were splattering on the windshield, and they ran inside through a welcome shower that hit the parched earth and was absorbed instantly as if by a sponge.

The turnout for the meeting was large, and the developers spoke first. Rain thundered on the roof as one of Morse's colleagues told how Citrus Farms was going to transform the San Gabriel Valley into the Garden of Eden.

To their credit, the ranchers sat in stoic silence and let him talk; there were no boos or catcalls, but no applause, either. When the chairman of the city council asked to hear from the Ranchers' Association, Tay stood up to a round of encouraging comments from his neighbors.

"I've been ranching in this county for ten years," Tay said. "And I'm opposed to the rezoning for the developments, and I'll tell you why."

Sharon sat at his side, listening.

"All the open country around here is getting swallowed up," he said. "Time was when you could drive from one spread to another and tell where one left off and the other began only from the color of the fences," he went on. "Now the housing developments are carving the West Coast into sections like a paring knife slicing into fruit. There's going to be no place left for the animals or for the people who tend them."

The ranchers nodded and murmured approval.

"Those people have to live somewhere, Mr. Braddock," the Citrus man said.

"They don't have to live here," Tay shot back.

"Braddock has the floor," the council chairman said mildly.

"Tell them what happened to you last night, Tay," someone in the back called out.

Tay ignored that and went on, talking of his love for the land and his respect for the area people who made a living on it. His speech was simple but eloquent, straight from the heart, and Sharon was moved by his obvious sincerity.

So was his audience. When the time came for a poll, the rezoning plan was defeated.

"Is that the end?" Sharon asked Tay as his friends came up to congratulate him.

He shook his head. "No way. They'll resubmit their plan and put it to a general referendum as soon as they can. This just stalls them off a little. But every bit helps."

"Why were they so eager to buy our place when they don't even know if they'll get the rezoning?" Sharon asked.

"They know," he replied. "Or they think they know. It's called confidence. They're confident they'll pay off or buy out whoever they have to in order to make this work. They've done it before elsewhere, I understand. They'll regard this as a setback, but hardly a defeat."

"A formidable opponent," Sharon said.

"Yes," Tay said evenly. "But so am I."

It was still raining hard when they left, and the townspeople delighted in the rare spectacle of an honest-to-goodness thunderstorm.

"You'd think they'd never seen rain before," Sharon marveled as they went back to the car.

"They don't see much of it," Tay replied.

"You were really impressive in there," Sharon said as they backed out onto the road.

"I just said what I felt."

"You said it very well."

"I feel like Peter putting my finger in the dike," he said, squinting through the streaming windshield. "What I did wasn't enough, but it's a start."

"Are you sure you should be driving?" Sharon asked nervously. She could hardly see a thing, and he was still favoring his side.

"I'm fine. I don't see how holding a steering wheel can affect my ribs."

He negotiated the return trip, and they dashed back into the house as forks of lightning split the sky. Sharon took off her wet raincoat and was shaking out her damp hair when Tay said, "I was surprised. You seemed one hundred percent with the ranchers."

He was wiping his damp face with the back of his hand. Touched by the eloquence of his plea at the meeting and feeling guilty about her meeting with Citrus Farms, Sharon faced him and said quietly, "I don't want to sell the ranch, Tay. I never did."

He stared at her, speechless. After a moment he recovered and said, "Then what was all that pussyfooting around with Morse?"

Sharon hesitated. Seconds passed, and then he held up his hand.

"No, wait a minute," he said. "I get it." He took a step forward, his dark eyes blazing. "It's really important to hurt me, isn't it?"

"Tay..."

"You despise me, don't you?"

"I don't despise you...."

But there was no stopping him now.

"That's the real reason you came back here, isn't it? The will provided you with an excuse to return and make me pay, get me back for what happened when you were a kid."

Sharon was silent. She wanted to contradict him, but there was an element of truth in what he was saying. He had hurt her deeply back then, and she hadn't been able to explain even to herself why she'd made it look as though she was entertaining Morse's offer.

"And when Sun City gets in touch with you, I guess you'll keep them on a string, too, to make me squirm a little more," he said softly.

She shook her head. "No, I'm calling Mr. Morse in the morning. I'll tell him and Sun City that I'm not interested."

"Oh, thank you so much. What caused this sudden change of heart? Is the lady of the manor taking pity on the lowly retainer begging to hang on to his parcel of land? Is this the same lady who walked away from the retainer without a backward glance or a word passing between them in all this time?"

"Tay, don't do this," Sharon said quietly, pained by the depth of the bitterness in his voice. She wasn't the only one harboring resentments through the years.

"You must really hate me," he said quietly.

"No," she whispered, her voice trembling.

"And the funny thing is, there's no need for it," he went on, his tone tinged with irony. "You think I rejected you that night in the bunkhouse." His eyes moved over her face, and she fancied she could feel their burning touch. "You'll never know how much I wanted you to stay."

She shook her head blindly, her eyes filling with tears. "You told me to go back to school, you said you responded to me the way you had to the whores in Saigon," she sobbed.

"What a memory. As it happens, I remember every word of that little speech, too. I've heard it drumming in my head ever since." He moved forward and took her arms, holding her fast when she struggled. "Don't you see that I had to say something bad enough to make you go?" he demanded roughly. "I had to get you to leave right then, or I would have begged you to stay."

Sharon stared up at him, tears running down her face.

"I don't believe you," she whispered. She wanted to believe him, desperately, madly, but the memory of that brutal rejection was too vivid in her mind.

"It's the truth," he said huskily, catching a tear on the end of his thumb. "Baby, it's the truth. I had never wanted any woman the way I wanted you that night." He closed his eyes, then opened them. "And I never have again," he added. "Until now."

She tried to say his name, but he bent his head and kissed her, stopping her mouth with his.

This time there was no audience and no pretense that they were performing for one. His clothes were damp and so were hers, and the heat of their bodies blazed through them as they embraced. He dropped his hand to her blouse and unbuttoned it as his mouth moved down her neck and on to the cleft between her breasts, his tongue leaving a trail of fire on her rain-cooled flesh. He tried to unhook her bra, but his fingers were shaking and clumsy, so he ripped it in frustration, making a sound of satisfaction low in his throat as his lips closed over a swollen nipple. Sharon gasped, then sighed, barely able to stand as he suckled one breast and then the other, binding her to him with one arm, as with his free hand he searched for the hem of her skirt. He found it, and his rough palm trailed over her bare thigh. He lifted her suddenly, backing to the wall and forcing her to lock her legs around his hips. She felt him hard and ready against her, with only the thin barrier of their light summer cottons between them, and she whimpered restlessly, eager for more.

They were so lost in each other that it was a while before they heard the pounding on the outer door. Tay finally raised his head and muttered, ''What's that? Do you hear that?''

''Someone's knocking,'' Sharon replied shakily.

''In this weather?'' He set her down gently and waited for her to arrange her clothes before he went through the hall, tucking in his own shirt, and opened the door.

Carlo Perez, one of the hired hands, was standing on the porch.

''Lightning,'' he shouted over the noise of the wind and rain. ''Hit the main stable. It's on fire.''

Chapter 7

"Did you call the fire department?" Tay yelled to Carlo as he dashed through the door.

"First thing."

Tay disappeared, calling back to Sharon, "Stay here."

Sharon ignored him and followed on his heels, trailing the two men at a safe distance. It wasn't difficult to stay behind them; they were running full out and she was hampered by a full skirt and heels. Hibiscus and jacaranda whipped against her legs, the shining leaves cold and wet, as she circled the house in the thinning rain.

The roof of the stable was ablaze, spewing a funnel of thick smoke. But as the rain tailed off, the flames increased, and it was clear that the storm wouldn't last long enough to put out the fire.

As Sharon got closer to the stable she could hear the fearful noise the horses were making; they could smell the smoke even though they couldn't see the fire spreading from the roof.

Tay and Carlo were pulling open the double wooden

doors, and as she watched, they ran to and fro, leading the stamping, frightened animals from the barn. Melody was the last to emerge, and Sharon could see that she was veering out of control, bucking wildly, her eyes rolling with terror. Tay was dragging on the tether, trying to handle her. He finally gave up and leaped onto her, riding bareback, digging in his heels and urging her forward with his head bent low, his mouth almost against the horse's ear. She responded and Tay rode her out, letting her jump a couple of fences until she wound down, trotting to a halt almost at Sharon's feet.

"I thought I told you to stay in the house," Tay said to her as he tied the horse to a tree. They could hear fire engines screaming in the distance, coming closer.

"I was worried, I wanted to see what happened."

Tay took her by the shoulders and looked down into her eyes. "Sharon, read my lips. I know you've made up your mind never to listen to a thing I say, but this is important. I don't want you to get hurt. This fire could spread. Now go back to the house and stay there. If you want to help, make coffee for the firemen. They're going to need it when they're through with this."

Sharon obeyed reluctantly and then compromised by standing on the back terrace to watch while the two engines attacked the fire with powerful streams of water. The rain had stopped, but droplets clung to all the plants and shrubs, bejeweling the foliage. A crescent moon emerged to hang over the landscape, veiled by smoke at first but becoming more visible as the fire subsided. The crews worked steadily to subdue the blaze, and after a few minutes Sharon went inside to make the coffee.

It was almost an hour before the men started coming to the house for refreshments. They kept her busy dispensing drinks in the Styrofoam cups Rosa stocked, until only one man remained behind while his colleagues returned to their truck.

Sharon glanced at him, lounging in the kitchen in his soot-stained clothes, and she looked at the clock. It was after one in the morning.

"Is there something else I can get for you?" Sharon asked the fireman.

He shook his head, taking a last sip of his coffee. "So you're the new missus, huh?" he said.

"That's right," Sharon replied, wondering how many times she was going to have this conversation.

"We heard down at the firehouse that Tay got married. None of us could believe it."

Sharon smiled vaguely, waiting for him to get on with the rest of it.

"Tay and I used to hoist a few together, back in his heavy drinking days," the fireman said. "He said he was burned once real bad, years ago, and I really thought that would put him off women forever."

"Is that right?" Sharon said, listening closely now.

The fireman seemed to realize that he might be telling tales out of school and said, "Hey, maybe this is classified stuff and I should shut up. I'm Rob Harris, by the way."

Sharon shook his extended hand. "Don't be silly, Rob. I'm aware of my husband's checkered past."

"Oh, then you know that girl Sharon really blew him out of the water."

Rob was looking for a place to put his empty cup, or he would have noticed the stunned expression on Sharon's face. She recovered and turned away from him, saying quietly, "I heard something about it. What did he tell you?"

Rob shrugged. "Not much. Enough to let me know he couldn't forget her. He was drunk that night and never mentioned her again. He just said that she was younger, a kid really, and came into his life at a bad time. He let her go and he was always sorry about it."

"Why didn't he go after her later?" Sharon asked softly.

"Like I said, he only talked about it the one time. Maybe she married somebody else or something."

"She didn't," Sharon said.

Rob looked at her.

"I'm Sharon."

A huge grin split his grimy face. "You been having me on, huh?"

"A little," she admitted.

"Well, I'm sure glad you guys worked it out," Rob said. "I can't wait to go and talk to old Tay—"

"Uh, Rob, don't say anything to him, please," Sharon said, interrupting with her most potent smile. "We wouldn't want to embarrass him or anything. He might feel funny if he knew we were discussing him behind his back."

"Okay," Rob said agreeably. "Anything for a beautiful lady." He looked out the window ruefully. "I'd better go. They're going to be packing up the hoses."

"It was nice meeting you," Sharon said to him.

"Same here. Good night, Sharon." He winked.

"Good night."

Sharon cleaned up the kitchen mechanically after he left, almost in a daze. She would never have believed that some casual remarks from a semistranger could provoke such a reaction within her, but she felt that everything had changed.

Tay had wanted her and regretted letting her go. She had guessed it, hoped it, wondered about it during recent weeks, but now she was sure. Tay would have no reason to lie to his drinking buddy, especially while under the influence. Liquor had loosened Tay's tongue, causing the buried truth to emerge.

About half an hour later Sharon heard the fire trucks leaving, and shortly after that Tay came back to the house. He was as filthy as the firemen, his hair damp, his face beaded with sweat.

"Fire's out," he announced. "We'll need a new roof,

but we saved the stable. The horses are bedded down in the other barns.''

"Tay, sit right here," Sharon said firmly. "You've been overdoing it. You just had that fight and your ribs aren't healed.''

He sat. "I'm all right," he said wearily, closing his eyes.

"I can see that," she replied dryly. She filled a cup with the last of the black coffee and put it in front of him.

"Drink that," she said.

He raised the mug obediently to his lips and grimaced at its bitterness.

"It's old," Sharon explained. "I'll make some fresh."

He shook his head. "Don't bother. I'm just going to turn in, I think." He stood, then sat down again, hard, looking puzzled.

"What is it?" Sharon asked.

"Little tired, I guess," Tay mumbled, rubbing his forehead.

"I'll bet you are," Sharon said grimly. But in a way she was glad for his distraction; she was feeling very nervous around him after her conversation with Rob Harris, but Tay was too exhausted to notice.

"I'll turn down your bed for you," Sharon said. "Just wait here until I come back."

He didn't reply, but he also didn't look as though he was going to move. Sharon hurried down the hall and entered his sparsely decorated room. She went over to his bed, pulled the plaid spread down, folded it and placed it at the foot. There was a light summer blanket covering a muslin sheet, and she turned them down invitingly.

She was gone no more than two minutes, but by the time she got back to the kitchen Tay was asleep in the chair.

She shook his shoulder gently. His eyelids lifted and he stared at her groggily.

"Time for bed," she said.

He nodded and stood, and she walked with him down

the hall. He sat on the edge of the bed with his hands between his knees as she tugged off his shoes.

"You're making a habit of this," he said.

"What?"

"Putting me to bed."

"Well, if you'd take better care of yourself, I wouldn't have to do it all the time."

"I had to fight the fire," he mumbled.

"I thought that's what the firemen were supposed to do," Sharon replied, unbuttoning his shirt.

"They did a great job, saved the stable," he said, yawning and shrugging out of the sleeves.

"I met some of them at the house. I talked to your old friend Rob Harris."

Tay smiled slightly. "How is Rob? I haven't seen him in a while."

"He's fine. He was surprised to hear you were married."

"No more surprised than we were, huh?" Tay said, looking at her candidly.

Sharon put a forefinger against his shoulder and pushed. He fell back against the pillows, grabbing for her wrist.

She eluded him, and as he sat up again, she slipped quickly through the door.

"Go to sleep," she said sternly, shutting off the light and pulling the door closed behind her. She listened for a few moments to see if he would come after her, but within seconds his breathing was deep and even.

Sharon went back to the kitchen.

She couldn't sleep for the rest of the night. She was sitting at the kitchen table, still wearing the clothes she had donned for the zoning meeting, when Rosa walked through the door at eight o'clock in the morning.

"I heard about the excitement here last night," she said, putting her purse on the counter. "I was going to come over, but then the report came that the fire was under control, so I figured I could wait until morning.'' She examined Sharon. ''Have you got an early appointment?''

''I never went to bed.''

''Why not? Fire engines kept you awake?''

Sharon shook her head. ''No, they were gone by one-thirty. But I did have a conversation with one of the firemen that gave me a lot to think about last night.''

''Which one?''

''Rob Harris. Slim. Sandy hair.''

Rosa nodded. ''I know him. Pilar once had a crush on his brother. But that's not exactly an exclusive club. Pilar once had a crush on everybody's brother. What did Rob say?''

''He said he used to go drinking with Tay.''

''Another less-than-exclusive club,'' Rosa commented acerbically, folding her arms.

Sharon ignored that and went on. ''Apparently one time when they were out together, Tay got drunk and started talking about a girl from his past.''

''Uh-huh,'' Rosa said, rattling pans.

''Tay said he could never forget this girl and always regretted letting her go.''

''Let me guess,'' Rosa said, assuming an air of concentration. ''The girl was you.''

Sharon stared at her. ''How did you know?''

''I'm psychic,'' Rosa said sarcastically. She dropped a pot into the sink and turned to confront Sharon. ''You know, I don't care how many degrees you have, you are the stupidest woman I ever met.''

Sharon's mouth fell open with shock.

''You needed Rob Harris to tell you that? You couldn't figure it out for yourself?''

''Rosa,'' Sharon protested.

Rosa was silent.

''I told you what happened back then, I told you what Tay said to me…''

Rosa held up a hand to forestall any further commentary. "I don't want to hear that. He didn't mean it when he said it, and it doesn't matter anymore anyway. All I have to say is that if you blow it again this time, you'll have no one to blame but yourself." She picked up the pot, which she had just dried, shoved it into a cabinet and marched out of the room.

Well, Sharon thought, stunned by Rosa's outburst. What does she expect me to do? Throw myself at the man's feet? Feeling slightly annoyed with Rosa's attitude and fuzzy with her own lack of sleep, she went down to her room to shower and dress.

When she emerged twenty minutes later, Rosa was dusting furiously, still in high dudgeon, and the door to Tay's room was ajar. Sharon pushed it inward, suspecting that the housekeeper had checked on him, and Sharon decided to do the same.

He was lying on his back, his lips slightly parted, the surgical tape on his ribs contrasting with his tanned skin. Sharon was reminded of the night she found him sleeping in the bunkhouse, Endymion slumbering on his hillside, waiting for Diana to pass in her chariot of moonlight. He was older now but still much the same, still beautiful, still the most desirable man she had ever met. Was Rosa right? Sharon wondered, tucking the sheet more closely about his waist. Did she have their fate in her hands at last? She stood looking at him for a moment more and tiptoed out of the room.

"I have some shopping to do in Glendora," Sharon said to Rosa as she passed.

Rosa nodded, not looking at her.

Sharon took the car and spent a couple of hours in the stores, buying some personal items, and returned just after noon. She came into the kitchen and called, "Anybody home?"

Rosa entered from the hall, looking worried.

"Is Tay okay?" Sharon said.

Rosa looked more worried.

"What is it? Is he ill?"

"He's not here," Rosa said.

"Well, where is he?"

"In jail," Rosa replied, shrugging helplessly.

"In jail!" Sharon said incredulously. "He's sleeping when I leave, I'm gone for two hours, and when I come back he's in jail? What on earth happened?"

"I told him to wait for you, but he wouldn't."

"Wait for me to do what?" Sharon asked, trying to absorb it.

"The insurance adjuster came right after you left," Rosa explained. "Tay got up and went out to the stable with him. The insurance man looked at the stable roof and said the company would only pay ten thousand to replace it. Well, that's a new roof, Tay had it put on a year and a half ago for fifteen. They got into quite a dispute about it, and Tay wound up punching him."

Sharon rubbed her forehead. "Let me understand this. Tay wanted five thousand more than the company man said the roof was worth, so Tay handled the argument by decking the guy?"

"That's about it," Rosa said uncomfortably.

"Why am I surprised?" Sharon murmured to herself, shaking her head wearily.

"The insurance man was furious, he marched straight in here and called the police," Rosa said. "He's charging Tay with assault. The cops came and took Tay away in a squad car. He's in the municipal lockup right now."

"Oh, God, I can't stand this," Sharon said. "What's his bail?"

"It wasn't set yet when I called."

Sharon sighed. "I'll go down there and try to straighten this out. Rosa, I'm sorry you had to be here for it."

"Don't worry about me, I was just afraid somebody was

going to get hurt. I wish Tay would think before he reacted so physically."

"Amen," Sharon murmured. She glanced at her watch. "I'll have to stop off at the bank and get some money. I doubt if the bail will be more than five hundred for simple assault, but I'll get some extra money just in case."

"There was nothing simple about it," Rosa said darkly.

"The jail is right behind the municipal building, isn't it?" Sharon said, fishing around in her bag for her wallet, which contained her bar association card.

Rosa nodded. "Do you want me to come with you?"

Sharon shook her head. "I can handle it. I'll call you if there's any problem."

Sharon hurried out to the car and drove back to town, pulling into the lot of the municipal building and walking around to the jail. A uniformed clerk looked up desultorily as she entered through the double glass doors.

"I'm here to post bail for one of your detainees," she said.

The woman jerked her head toward the rear of the room. "See the desk sergeant."

The desk sergeant was seated on a raised platform from which he surveyed the world like a ruling despot on a throne. He fixed Sharon with a gimlet stare as she approached.

"Something I can do for you, young lady?" he drawled.

"I'd like to post bail for Taylor Braddock," she announced.

The sergeant, whose name was Brady, shuffled through a pile of papers on his blotter. "Braddock, Taylor," he recited. "Assault and battery, civil complaint filed by one Steven Caldwell of 10 Elmhurst Street, Upton. Braddock's hearing is in two weeks on the tenth, 11:00 a.m. Six hundred and fifty dollars, please."

Everything was more expensive in California, Sharon thought as she got the money out of her purse.

"Cash?" Brady said.

Sharon handed the pile of greenbacks to him. He counted it with the precision of a bank teller; he obviously loved his job.

"And you are?" he said, his ballpoint poised above a form.

"His lawyer."

"ID?" The sergeant asked.

Sharon presented her bar card and driver's license.

"These are from Pennsylvania," Brady said.

"Yes, I know," Sharon said patiently. "I've only been out here a short time and…"

Brady waited.

"Look, I don't have to be admitted to the California bar to get him out of jail," Sharon said firmly. "Can we proceed with this?"

"Your name is Sharon Philips," Brady said, copying it precisely onto his form.

"Sharon Philips…Braddock."

"A relative?" Brady asked, noticing her hesitation about the name.

"I'm his wife. Legally." Sharon winced inwardly after she added the last word. Why had she said that? Cops hated lawyers.

"Is there any other way?" Brady asked, raising his bushy brows. "Spiritually? Metaphysically?"

"We're married," Sharon said flatly.

"So you're his lawyer and his wife? Isn't that a—what do you call it—conflict of interest?"

"Are you writing a book, Sergeant Brady?" Sharon demanded. "You have the money right here. Just let me sign the papers now and get him out of here."

Brady scribbled on his forms and pushed them across the desk for her signature. As she wrote, he pressed a button on the house mike at his elbow and said in a bored tone, "Bring Braddock up, his bail's in."

Sharon was tucking her license back into her wallet when Tay appeared, escorted by a female officer. He looked extremely pained when he saw her.

"Personal effects," Brady said, handing Sharon an envelope containing Tay's watch and billfold, and some other items that rattled when she took it. Tay walked past her and stopped by the desk.

"I'm free to go?" he said.

Sergeant Brady raised his hand and made a tightfisted gesture of farewell, like a baby waving bye-bye.

"That guy thinks he's a comedian," Tay muttered as they walked to the door.

"I noticed," Sharon said. When they were outside, she turned to face him.

"All right," he sighed. "Let me have it."

"Let's go across the way into the coffee shop," Sharon said tersely. "I don't want to make a scene in the street."

"Oh, I agree," he said, keeping pace with her. "Making a scene in a restaurant is preferable any day."

Sharon ignored that and waited until they were seated in a booth before saying, "Tay, I never want to bail you out of jail again. If this is the way you plan to handle your problems, in future I suggest you retain the services of somebody else."

"As lawyer or wife?" he countered.

"Very funny. You should work up a routine with Sergeant Brady, should be good for a few laughs."

"Are you going to let me explain?"

"Rosa already told me what happened. You got a low estimate on the roof replacement and responded by decking the insurance agent."

"That's not exactly how it went."

Sharon surveyed him with exaggerated tolerance. "Are you suggesting that Rosa lied to me?"

He shook his head. "She only told you what I told her. But it wasn't the whole story."

"So?" Sharon said.

"Crisp as lettuce, aren't we?" Tay said dryly.

"I'm waiting."

"I didn't want to go into it in front of the two cops," Tay said. "They were standing there listening to me when I talked to Rosa."

"I'm still waiting."

"The guy made a crack about us, okay?" Tay said tightly.

"Us?" Sharon said uncomprehendingly.

"Us. As in you and me."

Sharon closed her eyes. "Doesn't anyone around here ever talk about anything else?"

"Apparently not. When he told me he would only give me ten grand for the roof, I said it wasn't enough. I wanted to go into the house and get the bill for the roof replacement I had done just a year ago, but he said he couldn't understand why I was worried about money. After all, I had just married you to get the ranch, and with all you were worth, a bill for the roof was a drop in the bucket. That's when I hit him."

"Oh."

"He went nuts and ran back to the house, screaming that he was calling the cops. By then I felt like a jackass about it, and so I just waited for the police to show up and went along to the station."

"I didn't realize we were so famous," Sharon murmured.

Tay shrugged. "The ranchers in the valley are a closed community. I guess this guy had been hearing the gossip." He shook his head. "I shouldn't have reacted that way, but our...uh...situation is kind of a sore subject with me."

Sharon merely looked at him.

He met her gaze and glanced away.

"Was he hurt?" Sharon asked.

"Nah. I didn't hit him that hard. His pride was damaged

more than anything. He didn't see it coming, and it landed him in the dirt in a rather undignified position.''

"How nice," Sharon said evenly. "I'm so sorry I missed it."

"So you're pretty mad at me, huh?"

"Whatever gave you that idea?"

He fiddled with the packets of sugar in the metal stand on the table. "Look, Sharon, I know you think I'm a hothead..."

"No!" she said, feigning astonished disagreement.

He held up his hand. "Let me finish. I've been trying, I really have. But can you imagine how it makes me feel when I'm reminded that everyone knows why you married me? I see the look on their faces, the tone of their voices. They might as well say that a woman like you wouldn't have me, gilded, except for your father's will. I know what they're thinking."

"Oh, Tay, we've been over this before. You're too sensitive."

"It wasn't a thin skin that caused me to react today," he said quietly. "That insurance agent was pretty direct."

"Can't you overlook that sort of remark?"

He dropped his eyes. "Not when it's true," he said quietly, his expression grim.

The waitress arrived to take their order. Sharon, nonplussed by his last statement, asked for coffee. Tay nodded that he would have the same. The woman left.

"Tay," Sharon said guardedly, "I don't think this is working out."

His head came up sharply. "What do you mean?"

"I seem to have brought you nothing but trouble. Maybe I should just go back to Philadelphia. I don't have to stay here for us to inherit the ranch. It will come to us as soon as the will is probated, and then I can file for divorce in absentia."

His face became veiled, withdrawn. "Is that what you want?" he said flatly after a long pause.

She shrugged. "We're just torturing each other this way, creating uncomfortable circumstances. Don't you agree with me?"

"Whatever you say." He wouldn't look at her.

"Do you want me to stay here?" she asked directly.

"I want you to do whatever suits you," he replied, his tone deliberate.

The coffee arrived and they stared at the cups morosely, equally miserable.

"Will you take me to the airport if I book a flight?" Sharon ventured at length in a small voice.

"I'll take you wherever you want to go," he answered, staring past her head.

"Good."

They pretended they were interested in their drinks a little while longer, and then they got up and left.

Rosa was sipping tea in the kitchen as they entered by the back door. She looked up apprehensively and said to Tay, "Are you out of jail for good?"

"I'm out on bail," he said. "I have to appear for a hearing."

The two women exchanged glances.

"I'm glad it was no worse," Rosa said.

"It was bad enough," Sharon said darkly.

"Nothing like Army jails," Tay said, shaking his head.

"Did you spend a lot of time in jail when you were in the Army?" Sharon asked archly.

"I did a couple of turns in basic training," he replied. "After that I learned that Uncle Sam is always right, and we got along just fine." He scratched the back of his neck. "And to tell you the truth, after the prison camp, nothing else seems like jail to me. The Glendora lockup is a country club by comparison."

Neither woman answered, and he walked through the kitchen and into the hall. Seconds later they heard his door close.

"I can't tell you what a wonderful time I've been having today," Sharon said dully, sliding into the chair across from Rosa.

"Tay doesn't look any happier than you do."

"I'm thinking about going back to Philadelphia," Sharon said bluntly.

"What?" Rosa said, sitting up straight.

"You heard me."

"So you're just going to give up on him?" Rosa demanded.

"Rosa, what can I do? You see what's happening. Today he wound up in jail because of me."

"He wound up in jail because he has a bad temper. He'll still have a bad temper if you leave, and you know that. What's the real reason?"

"I can't stand it," Sharon whispered.

"You can't stand what?"

"Being around him all the time. Seeing him, hearing him, and knowing that it will all end. The longer I remain, the worse it will be when I finally get the divorce and have to leave."

"Who says you have to leave?"

"Do you think I would stay here and continue this... farce?"

Rosa put her hand on Sharon's arm. "Go to him. Talk to him."

Sharon shook her head mutely. "I still have some pride left. I'm going to gather the shreds of it around me and go home."

"Your home is where Tay is," Rosa said.

Sharon shook her head, tears gathering in her eyes. "I hoped I could make that come true, but all I've done is cause problems."

"Sharon, I know he wants you."

Sharon nodded slowly. "I believe that now, but it's not enough. He wanted me ten years ago, but even then I brought out the worst in him. And it's happening again. Can't you see that?"

"No. I see a man who's in pain because he's afraid, quite rightly, that it will not work out between you. Again."

Sharon didn't answer.

"Think about it," Rosa added. "And don't go anywhere, don't do anything without talking to me."

"Fine, Rosa, but—"

"No buts," Rosa said firmly, putting her teacup in the sink. "I'll see you tomorrow."

Tay emerged from his room as Rosa was leaving. He had changed to a T-shirt and cords with chukka boots.

"I thought you weren't going to work until your ribs healed," Sharon said to him.

"Jensen's coming over to deliver a colt," he replied tersely. "I'm not going to do anything strenuous."

"See that you don't," Rosa said in parting, and he followed her out the door.

Sharon tried to busy herself putting away the morning's purchases and straightening the house, but Rosa had left very little for her to do. Her mind was racing, and after being so busy for so long in Philadelphia, she found leisure time almost a chore. The afternoon dragged on, and when Tay didn't return by dinnertime, Sharon wrapped a sandwich in waxed paper and went to look for him. She had a notion that his idea of strenuous did not exactly coincide with hers, and she wanted to make sure he wasn't overdoing it.

The sun was still bright and hot, though descending toward the horizon, as she made her way back to the small ancillary barn the hands used for veterinary work. As she walked through the door, she could see that something was wrong.

Tay was kneeling in one of the stalls on a stained mess of hay, his arms and hands covered with gore and blood. Miguel knelt next to him, and they were both trying to assist the straining mare in her delivery. She was shivering and groaning, her coat matted with sweat, her eyes large with pain and fear.

"What is it?" Sharon asked, leaning over the half wall of the stall.

"Breech," Tay answered, gasping as he struggled with the horse. "Can't turn the colt."

"Where's George Jensen?" she said.

"An emergency delayed him," Miguel replied. "He's on his way."

"This looks like an emergency to me," Sharon said, walking around to stand behind them. Tay's face was weary, and his shirt was stuck to his back with sweat. It was clear they had been at this for a while to no avail.

"Let me take your place," Sharon said, crouching next to Tay.

He glanced at her. "You don't have the strength to do this."

"Neither do you, anymore. You look about played out. Now show me what to do."

Tay must have been as tired as he looked, because he obeyed. He moved over to demonstrate how to manipulate the horse's lower abdomen in concert with Miguel to try to get the colt into proper position. She was just getting the hang of it, as Tay looked on, when George Jensen burst through the door, his bag in hand.

"Out of the way," he said brusquely as Sharon gladly gave up the field to the expert.

"How long has this been going on?" George said to Tay.

"Hard labor for about three hours," Tay replied, and they fell into an anatomical discussion Sharon couldn't follow. She went over to the far wall and retrieved a grooming rag from a nail to wipe her hands, feeling weak and drained.

She could only imagine how Tay felt after his long ordeal with the horse. She turned as he came up behind her and put his hand on her shoulder.

"Thanks for the help," he said quietly.

"Will the mare be all right now?"

He nodded. "I think so. George has handled this type of thing hundreds of times."

"Tay, you really look beat. Let's go back to the house. George will call there if he needs you."

He went along without protest.

The sun was setting in a sky streaked with orange and lilac and red, and a silvery-white slice of new moon rose behind it, pale and ethereal. A fresh breeze came up, ruffling Sharon's damp hair, and as they passed the main stable with its blackened roof, Tay said, "I guess that fire wound up costing me more than I thought."

"You mean to fix the damage?"

"Not exactly," he replied, but when Sharon looked at him quizzically, he wouldn't elaborate.

They went into the house and Tay said, "I'm going to get cleaned up, I'll take a shower."

"Would you like something to eat?" The sandwich she'd brought out to the stable had been forgotten.

He nodded. "Sure. Thanks." He walked off down the hall and seemed so dispirited that Sharon looked after him. He's just tired, she thought; he had a long, grueling day, and he wasn't well at the start of it.

The phone rang while she was tossing a salad, and she answered it distractedly.

"Hello?"

"Sharon, it's George. Tell Tay that Sandpiper delivered a healthy colt. He's on his feet right now, Miguel is wiping him down. I've medicated the mother, but Tay should check on her during the night. She should sleep through it."

"Oh, thanks, George. Tay will be relieved to hear it."

"I'm going home. He can call me there if he has any questions, it doesn't matter how late."

"I'll tell him. Good night."

"Goodbye."

Sharon was anxious to convey the message, but she could still hear the water running in Tay's bathroom. She finished the salad and grilled a porterhouse medium rare, the way she'd heard him order steak in restaurants. She sat and waited, but twenty minutes passed with no sign of Tay. Wondering if he had fallen asleep, she set the kettle to boil to make a cup of tea for herself and left the food on the table, going to his door.

"Tay?" she said, tapping lightly.

There was no answer.

"Tay, I heard from George."

"Come on in." His voice was subdued.

Sharon pushed the door inward gently. He was seated on the edge of the bed, wearing nothing but a towel wrapped around his hips. His hair was wet and droplets of moisture clung to his upper arms and torso. The tape on his ribs was already gray at the edges and fraying badly. He was staring at the floor.

"George said the horses are fine," she told him. "You should check on Sandpiper during the night, Miguel is taking care of the colt. It sounds like everything is under control."

Tay nodded. "Good."

"I made dinner for you."

He nodded again silently.

"Tay, what is it? What's wrong?" Sharon asked softly.

He lifted one shoulder. "What's right?" He raised his eyes to hers and said, "When are you leaving?"

"Um...I don't know," Sharon replied, startled.

"Tomorrow? The next day? I'd like to know, I'd like to be ready for it."

"Ready for what?"

"The emptiness. The loneliness."

Sharon stared at him, afraid to breathe.

"For ten years I waited to see you again. I told myself that you had a life of your own and there was no place for me in it. But inside I always wondered, always hoped...." He sighed, swallowing. "But when you leave this time, there won't be any hope left. There'll be nothing but the knowledge that it's really finally over and I have to go on by myself."

Sharon took a step forward. Her knees were shaking.

He searched her face. His eyes were bleak in the lavender twilight filling the room; every line of his posture bespoke resignation and defeat.

"Sharon, please don't go," he said huskily. "Please."

Sharon crossed the distance between them in a second. She pulled him to her and he wrapped his arms around her waist.

"I love you," he murmured, his eyes closing as she cradled him against her breast. "Oh, God, I love you. I always have."

His whole body shuddered with the relief of saying it at last, and Sharon's throat closed with emotion. She clutched him tighter, and he pulled her onto the bed with him, pinning her to the mattress.

She opened her lips as he bent to kiss her. The scrap of terry cloth he wore did little to mute the impact of his muscular arms and legs, the lean strength of his body. His mouth was hot, his hands restless, in her hair, at the buttons of her blouse, the fastener of her skirt. She turned to help him, and then they both heard the piercing whistle of the teakettle as it started to boil.

"What the hell is that?" he muttered, his lips against her neck.

"The tea kettle."

He propped himself on one elbow and stared down at her. "You chose this moment to make a cup of tea?"

"Well, I thought you were coming out to have dinner. I'd better go turn it off."

"Nothing doing," he answered, his arms becoming like steel bands to restrain her. "You're not going anywhere."

"Tay, it will burn through the bottom to the heating coil. It could easily start a fire."

He groaned with real feeling and rolled off her. "Not another fire."

"I'll be right back," she whispered.

"I'll come after you if you're not," he replied, watching her departure with hungry eyes.

Sharon scampered to the kitchen and turned off the current, moving the kettle to a back burner. She was turning to go back to the bedroom when she caught sight of a man standing at the back door.

He was waving to her and smiling.

The man was Pete Symonds.

Chapter 8

In one panic-stricken instant Sharon considered several alternatives. The first was giving way to unrestrained hysterical screaming. The second was bolting like a vampire confronted by a crucifix and locking herself in with Tay. And the third was answering the door.

She decided to answer the door. Pete was very persistent and, having seen her, would knock until his fist fell off. She checked her buttons and snaps as she walked through the kitchen to let him in and found that everything was in order.

"Pete," she said, pulling open the door and manufacturing a smile. "What are you doing here?"

"Hi!" he said, grinning as he entered the house. "Surprised?"

"I sure am," Sharon said desperately, glancing over her shoulder.

"Well, I was missing you and I thought, I'll just take a few days off and hop on a plane, why not?"

"Why not?" Sharon echoed.

"So, this is your father's place?" he asked, looking around.

"It was, yes."

"Nice spread."

"Yes. As a matter of fact, why don't we go outside right now and take a look at it?" Sharon said hastily, attempting to shove him back out the door.

But she was too late. Pete's gaze was fixed over her shoulder at a point about seven inches above her head.

"Who's that?" he said.

Please let him be wearing a towel, Sharon prayed silently. She turned to face Tay.

He was wearing a pair of pants.

"Who the hell is this?" Tay demanded, hands on narrow hips.

Sharon tried very hard to vanish, but she was neither supernatural nor Harry Houdini. She was still standing there several seconds later, with the two men glaring at each other. She finally said, "Tay, this is my colleague from the district attorney's office, Pete Symonds. Pete, this is Taylor Braddock."

Tay made no move to shake Pete's extended hand.

Sharon said nothing.

Pete dropped his hand.

"What are you doing here?" Tay said to him.

"Sharon just asked me the same question," Pete said, smiling weakly. "Maybe I should have called first."

"Answer the question," Tay advised coldly.

Pete looked from one to the other in confusion and decided to tough it out.

"I've come to ask Sharon to marry me," he announced, stepping forward and putting his arm around her.

Sharon stared at him in horror, astonished.

"Is that right?" Tay demanded, his mouth a grim line.

"Wait, Tay," Sharon interjected, "this is a mistake...."

"I think I'm the one who made the mistake," he replied tersely, looking at her.

"There's no mistake," Pete said.

"Could be," Tay said to him flatly. "I think you're a little late for a wedding, pal." He turned on his heel and strode from the room without looking back.

"Tay, wait," Sharon called after him.

There was no answer.

"Sharon, what's going on here?" Pete said, examining her anguished face.

"I...it's complicated."

"It must be."

"Pete, let's get out of here. I want to explain, but it would be better if we left and talked someplace else."

They went out to Pete's rental car and he drove into Glendora, where they stopped at the same coffee shop Sharon had patronized with Tay. When they were seated in a booth and had ordered, Pete said, "I think you'd better start from the beginning and tell me all of it."

Sharon folded her hands on the table in front of her. "I wasn't entirely frank with you about the reasons for my trip out here."

"Somehow I sensed that."

"I told you that I was going to California to settle my late father's estate."

"Right."

"I didn't tell you that his will required me to marry my stepbrother in order for us to inherit the ranch."

"Tay? The guy back at your house?"

She nodded bleakly.

"You married your stepbrother?"

"As soon as I got here."

"Sharon, why? You know a piece of Victoriana like that will would never stand up in court today. You could have contested it easily."

"I know, but contesting it would have taken a long time,

and the ranch is Tay's livelihood. I didn't want to tie it up in a long legal wrangle that would have left him unsettled indefinitely.''

''Or maybe you really wanted to marry the guy,'' Pete said, watching her expression.

''Not at first,'' she said slowly.

''But now?''

''Now, I...'' She gestured helplessly, leaving the sentence unfinished.

Pete stared at her. ''Sharon, I came out here to propose. I have a ring in my pocket. Now you tell me you've married somebody else because of some antiquated will and, even crazier, that you want to keep it that way?''

''I know it all sounds...odd,'' she said weakly.

''It's clear I jumped to a conclusion here.''

''Pete,'' Sharon said gently, ''I'm sorry if you mistook my feelings, but I don't recall doing or saying anything that would have led you to believe I was ready to marry you.''

''No,'' he admitted.

''What, then? What brought this on?''

He shrugged. ''I guess it was impulsive. I want to get married, I want to have children, and we've always gotten along....''

''Do you love me?''

He looked abashed. ''I guess so. I, well, I don't know.''

Sharon remembered the passion in Tay's husky voice as he said, ''Oh, God, I love you. I always have.'' She dropped her eyes.

''I know that's not a statement to sweep you off your feet,'' Pete admitted, ''but I'm afraid I'm not sure what love is exactly.''

''You'll be sure when it happens to you,'' Sharon said quietly.

''Has it happened to you?''

She nodded.

The waitress brought their iced teas, and Pete waited until she left before saying, "So fast?"

"Not so fast, really. I knew Tay years ago when I was just a kid. I fell in love with him then, and it has never changed."

"And he feels the same?"

"He says so."

Pete sighed heavily. "You were making love with him when I arrived, weren't you?"

"Not exactly."

"No?"

"I've never slept with him."

Pete looked properly bemused. "I know I shouldn't pry, but that strikes me as a singularly taxing situation."

"Tell me about it," Sharon said fervently.

"You've been living in the house with him?"

"I've been living in the house. But not with him."

"And he hasn't tried anything?" Pete couldn't believe it.

"We sort of agreed in the beginning that it would be a marriage in name only. We thought we could stick it out long enough to inherit the ranch and then go our separate ways."

"But it hasn't worked out like that."

Sharon shook her head.

"I guess my timing's not so hot, huh?" Pete said sheepishly.

Sharon had to laugh.

"Are you going to stay with him?"

"I want to, but after today, I don't know what's going to happen."

"You're afraid he'll think you were using him to get the estate settled quickly, all the time planning to marry me?"

"Bingo."

"Is he that suspicious?"

Sharon shrugged. "You don't understand. We have a

long history of hurting each other. He's very sensitive where I'm concerned and very..."

"Jealous?" Pete supplied.

"Yes."

"Why don't I talk to him then? I could tell him that I decided to come out here on my own, that you knew nothing about it. Surely he's not that unreasonable."

"He's pretty unreasonable," Sharon said darkly. "I think I should talk to him alone. I don't want you to get hurt."

Pete's spine stiffened. He was not the man of her dreams, but he was no coward, either.

"I'll take my chances," he said tightly.

"Why don't you just drop me off at the house?"

"I'll go in with you," he said firmly. "I saw the tape on his ribs. He was in a fight recently, wasn't he?"

Sharon nodded.

"Is he violent?"

"He's...testy."

"Would he hit you?" Pete asked worriedly.

"Me! No, of course not, Pete. He might hit *you*, though. That's what I'm worried about. I don't want you to get in the middle of this awful mess."

"I already am in the middle of it," he said. He hesitated and said, "Are you sure you want to stay with this guy? He sounds...questionable."

"I've loved him for more than a third of my life," Sharon replied simply. "I can't give up on him now."

"If you say so," Pete answered doubtfully. "But I'm still going back there with you."

Sharon didn't have the strength for another debate, so she let that pass. "I'm sorry this didn't work out the way you wanted it to, Pete," she said.

He made a dismissive gesture. "It was a shot in the dark really. I guess I knew you weren't in love with me, and if

I asked you to marry me directly, you would say no. Blind-siding you didn't exactly improve my chances, did it?''

She smiled noncommittally.

"I hope my arrival didn't ruin things for you," he said sincerely.

I hope so, too, Sharon thought. "So how are things at the office?" she asked brightly, diverting herself from that unhappy thought.

"Nuts, as usual. Everybody's overworked, and we just got a memo about new staff cutbacks taking place next month."

"Cutbacks! We've got the paralegals doing briefs, as it is."

"The secretaries are going to be doing them next. Real estate is looking better every day."

"Are you really thinking about leaving?"

He nodded. "And the offer is still open for you, even if you don't marry me," he said, smiling.

"I'll bear it in mind. But I may be staying here."

He nodded again. "Well, I guess we'd better get back and face the music, huh?"

Sharon agreed and stood up. Pete paid the bill and they walked out into the balmy night.

"I feel like I should reimburse you for the plane fare or something," she said inadequately as they walked to his car. "You came all the way out here for nothing."

"Don't be silly. I'll take a vacation. I've always wanted to see Carmel and Monterey, Big Sur. I'll drive up there and play tourist. Who knows, maybe I'll meet a friendly lady who'd like to show me around."

Sharon turned and hugged him impulsively. "You're a nice man, Pete."

"Nicer than your wonderful Tay?"

"In some ways, yes," she admitted.

"But no chemistry?"

She didn't answer.

"Unfair question," he said as he opened the door for her. "No lady will tell a man to his face that there's no chemistry between them."

"It takes two, Pete. I'm sure you'll have marvelous chemistry with somebody else who'll be far better for you than I could ever be."

"Can you guarantee that I'll meet her?" he asked.

"Give it time."

"I'll try," he said, walking around to get into the driver's side of the car. "But I'm lonely."

"I know the feeling."

"And you're not lonely with Tay?"

"No. Furious, exasperated and terribly upset, but not lonely."

He grinned. "Sounds...interesting."

"Oh, it is. No one could ever accuse Tay of being dull."

He pulled the car out of the lot and headed for the ranch. "He's a good-looking guy," Pete observed generously.

"He's better looking without the scowl," Sharon offered.

Pete laughed. "Do you ever see him without it?"

"Occasionally."

"He really looked like he wanted to murder me."

"Well, to be fair, he didn't know anything about you. I never told him I was dating anyone back in Philadelphia. I just figured it was better not to discuss it."

"I can see why."

The drive home was short, and the house was dark when they pulled up in the driveway.

"Do you think he went out?" Pete asked.

"His car is here."

They entered together, and Sharon snapped on the kitchen light. She was about to go into the living room when Tay entered from the hall, a half-finished drink in his hand. He was wearing the same pants as before, with a loose cotton sweater.

"Well, if it isn't the happy couple," he said, toasting them with his glass.

Sharon and Pete exchanged glances.

"So when's the joyous day?" Tay asked, polishing off his drink in one gulp.

Sharon said nothing, trying to determine how to handle him.

"Cat got your tongue?" Tay said to her. "I would think that such felicitous tidings would be just bursting from your lips."

Pete moved in front of Sharon.

"I'll bet you thought that only you lawyers could talk like that," Tay added. "Speaking of the law, I have a question. Was the blushing bride going to wait until our divorce to marry, or was bigamy part of the plan?"

"There was no plan," Pete said.

"You're drunk," Sharon said.

"Couple drinks," he replied. "Just enough to help assua...assu...comfort me in my disappointment." He threw his empty glass against the wall, where it shattered noisily.

Pete took a step forward.

"Isn't this touching, Sharon?" Tay said sarcastically. "Your knight in shining armor is going to protect you."

"Somebody should protect her from you, bud," Pete said stiffly.

"Pete, don't," Sharon said, aware that such intervention would only worsen the situation.

"Listen to the lady, Pete," Tay said softly. "Otherwise I might have to rearrange your face."

It was obvious that Pete's usual good humor was dissipating rapidly. "You'll probably fall down plastered first, big man," Pete sneered.

"I'm still standing," Tay said, closing in on him.

"Oh, you're so macho," Pete taunted him, now furious himself. This was exactly what Sharon had wanted to avoid.

"You like the macho type, sweetie?" Tay said to him.

Pete's face suffused with color. "You're all talk, Braddock. Nobody witnessing this performance would believe that you've had this beautiful girl here all this time and never laid a finger on her. What's the matter, you afraid of women?"

Tay lunged for Pete, but Sharon, expecting it, was lighter and quicker. She launched herself at Tay, whose liquor-inhibited reflexes were slowed. He stumbled against her, and she flung her arms around his neck, bringing him to an awkward stop.

"If you do anything to him, I swear I will never speak to you again as long as I live," she said vehemently, looking up into Tay's face.

Her intensity got through to him, and he backed away, shrugging off her hold.

"I'm impressed," he said hoarsely. "Your instinct to shelter your beloved is as strong as his."

"Oh, for heaven's sake, will you listen to how ridiculous you sound? If you'd stop hurling insults long enough for me to explain, you'd realize how foolish you're acting."

"He doesn't deserve an explanation," Pete said tersely.

"Shut up," Tay said to him.

"Pete, I think you'd better go," Sharon said.

"Yeah, Pete, why don't you go?" Tay said.

"I'm not leaving you alone with him," Pete announced. "I don't know what he would do to you."

"Oh, please, let me hit him just once," Tay said, brushing past Sharon.

"Tay, stop it," Sharon barked.

He halted.

"How would you do without your little watchdog to run interference for you?" Tay demanded of Pete.

"I'd love to show you."

"Pete, just go. I told you this would happen. Can't you see that you're making everything worse?"

Pete hesitated.

"I'll call you later," Sharon said quickly, observing his indecision. "Where are you staying?"

"At the Palm Court, in town."

"Go. I'll be fine."

"You promise you'll call me?"

"I promise."

"Over my dead body," Tay said.

"That can be arranged," Pete replied.

"Tay, do you want him to leave or not?" Sharon demanded.

Tay didn't answer.

"If you'd stop antagonizing him, he'll go."

"Don't talk about me as if I weren't here," Pete said angrily. "And don't count on my leaving."

Sharon was ready to cry. She felt as if she were keeping two hungry lions from fighting over a piece of meat.

And she was the sirloin.

"Pete, I'm begging you," she said, and the incipient tears were evident in her voice. "I can handle this if you would just leave it alone. He's not going to hurt me."

Tay looked at her and turned away.

"If you're sure," Pete said, not wanting her to break down.

"I'm sure."

He threw Tay one more challenging glance before he strode purposefully out the door.

"I'm seriously afraid your boyfriend is a sissy," Tay said, watching him go.

"He's not my boyfriend and he's certainly not a sissy," Sharon replied angrily. "But you definitely are an idiot."

"Yeah, well, let's not discuss what you are right now."

"What is that supposed to mean?" Sharon demanded.

"I have to hand it to you," he said, leaning back against the kitchen counter and surveying her dispassionately. "It gives me a whole new respect for the workings of the legal mind."

"I don't know what you're talking about."

"I thought you had planned the perfect revenge by dangling the threat of the developers over my head, but this is better. This is perfect. You worked on me just long enough to get me to admit it, didn't you, and then up pops the fiancé, right on cue."

"Admit what?"

"That I love you," he said as if the words were torn from his soul. "It must have been such fun, listening to me begging you to stay with me, when all along you knew you were getting engaged to him." He jerked his head in the direction of Pete's departure.

"I'm not engaged to him!" she shouted, shaking her fists.

"Oh, right, I guess not. Since you're married to me."

The tears were very close to the surface now, and Sharon's hands trembled as she pulled out a chair. "Tay, please sit down. I have to talk to you, and I'm asking you to listen."

"Have I ever denied you anything?" Tay asked archly.

Sharon pulled out a chair for herself and sat, waiting.

"I may need another drink for this," he said.

"No more drinks," Sharon warned.

He sat across from her, watching her warily.

"You've gotten the wrong impression about Pete and me," she began.

"Oh, I see. He's a perfect stranger who wandered in here under a spell?"

"Could you cut the sarcasm and let me talk?"

Tay was silent.

"I work with Pete in the D.A.'s office."

"He's a colleague."

"That's right."

"A colleague who took it upon himself to fly two thousand miles out here and propose to you."

"Essentially, that's correct."

"What does essentially mean?"

"Oh, what is this? A quiz show?"

"Answer the question," Tay said humorlessly.

"I've been dating him," Sharon admitted.

"Dating?"

"Yes."

"That's all?"

"That's all," she replied, emphasizing the second word.

"For how long?"

"About six months."

"You've been keeping that guy on a string for six months?"

"I haven't been keeping him on a string, as you put it. I just couldn't make the commitment that he wanted."

"So you're telling me he came out here to make a grand gesture and impress you into marrying him?"

"I guess that's about the size of it."

"So he didn't know about us."

"I didn't tell him."

"You thought you could come out here and marry me, get the ranch and then shed me like a skin before returning to his waiting arms?"

Sharon put her face in her hands. "I had no intention of marrying him, Tay. I didn't know what was going to happen when I got here. It was a sticky situation and I just didn't want to go into it with him. Can you blame me for that?"

"You mean you wanted to keep him hanging around, since our previous encounter had been less than successful."

"That is *not* what I mean."

"No?"

"You don't believe me," Sharon said miserably.

"I believe that I don't stack up to much next to a fellow lawyer."

"Oh, please, not that again. Tay, I was about to make

love with you when Pete showed up at the door. Do you think I would have done that if I were expecting him to come here?''

"I don't know, would you?" he said, eyeing her levelly.

There was a shocked silence. Then, "You don't think very much of me, do you?" Sharon asked, stung.

"I thought a lot of the girl I used to know." His voice dropped an octave. "She loved me."

"Yes, she did," Sharon whispered.

"But you're not that girl anymore."

"Thank God. You treated her like dirt," Sharon said bitterly.

"I never meant to," he said quietly.

"Thanks a lot. That helps a bunch. Do you know what it was like to lie awake night after night, wanting you, needing you so much I could taste it?"

"Yes," he said quietly.

But she wasn't listening, lost in the past. "Do you remember those white jeans you used to have?" she said dreamily. "I guess they weren't white, they must have been beige, but they'd been washed and bleached so much they looked white. They fit you like a coat of paint, and you used to work outside in them, perspiring in the sun until the waistband was dark with sweat. You'd take off your T-shirt and work half-naked all day, and I'd have to walk past you, wanting to unsnap the snap and pull down the zipper...."

"Jesus," Tay said hoarsely, his hands gripping the edge of the table.

"I wanted to lick every drop of sweat from your body and kiss the place where it had been. I could imagine the taste of your skin, the smell."

"Sharon," Tay said wildly, kicking back his chair and standing, reaching for her.

She held up her hand. "And when I went to you in the bunkhouse," she continued, "I was not disappointed. You were everything I imagined, and more. But of course you know how that ended.''

Tay stopped moving.

"That has haunted me for ten years,'' Sharon said slowly. "I've only been with one man in my life, a student I planned to marry when we were both in school. The experience of sleeping with him was so pale by comparison with just the memory of the preliminaries with you that I couldn't go through with it.''

Tay swallowed hard, his dark and luminous eyes fixed on her face.

"That was his only problem, you know,'' Sharon said quietly. "His and Pete's. Neither one of them was you.''

He put his fingers over hers on the table. She snatched her hand back.

"And now you're going to tell me that I was taking advantage of *you*, leading you on while I was keeping Pete on the back burner? Pete never had a chance, and thanks to you, Taylor Braddock, neither do I.''

She stood clumsily, blinded by tears, and he caught her against his chest.

"Let me go,'' she said, struggling weakly.

"Why?'' he said, kissing her face, her neck. "Didn't you just say you love me?''

"I love you, all right, you creep, for all the good it's ever done me. You've made me more miserable than anybody else in my life, including my mother, and that's saying something.''

He scooped her up in his arms. "Then don't you think we've wasted enough time?'' he asked quietly.

"Tay,'' she whispered.

"You're my wife, Sharon,'' he added, silencing her with his mouth.

She closed her eyes as he carried her into the bedroom.

Chapter 9

It was dark in Tay's room, but he left the door ajar to catch the light from the hall. He set her on the edge of the bed and then joined her, drawing her down with him onto the pillows.

Tay could not wait, and he carried Sharon along on the tide of his urgency. He kissed her gently and then not so gently, unable to reign in the ten years' longing about to be satisfied. He fumbled with the buttons on Sharon's blouse, his usually nimble fingers stiff and clumsy, until he gave up trying, releasing her and sitting up.

"My hands are shaking," he said huskily, holding them before his face in the gloom. "I feel like I'm fourteen years old."

"I'll do it," Sharon said, reaching for her collar.

Tay shook his head. "I'm afraid I'm going to hurt you."

"Oh, Tay, how could you hurt me?" Sharon said softly.

"You may have noticed that control is not exactly my long suit," he said dryly. "I couldn't bear it if..."

"If?"

"This wasn't right for you. After waiting so long."

"It will be right, it couldn't be anything else," Sharon said, moving next to him and embracing him. "Now why don't we start by getting rid of this sweater?" She tugged at its folds and pulled it over his head as he lifted his arms to assist her.

She dropped it onto the floor.

"Getting kind of bold aren't you, Mrs. Braddock?" he murmured.

"Only with my husband, Mr. Braddock." She slid her arms around his neck luxuriously and rubbed her cheek against his smooth shoulder. "Nobody else feels like you," she whispered.

"You have determined this from your vast experience of one previous lover?" he said lightly, resisting the temptation to push her back on the bed.

"Nobody else *could* feel like you," she answered, closing her eyes and running her tongue down to his flat nipple, obscured by a mat of dark hair.

Tay seized her and bore her down to the mattress. There was only so much mortal man could be expected to endure. He kissed her again, his tongue exploring her mouth, and she responded in the same vein, taking the weight of his body easily, turning her head when he moved his lips to her throat. She unbuttoned her blouse rapidly, anticipating him, and he followed the motion of her hands, mouthing the soft flesh of her neck and the cleft between her breasts. He pulled the blouse off her shoulders and lifted her to unhook her bra, working surely now, taking the clothes from her body with practiced ease.

When she was naked to the waist, as he was, he rolled onto his back and pulled her on top of him. He took one breast and then the other into his mouth, running his callused hands across the satiny surface of her back, lost in the scent and feel of her. Sharon's breath was coming in short gasps, and as he teased a swollen nipple with his teeth she moaned aloud, clutching him to her convulsively. In-flamed by her response, he dropped one hand and unfastened her skirt, then pushed it clear of her bare legs. There was nothing left but the scrap of her panties, and he shifted her off him, bending to caress the silk of her abdomen.

Sharon felt as helpless as a rag doll as he dragged his lips across her navel and lowered his head to the tender skin of her thighs. His breath was hot, seeming to scorch her, and she tangled her fingers in his hair, soundless with emotion as he lifted one smooth leg and kissed the calf, the delicate, slender ankle.

He looked up at her, supine and limp with pleasure, her upper lip misted lightly, her eyes huge in her shadowed face.

"Yes," Sharon said in a drugged, husky voice she hardly recognized as her own. "Oh, yes."

His unasked question answered, he removed the thin silk briefs in a second. She gripped the blanket and twisted it, making a sound of pure satisfaction as he grasped her hips and caressed her with his mouth.

Sharon never knew that her body was capable of such response; she whimpered and surged against him, digging her nails into his back, finally begging, "Now, Tay. I can't wait anymore."

Neither could he. He stood and undressed fully, dropping next to her on the bed and enfolding her completely. She sighed as she felt him entwined with her, fitted to her like a glove. His body was lean and hard, and she reveled in it, hooking her slim legs around his longer, sturdier ones, her breath catching in her throat as she felt his arousal.

"Touch me," he said hoarsely. "I want you to."

Sharon obeyed him, encircling him with her fingers, feeling him throb and pulse in her hand. He groaned and dropped his head to her shoulder, pulling her tighter against him. After a second he loosened his hold and slid his body along the length of hers, positioning her. She followed him naturally, turning as he rose above her, arching to meet him.

"Tay," she said. It was a sigh.

"I know," he murmured. "I know."

He entered her in one smooth motion, and they made a sound of completion together, breath mingling with breath. Sharon closed her eyes and let her head fall backward as he moved within her.

"Oh, baby," he said brokenly, "why did we wait so long?"

Sharon couldn't answer, clasping him to her as they made up for lost time.

The room was still dark but striped with moonlight when Sharon awoke. Tay was lying next to her in the bed, staring down into her face.

"Hi," he said softly.

"Hi, yourself."

"How are you feeling?"

"Spectacularly wonderful."

"Me, too."

"What were you doing when I woke up?" she murmured, reaching up to touch his cheek.

"Looking at you."

"I could see that. Why?"

"I like to look at you. I always have. Now I can do it without worrying that you'll think I'm staring or being rude."

"I see. Your status has changed?"

"You bet. Now I'm your lover."

Sharon smiled tenderly and stretched, replete. "You certainly are."

"I should have been your lover long before this," he said quietly. "I should never have let you leave me that summer. I have never regretted anything so much in my life."

Sharon covered his large brown hand with hers. "Tay, you have to let that go. We both must let go of the past and live for the future now."

"I know that," he said quietly. "But I keep thinking that I could have done something a few years later, after you graduated from school and I got established here. I could have come after you then."

"Why didn't you?" she asked.

He shrugged. "I don't know. Pride, I guess. I didn't know what kind of reception I was going to get after the way we left things between us. Then your father started telling me about your plans to go to law school, and I really felt outclassed. And when you got there and I heard about your dates, and then the fiancé, it seemed like it was all over, period. You had gone on with your life without me."

"You don't know how I prayed for a letter, a phone call, anything," Sharon said softly.

"About as hard as I tried to forget you with any woman who would look at me."

"And there were quite a few who looked, I hear," Sharon couldn't resist saying.

"Too many," he agreed morosely. "Too many people I hurt because they couldn't possibly be what I wanted." He lifted her fingers to his lips and she was struck by the contrast of their skins.

"You're so tan," she said.

He examined her hand. "Snow white," he said gently.

"I have rarely managed to get a decent tan," she said ruefully.

"You got one the summer you were out here."

"Oh, I worked very hard on that, trying to get your attention."

"You got it," he said dryly.

"Did I?"

"Come on. I took so many cold showers I was growing icicles on my eyebrows."

Sharon laughed. "I wish I had known that then. My delicate ego could have used the reinforcement. Every time I saw you with a woman, I went into a black depression." She sighed elaborately. "I was usually depressed."

"You shouldn't have been. I wanted you."

"I'll bet that would have come as a surprise to Eloise Randall."

"Who?"

"Don't play dumb with me. You remember Eloise. She favored red cocktail dresses and stiletto heels? You left your mother's wedding party with her?"

"Oh, yeah. Eloise. Boy, you have quite a memory."

"The image of you following her out the door like a lemming marching into the sea was engraved into my brain. I was so jealous that I didn't know whether to kill her or you or myself."

"You should have killed her," he said, grinning. "That would have left the two of us alone."

Sharon punched him. "Don't make fun of me! I really suffered. Don't you remember what it's like to be that age and fall in love for the first time?"

He shook his head, turning serious. "No. At that age I was too busy making war to fall in love."

There was no reply to that, and Sharon made none.

Tay peeled the sheet down to her waist and crawled on top of her, nuzzling her breasts. "Mmm, delicious," he murmured, licking them lightly.

"But too small," Sharon said mournfully.

"Who says?" he asked, lifting his head.

"Everybody."

"Aw, what do they know? You have always looked perfect to me." He lay back down and closed his eyes contentedly.

"I feel the same. People used to say you were too skinny, but I never thought so."

"I *was* too skinny."

"You were gorgeous," Sharon said firmly.

He smiled without opening his eyes. "Far be it from me to argue with so relentless a romantic."

"You were!" she protested. She smiled suddenly. "When I came back here I was half hoping you had gotten fat. Or gone bald."

He chuckled silently, his shoulders shaking. "Well, if I keep on the way I've been going, I'll probably manage to knock out a few teeth," he offered. "How's that?"

"Poor Pete," Sharon said, reminded of him by the turn of the conversation. "I'm sure he thought you were going to maim him for life."

"I guess I owe him an apology," Tay mumbled.

"Based on your inexcusable behavior, I'd say you owe him a Porsche, but I suppose an apology will have to do."

"He said he was going to marry you," Tay growled. "How did you expect me to react?"

"Tay, really. If you had just listened to me..."

He raised himself on his forearms and kissed her on the mouth. "Do we have to talk about Pete right now?"

"I guess not," she said against his lips.

"I have an idea," he said, now kissing her neck.

"Uh, oh."

"No, you're going to like this one."

"Shoot."

"Let's have a wedding."

Sharon groaned and pulled the sheet over her head. "That is the one subject I would have thought we'd exhausted," she said weakly.

"No, I mean a real one, now that we're planning to stay married."

"Are we?" she asked, dropping the sheet and looking at him.

His face changed, and he turned away from her. "Aren't we?" he said dully.

Sharon sat up. "Tay, I didn't mean...don't...I was only kidding," she concluded hastily, alarmed by his reaction.

He embraced her immediately, his bare arm strong and warm around her. "Don't scare me like that," he said tensely. "If this fell apart now, I don't know what I'd do."

"It's not going to. You're stuck with me. For good."

"Is that a promise?"

"It's a promise," she whispered.

He lowered her to the bed and pulled the sheet down to their feet.

"No clothes," he murmured, running his lips along the line of her shoulder. "I like this."

"Yes, I noticed you had a little trouble with my clothes," Sharon replied, smiling.

He raised his head. "Are you suggesting that my technique was less than polished?" he said archly, then kissed the tip of her nose.

"Your technique was, is, wonderful," she answered, sighing as he rasped her nipple with his thumb. It hardened at his touch.

"Glad you appreciate it, because it's the only one you're going to experience for the rest of your life."

"Is that so, sir?" she said, closing her eyes as he moved over her, lifting her hips to his.

"That's so, madam," he replied, and gave her another sample of his technique.

When Sharon awoke she could tell by the quality of the light that it was very early. She was alone in the bed and could smell something burning. She slipped into her own room to get a robe and she joined Tay in the kitchen.

He was barefoot, wearing only a pair of jeans, stirring something on the stove. Sharon came up behind him and kissed the back of his neck. He had showered and he smelled clean and soapy.

He turned and embraced her. "I didn't mean to wake you. I was going to surprise you with this."

"With what?"

"Breakfast." He looked back at the mess of runny eggs in the pan and said ruefully, "Or what should have been breakfast."

"What's burning?"

"The toast. I guess I should have waited for Rosa, huh?"

"I guess so," Sharon said, turning off the heat under the pan.

"I'm starving," he confessed. "I drank my dinner last night after you walked out with Pete."

"I remember."

"And I kind of worked up an appetite later," he added, nibbling her earlobe.

"I remember that, too. Vividly." She slipped out of his arms and said, "Sit down. I'll feed you. What would you like?"

"Pancakes?" he suggested hopefully.

She looked at him.

"Of course, if that's too much trouble," he added, shrugging, casting her a sidelong glance.

Sharon shook her head, smiling. "You are an operator, Mr. Braddock."

He sat at the table, sliding down onto his spine. "You want to keep my energy up, don't you?" he said slyly.

"I have never known it to be down," she replied crisply, looking for the flour.

"Not where you're concerned," he answered. He watched her moving about the kitchen and said, "This reminds me of the first time we met. You cooked for me then, too, remember?"

"Yes. You arrived looking like a road bum and proceeded to eat everything you could find until I made you an omelet."

"I thought you were awfully cute." He sighed. "But awfully young."

"And I thought you were challenging and interesting and...different."

"I'd been wearing the same clothes for three days," he said dryly. "That must have been different."

"Well, you were quite a change from the boys in my high school. You were..."

"What?"

"A man."

He regarded her fondly as she located the flour and reached for the measuring cups. "I was acutely aware of that fact every time I looked at you," he admitted. "You were always so clean and neat and pretty, with your tan hair hanging down over your shoulders like that princess in the fairy tale."

"Which one?" Sharon asked, indulging him.

"You know, the one where she's locked in a tower."

"Tay, they are always locked in towers. That's a staple of the fairy-tale market."

He shook his head. "No, no. The one where the prince comes and stands below her window and calls, 'Da-da-da, Da-da-da, let down your hair.' And when she does, he climbs it like a rope to see her."

"Da-da-da?" she said, teasing him.

"You know," he insisted.

"Rapunzel," she said, ending the suspense.

He snapped his fingers. "Rapunzel! You knew it all the time."

She put her hand over her heart. "I confess. I knew it all the time. The sugar canister is empty, do you know where Rosa keeps the big bag?"

"Under the silver drawer," he replied.

Sharon bent from the waist to get it, and he watched as the action lifted her shortie robe and displayed a smooth expanse of creamy leg, stopping just short of what he most wanted to see. His eyes narrowed to slits and his breathing quickened. Sharon held the position as she searched, unaware of his reaction, until he finally stood abruptly, shoving aside his chair and covering the distance between them in two long strides.

He embraced her from behind just as she straightened with the bag in her hand.

"I bet I can make you drop that," he said softly, untying the sash of her robe.

He was fully aroused, and Sharon leaned back into him, closing her eyes.

"No bet," she replied, letting the bag fall into the sink.

He pulled the robe off her shoulders and let it fall, cupping her breasts in his hands as it slid to the floor. She rotated her hips, pressing and rubbing against him, and she was rewarded by his deep moan of pleasure.

"Temptress," he said in her ear.

"I'm trying."

"Seductress."

"I hope so."

He released her long enough to unfasten his jeans and step out of them, then pulled her to him again, spinning her around and bracing her against the counter.

"Just...lift," he said, grunting as he held her up and she locked her legs around his hips. He entered her standing, and they raced to a swift conclusion that left them drained and panting. Sharon let her head fall to Tay's shoulder, and it was several seconds before he realized that she was laughing.

"What?" he said.

"I can't believe we just did that," she said, looking up at him.

"Why not?"

"What if Rosa had walked in?"

"Knowing Rosa," Tay said, kissing her damp temple,

"she would have applauded and said, 'It's about time, *no es verdad*?' "

Sharon giggled. "You're probably right."

Tay stepped back and Sharon put her feet on the floor. "So, what about those pancakes?" she said briskly, reaching for her robe.

Tay snatched it out of her grasp. "You won't be needing this," he said, tossing it into a corner.

"I thought you wanted breakfast," Sharon protested as he took her hand and began leading her back to the bedroom.

"Breakfast can wait," he replied. "I just remembered what I'd rather do."

"You don't feel weak or faint or anything, do you?" she said as he dragged her through the door. "From lack of food, I mean?"

He picked her up and tossed her, squealing, onto the bed.

"If I pass out, just slap me a few times and I'll come around," he said, sprawling on top of her, catching his weight on his hands at the last second.

"I'll keep you awake, Braddock," she promised, scrunching down in the bed and planting a row of kisses on his hip, working inward.

"I'm awake, I'm awake," he said huskily, turning to accommodate her.

They both fell silent, and he proved to her that he was indeed awake.

When Rosa entered the house an hour later, she found Sharon's robe crumpled behind the kitchen table and Tay's jeans on the floor in front of the sink. She stared for a few seconds, and then, grinning to herself, picked the clothes up and folded them neatly.

Sharon emerged from the bathroom minutes later, wearing her terry beach cover-up, her hair wet from the shower.

She stopped short when she saw Rosa standing in the kitchen, putting the flour back in the cabinet.

"Hello," Sharon said sheepishly.

"Well," Rosa greeted her, "it looks like a few things have changed around here."

"Can't fool you, huh?" Sharon said.

"The clothes on the floor were my first clue," Rosa said dryly.

"Oh. We forgot them."

"Obviously. And I also noticed the ingredients of... something scattered around the kitchen. Never got around to cooking it, huh?"

"I was going to make pancakes. I was...interrupted."

"I'll bet. Where's Tay?"

"Sleeping."

"I'm sure he's tired," Rosa said solicitously.

"Stop looking so superior, Rosa, this is what you wanted."

"No, it's what *you* wanted," Rosa replied, plugging in the coffeepot.

"Is that coffee?" Sharon said, sitting down and trying to change the subject.

"No, it's beer. Don't change the subject. May I ask how this miracle came about?"

Sharon sighed. "It's a long story."

Rose spread her hands. "I have nothing but time."

Sharon faced the inevitable. "Last night a friend of mine from Philadelphia showed up here to see me."

"A friend?"

"A man I had dated, someone I work with at the office."

"I see."

"Tay got upset."

"I would think so."

"Especially since Pete—that's the friend—announced that he wanted to marry me."

Rosa turned to look at her.

"Yeah, it was pretty bad," Sharon agreed.

"Is the friend still alive?"

"Tay...explained to him that we were already married. In a manner of speaking."

"I'm so sorry I missed this," Rosa observed, removing cups from the dishwasher."

"I wish I could have missed it."

"Did this Pete think you wanted to marry him?"

"He conceded that he wasn't thinking much at all. I told him my situation with Tay and he accepted it, but his arrival sort of brought things to a head between Tay and me."

"I can imagine," Rosa murmured.

"We had a big fight."

"And a bigger reconciliation."

Sharon nodded, coloring.

"And you both admitted that you had loved each other all along."

Sharon nodded again.

"Well, it's about time."

Sharon grinned.

"What?"

"Tay said you would say that."

Rosa removed the incinerated remains of Tay's toast from the toaster and fed them to the disposal. "I haven't exactly made a secret of my feelings on the subject. But you two have been as obstinate as mules since you got here. I never saw such foolish behavior in my life."

"That's because you weren't here last night when Pete arrived," Sharon said, wincing. "It wasn't Tay's finest hour."

"Taking my name in vain?" said the man himself, coming into the kitchen. He was wearing the sweater Sharon had removed the night before and a fresh pair of jeans.

"Good morning!" Rosa said, beaming. "My, don't you look relaxed."

Tay glanced at Sharon.

"She knows," Sharon said.

Tay flushed slightly, walking past Rosa to the coffeepot, which was bubbling to a noisy conclusion.

"Isn't that cute?" Rosa said to the air. "He's embarrassed."

Tay poured himself a cup of coffee and turned to face them. "You're a riot, Rosa," he said darkly.

Rosa smiled and flicked her dish towel at him. "I've been waiting a long time for this," she said. "You can't blame me for enjoying it."

"I enjoyed it," Sharon piped up, and Tay choked.

Rosa slapped his back. "Take it easy there," she said.

The phone rang.

"I wonder who that is," Sharon said, reaching for it.

"Probably George, checking on the horse," Tay said. Then he slapped his forehead. "The horse! I was supposed to look in on her last night."

"I'm sure she understands that you were busy," Rosa contributed.

"Hello," Sharon said into the receiver.

"Hi, Sharon, it's Pete."

"Oh, hi, Pete."

Tay looked up, his expression guarded.

"Are you okay?" Pete asked.

"I'm fine," Sharon responded.

"More than fine," Rosa corrected.

"You said you were going to call me."

"Oh, Pete, I'm sorry. I forgot."

"I was worried."

"I'm sorry that you were worried, but I'm perfectly all right. Really."

"Is your...husband still there?"

"Yes," Sharon answered carefully. Tay was listening to every word.

"I wanted to come over to say goodbye," Pete said.

Sharon glanced nervously at Tay. ''You want to come here?''

Tay watched her.

''I don't know if that would be such a good idea,'' Sharon said hesitantly.

''Let him come,'' Tay said indulgently, draining his cup. ''I'll be good.''

''He'll be good,'' Rosa seconded.

Tay shot her a dirty look.

''I won't cause any trouble. I just want to see you before I leave,'' Pete said.

''All right,'' Sharon agreed. ''What time?''

''I can leave right now, be there in about twenty minutes.''

''Okay. See you then.''

''Goodbye.''

Sharon hung up the phone to the heavy silence in the room.

''He'll be here soon,'' Sharon announced.

''I've got work to do,'' Tay replied. ''I'll make myself scarce.''

''I'd appreciate it,'' Sharon said gratefully.

''He doesn't threaten me anymore,'' Tay said, putting down his cup. He walked over to her and kissed her cheek. ''I got the girl.''

''Hurray!'' Rosa said and threw her dish towel into the air.

''Give me that thing,'' Tay muttered, grabbing for it. Rosa danced out of his reach, laughing.

''I'll be down in the foaling barn if you need me,'' Tay said to Sharon.

She nodded.

''For anything,'' he added, grinning wickedly.

''Get out of here,'' Rosa said.

''I'm going,'' he said, holding up his hand. On the way

out he grabbed two of the sweet rolls Rosa had brought with her and popped one into his mouth.

"I guess that's his breakfast," Rosa said resignedly.

"He'll make up for it at lunch," Sharon said.

"Don't you think you'd better get dressed?" Rosa said pointedly, examining Sharon's sketchy outfit.

"Right." Sharon stood and headed for her bedroom.

"I'll make you something to eat," Rosa called after her.

"Don't bother, I'll get a sandwich later," Sharon answered.

"I don't know what I'm doing here, nobody ever consumes any food in this house," Rosa muttered to herself.

Sharon dressed quickly and was waiting for Pete when he arrived. Rosa withdrew discreetly to do the laundry.

"You look lovely," Pete said to her as they sat in the living room.

"Thank you."

"Where's Tay?"

"Down with the horses."

"Avoiding me?"

"I don't doubt it."

"So I guess you made it up with him last night," Pete said.

"How can you tell?"

"You're glowing, just like the advertisements say. Except I don't think it's face cream, is it?"

"No."

Pete sat forward and clasped his hands. "Well, the way things were going, I figured he'd wind up either killing me or making love to you."

"I'm glad he chose the second alternative."

"Are you happy?"

"Yes. Very."

He nodded. "I could see that, but I had to ask."

"Pete, I'm sorry about the way things turned out for you."

"Don't be. I know when I'm beaten. Even when you were furious, I could tell by the way you were looking at him that you were crazy about him."

"We've caused each other a lot of pain."

"That goes with it sometimes."

"So what are you going to do now?" Sharon asked, trying to get him to talk about himself.

"Finish my vacation. Then go back to Philly and resign."

"Really? You've made up your mind?"

He nodded. "I've got to do something for my future, I'm just spinning my wheels with Desmond."

"I hope it works out for you."

"Do you think you'll be staying here?"

"Yes."

Pete stood. "Well, I guess that does it." He kissed Sharon's cheek. "Be happy."

"I'll try."

As Pete was turning for the door, it opened, and Tay walked into the room.

The two men confronted each other, and Sharon tensed.

Tay wiped his palm on the thigh of his jeans and extended his hand to Pete.

"I wanted to see you before you left, and I noticed your car was still here," he said. "Please accept my apology for the way I behaved last night. I was a little drunk and a lot jealous. I'm sorry."

Sharon watched in amazement as Pete took Tay's hand and shook it.

It seemed that no one was immune to Tay's charm when he chose to exert it.

"Forget it," Pete said. "I was barging in where I didn't belong, I realize that now."

Tay nodded.

"I was just concerned about Sharon," Pete added.

"I'm glad she has such good friends."

Why don't they kiss each other, Sharon thought dryly, suspecting that they were overdoing it for her sake.

"Goodbye, Sharon," Pete said, turning to her.

"Goodbye, Pete. Have a safe trip."

After Pete left, Tay said, "He isn't such a bad guy."

"Last night you wanted to vivisect him."

"That was last night," he replied, moving closer and putting his arms around her. "Before you declared your undying love for me."

"And demonstrated it."

"Very capably."

"How is Sandpiper?" Sharon asked.

"Okay, no thanks to me. Miguel looked after her." Tay held her off and looked down into her face. "I had an idea."

"Another one?"

"Don't get smart. Remember that Italian place we went on your birthday, the night Rae and your father were at the auction?"

"How could I forget? The dinner didn't go so well, but you took me for a hamburger later that night and I started to fall in love with you."

"Because of the hamburger?" he said teasingly.

"Because you were so nice to me."

"Was I?"

"You didn't treat me like a kid, although I'm sure I was acting like one."

He shook his head. "No, I thought you were very mature. That's why it was so hard for me to remember your age sometimes." He traced her nose with a blunt fingertip. "I thought we could go back to that restaurant tonight if you like, do it right this time."

Sharon grinned. "I still won't be able to read the menu."

"I might not be able to, either. It's been a while, my Italian is a little rusty."

"Make the reservation. It'll be fun to go back there."

"Okay."

He started to walk away, then turned back to her and kissed her.

"I can't seem to stop doing that," he said.

"I'm not complaining."

"I'll make the reservation for eight. I'm going to town with Carlo, but I'll be back in plenty of time."

"Good."

He winked and left. She heard his footsteps go through the kitchen and out the door.

Sharon hugged herself, wondering if anyone deserved to be this happy.

A few minutes later Rosa tiptoed up the cellar stairs, peering around her overflowing laundry basket.

"Any fireworks?" she asked Sharon when she saw her.

Sharon shook her head. "Pete's gone. Tay apologized to him, and I must say they were very civilized about it."

"Tay apologized to him?"

"Yes."

"I would have paid good money to see that."

"How could you see it when you were hiding in the cellar."

"I wasn't hiding," Rosa said indignantly. "I thought you wanted some privacy for your meeting with Pete. I didn't know Tay was going to come back."

"Neither did I. Do you think he was trying to impress me with his self-control?"

"Probably. It worked, didn't it? Besides, I think he often regrets his fits of temper." Rosa opened a kitchen door and tucked a stack of dishcloths into it. "Sharon, have you discussed your job with Tay?"

"My job?"

"Yes, your job in Philadelphia. Are you planning to quit it?"

"I guess," Sharon said uncomfortably.

"Well, I hate to point this out to you, but you can't be in Pennsylvania and California at the same time."

"Thank you."

"Tay will never leave this place."

"I know that."

"So what are you going to do?"

"Get a new job?"

"You'll have to take the bar exam all over again for this state. That's a lot of work, and you could fail. It's been how many years since you took the first one?"

"Rosa, sometimes I wish you didn't think so damn much," Sharon said irritably. "Can't I be happy for one day before I start worrying about things like that?"

"Fine. One day. But then you'd better start thinking, because Tay is planted on this ranch like a tree, and he's not one for bicoastal romances. He'll want you here with him."

Sharon helped her put away the rest of the laundry and they talked about other things, but Rosa's words of warning haunted her for the rest of the day.

Rosa went home at about four, and an hour later Sharon was taking a bath when she heard Tay come in and shout for her.

"In here," she called.

He opened the bathroom door and paused on the threshold.

"Isn't that a picture?" he said softly.

"Care to join me?" Sharon said, raising her arm covered with suds from the bubble bath in a beckoning gesture.

He sat on the edge of the tub and embraced her.

"God, you smell good," he said, sighing.

"You always say that."

"It's always true," he murmured, running his hands, now slick with soap, over her body.

She hooked her arms around his neck and pulled him into the foaming water.

Chapter 10

"Hey!" He was laughing, trying to keep his head above water as Sharon climbed on him, bearing him down. He gripped the edge of the tub with one hand and grabbed her with the other, wrestling her into submission.

"Uncle, uncle!" she cried, pretending to surrender. When he released her, she splashed suds into his face, giggling maniacally.

"Oh, you're going to pay for that," he said, kneeling and hauling her upward with his hands under her arms. He flipped her over the edge of the tub and dumped her unceremoniously on the bath mat, as if he were a camp counselor bathing a five-year-old. Then he vaulted after her, pinning her before she could scramble to her feet.

"Now I have you at my mercy," he pronounced in a deep theatrical voice, twirling an imaginary moustache.

"Oh, please, sir, take pity on a poor serving girl with nary a penny to her name," Sharon whimpered in a cockney accent, batting her lashes.

"A poor serving girl?" Tay said, dropping the act. "Isn't that a bit much?"

"I thought it was a nice touch. You can get off me now."

"Really?" He was holding her down with one hand spread flat on her abdomen. It didn't seem as though he was exerting much force, but when she tried to move, she couldn't.

"You're dripping on me," she pointed out to him.

"Whose fault is that?" he asked. "Anyway, you were wet already." He shook his head like a dog coming in from the rain and splattered her with droplets.

"And now I'd like to get dry," Sharon said.

He sprawled next to her, still holding her down, and licked a rivulet of water from her shoulder. The warmth of his skin came through his wet clothes like steam through a damp towel.

"I'll dry you off," he murmured, lowering his head to her breasts.

"Oh, thank you," she sighed, closing her eyes. She was no longer trying to get him to release her.

"Still a little wet here—" he sucked on a nipple "—and here." He trailed his tongue down to her navel.

"This is a lovely service you provide," Sharon whispered, holding his head against her.

"Any time." He sat up and tried to pull his shirt over his head, then subsided, frustrated.

"This damn thing is stuck to me," he said. The absurdity of it struck them and they both started to laugh.

"Some Casanova I'm turning out to be," he said ruefully.

"Never mind," Sharon said, reaching for the waistband of his jeans. "I think we can make a success of this with a few minor adjustments." She unzipped his fly and climbed into his lap. He shifted to accommodate her.

"How's that?" she murmured as he settled her onto him.

"Clever girl," he said huskily, closing his eyes.

"That's what I've been trying to tell you," she replied, shivering with delight.

Some time later they became aware that they were lying in a puddle.

"Do you think we should move?" Sharon said dreamily.

"I guess that might be a good idea," Tay replied, yawning.

"If we fall asleep here we'll both get pneumonia."

"It might be worth it," he replied.

"You won't think so when you're in an oxygen tent," Sharon replied. "Now who's going to get up first?"

"You?" he suggested.

"What an unchivalrous attitude," she chided him.

"I'm not the one who started this," he reminded her.

"Tay, we're going to miss dinner. And I, for one, am starving. I've heard it's possible to live on love, but I don't feel like putting it to the test tonight."

Grumbling under his breath, he stood awkwardly and helped her to her feet. They both looked around them. The tile floor of the bathroom was awash, Sharon was naked, her hair in a damp tangle, and Tay was half in and half out of his sodden clothes. Drenched towels were bunched at their feet like cold lumps of mashed potatoes.

"Geez, what a mess," he observed.

"I'll get the mop," Sharon said.

She left him puttering around, and by the time she returned he had drained the tub, wrung out the towels and hung them up to dry on the racks. She mopped up the remaining water and wiped out the tub.

"I like that maid's uniform," he said, observing her.

"It's transparent, like the emperor's new clothes," Sharon said, grinning.

"Yeah, well, you'd better cover it up or we may never get out of this bathroom," he said dryly.

Sharon dashed past him and returned the mop to its bucket in the kitchen closet. When she went back to the hall, he was waiting for her.

"I have a proposition to make," he said.

"I think I've heard all of your propositions," Sharon replied, laughing.

"You haven't heard this one. When we're home alone together, I'd like you to stay like this all the time."

"Don't you think I'd get a little chilly in the winter?" Sharon asked.

"The house has heat. We usually don't have to use it, but for you I'd turn it up full blast."

"I'll consider it," Sharon said and tried to brush past him into her room. He caught her about the waist and held her.

"Where are you going?" he asked.

"To get dressed. I don't think I can go to the restaurant like this. Not unless you want *me* to wind up in jail this time."

"Let's stay home," he said, nuzzling her. "We can send out for a pizza."

"Tay, for heaven's sake. You're like an adolescent who just discovered sex."

"I just discovered sex with you."

"But you don't want to do anything else."

"Do you?" he asked, smiling.

"That's beside the point," Sharon replied with mock severity. "I am not going to live on fast food for the rest of my life just because we…"

"We?" he prompted, deadpan.

"Have found each other," she finished lamely.

"Can't keep our hands off each other," he amended.

"Speak for yourself," Sharon said tartly.

He burst out laughing, not exactly the reaction she had anticipated.

"What?" she demanded.

"Who was that unzipping my pants back there in the bathroom?" he asked, his eyes widening. "Miss Sadie Thompson?"

"Well, that was just..."

"Just?"

"Unbridled lust," she admitted, sighing heavily.

"Ah, that's what I like to hear," he said.

"It's embarrassing," Sharon said, propping her chin on his collarbone. His clothes were drying now, smelling of her bath salts.

"What is?"

"How much I want you."

"Why should that be embarrassing, baby? It's natural."

"It's not natural for me. I'm kind of a businesslike type."

He managed not to laugh again, but his smile was roguish.

"I mean," she went on, "it seems like in less than a day my whole life has changed."

"It has. Mine, too."

"But I can't believe that you're with me and I can touch you and have you any time I want."

"You certainly can. I am completely and utterly at your service," he said. He stepped back from her and bowed.

"Stop teasing me. I'm trying to make a serious point here."

He assumed a serious face.

"Despite the fact that I am addressing you while stark naked," she added.

"Despite that," he agreed, his lips twitching.

She moved close to him again and he embraced her lightly.

"It's a little scary to get what you've always wanted, isn't it?" she asked him.

"A little," he replied, kissing her hair.

"'To have that which you fear to lose,'" she murmured.

"What's that?"

"Shakespeare. One of the sonnets, sixty-something, I think."

"How does it go?"

"'This thought is as a death, which cannot choose/But weep to have that which it fears to lose.'"

"Don't worry," he said soothingly. "No weeping is on the horizon. Neither one of us is going to lose this time."

Sharon glanced at the clock on the living room wall, just visible over his shoulder. "But we are going to lose those reservations if we don't hurry."

He released her reluctantly.

"You're sure you have to get dressed," he said.

"Positive."

"All right. I think it's a stupid custom, but I'll go along with it. Tonight."

Sharon went into her room to dress, hurriedly selecting a blue sheath, adding a gold chain and earrings. She applied lipstick and eye makeup and combed her hair, which was drying in flyaway strands. Finally she stepped into medium heels, snatched her bag from her dresser and slipped out to meet Tay.

As quick as she was, he was quicker, waiting for her in the living room. He was wearing a navy suit with a white shirt and a brick-red tie. She stopped short when she saw him.

"What's the matter? My face green?" he said testily.

"No. You look..."

"Well?"

"So...nice."

"Listen to how surprised she sounds."

"Tay, other than the wedding I haven't seen you in anything except work clothes since I got here. You're dazzlingly handsome in a suit."

"You don't look so bad yourself. What shade of blue is that? Royal?"

"Della Robbia blue," Sharon replied. "The painter used it all the time in his work and so it was named after him."

Tay stared at her for a moment and then looked down. He seemed disturbed.

"What's the matter?"

"Nothing."

Sharon walked over to him and kissed the tiny mole at the corner of his mouth. "Don't give me that. Something's wrong. Now fess up."

He hesitated a moment before he said, "There's such a gulf between us. You're quoting Shakespeare and talking about some painter I never heard of, all in the space of ten minutes. What's going to happen when I get together with your friends, the people you work with every day? Do you think we'll have anything to say to each other?"

"The women will be too busy mentally undressing you to talk," Sharon replied, hugging him.

"I mean it," he said over her head. He held her off and looked at her. "I've been thinking about this all day, so I might as well say it. What are you going to do about your job?"

"Rosa asked me that this morning."

"And what did you tell her?"

"I haven't really thought about it."

"Think about it now," he said flatly.

"Tay, we're going to be late."

"Sharon, you're starting to sound like the white rabbit in *Alice in Wonderland*. The restaurant will still be there when we arrive, I promise you."

Sharon was silent.

"I won't expect you to stay home and knit, you know," he said gently.

She looked at him. "I don't have to work as an assistant district attorney, but I do want to work," she said.

He nodded.

"I want to be with you, but..." She hesitated. "I've been

thinking about opening up my own practice," she said in a rush.

"Here?"

"Yes."

"Great," he said, smiling.

"Maybe not so great. I'd have to take the California bar."

"So take it."

"I could fail it."

"You'll pass."

"Even if I get the general section waived, I'd still have to deal with the state part."

"And?" he said, aware that she wasn't telling him everything.

"It's expensive to open a practice," she said, wincing. "Very. I have some money saved, but not nearly enough."

"I'll finance it," he said.

"The books alone cost thousands. Not to mention type-writers and Dictaphones and probably a computer."

"We'll get what you need," he said.

"A secretary," she went on, "maybe a paralegal. Stationery and a copying machine."

"I see that you've been giving this some thought," he said.

"I considered it even back in Philly. The job there was getting intolerable. Pete is going to leave, too."

"So why were you dodging the issue when I brought it up?" he asked.

"I wasn't sure how you would feel about it," she said honestly. "We were getting along so well I didn't want to spoil anything."

"What did you think I was going to say?" he demanded.

She shrugged. "You were the one just talking about the gap between us."

He came to her and took her by the shoulders. "Sharon,

you can do whatever you want, I won't stand in your way. I just don't want you to be ashamed of me."

Sharon threw her arms around his neck and laughed with relief. "You idiot, how could I ever be ashamed of you?"

"You're much better educated."

"Oh, who cares? If I wanted another lawyer, I would have married Pete. I want you."

"People around here know that this place was your father's."

"Are we back to that again? He was married to *your* mother, and she put her money into it when she sold her own place. If you like we can print up an accounting of who paid for what and distribute it to the neighbors."

"You make it sound ridiculous."

"It *is* ridiculous. Darling, I love it that you're proud and don't want people to get the wrong idea, but you're carrying a good thing too far. The hell with everybody else, anyway. As long as we're happy, forget about them."

"You won't care that I don't know what anyone's talking about at the Los Angeles County Bar Association Christmas party?" he asked.

"What do they know about horses?" she countered. "Who says one kind of knowledge is any better than another?"

"Lots of people."

"Then they're wrong." Sharon drew away from him and met his eyes. "Do you think I feel that way?"

After he looked at her for a long moment, he shook his head. "No."

"Good. Then it's settled." She snuggled back into his shoulder.

"I'm glad we talked about this," he said.

"Me, too." She raised her head. "Now can we eat?"

He glanced at his watch. "Let's go."

The restaurant was the same as Sharon remembered it. Even the wallpaper looked like the fleur-de-lis pattern she recalled from their last visit. The musical group was already in place, playing an abbreviated version of Pachelbel's *Canon in D*.

"It was really thoughtful of you to select this place," Sharon said to Tay as they were seated. "It brings back memories."

"I wondered if I should take you here. I know some of those memories aren't the best."

"You were very unhappy then," Sharon said quietly.

"I have a vague recollection of jumping some poor kid who asked you to dance."

"You had just found out you'd lost your job."

"And I didn't want to be dependent on your father."

Sharon nodded.

"Funny, isn't it? My association with your father was the best thing that ever happened to me. It introduced me to you and straightened out my life."

"You couldn't have known that then. You just didn't want to take charity."

He shrugged. "I wasn't used to getting a chance like that, free, for nothing. But then, I'd never met a man like your father." He paused. "I miss him."

"So do I," Sharon said softly, looking down at her hands. She looked up again. "But you paid him back. You helped him when your mother died and he couldn't help himself. I know that meant a lot to him."

"He engineered this, you know," Tay said, smiling slightly, gesturing at the two of them seated across from each other. "He wanted that will to bring us together. I think he had an idea what would happen when it did."

Sharon smiled, too. "Was he that smart?"

Tay nodded sagely. "My interest in your activities over the years was not lost on him."

"I think he knew I fell in love with you that summer," Sharon said. "And he respected you for not capitalizing on that with a young and innocent girl.'' She grinned suddenly. ''Although he wouldn't have thought me so innocent if he had seen me sneaking into the bunkhouse with my teenage seduction routine.''

''Don't make light of it. You were very successful,'' Tay said grimly. ''You almost got exactly what you were looking for.''

''Our lives would have been so very different if I had,'' Sharon said softly.

The musicians segued into Vivaldi.

''This place has gone a little highbrow, hasn't it?'' Tay said, glancing over at the dais. ''Do you think they know any Grand Funk?''

''I doubt it,'' Sharon said, laughing.

The waiter arrived and Tay ordered a Lambrusco to go with the meal. Sharon decided on Veal Française and Tay got the scalloppine, a specialty of the house.

When the waiter left, Tay reached over the table and took Sharon's hand in his.

''Do you know how many times I've been in a place like this with a woman, looked across at my date and wished she were you?''

''I'm here now,'' Sharon said, twining her fingers with his.

''And in honor of the occasion, I'm going to tell you about the big deal I have pending,'' he said, smiling mysteriously.

''What big deal?''

''I've been negotiating with one of the banks in Glendora for a loan to buy a brace of Arabians. It just came through last week.''

''Tay, that must involve a lot of money.''

''It does. But the ranch has been doing well, and I had the down-payment money, so they gave me the go-ahead. It should mean about ten or twelve horses, all blooded, nothing but the best.''

"That's wonderful."

"It's a big step for me," he said. "I'm taking a chance branching out like this, but it was a move I had to make sooner or later."

The waiter brought the wine for Tay to sample and left the bottle when it was approved.

"A toast," Tay said, filling their glasses.

"To your upcoming purchase," Sharon said.

"And our future together."

"Hear, hear."

They drank deeply.

The band changed again, to a slow tune popular a few months earlier.

"That's more like it," Tay said, pushing back his chair. "Would you care to dance?"

Sharon nodded.

He walked around, held her chair as she stood and led her to the dance floor. She slipped into his arms and followed him easily, enjoying his closeness as she always did.

Please let it stay like this, she prayed silently. Please let nothing happen to change it.

She closed her eyes and let her head fall to Tay's shoulder, drifting to the music.

When they got back to the house, Tay said, "Do you plan on leaving your little duds in your own room?"

"Sure. Why move them?" She hooked her arms around his neck. "But I'm moving myself into your bed. Permanently."

"Sounds good to me." He reached behind her and ran her zipper down its track. He pulled her sleeveless sheath off her shoulders and it dropped to her feet.

"That's the kind of dress I like," he said, kissing her neck. "Easy to remove."

"I'll buy some more of them."

"Do that." He started to work on her one-piece teddy,

pulling the straps down and pushing the silky material to her waist.

"Don't like this so much," he said judiciously. "Let's get rid of it."

"I agree." She tugged it over her hips and it puddled on the floor.

"Time to adjourn to the inner chamber," he said huskily, scooping her up and walking down the hall to deposit her on his bed. She sprawled in a deliberately seductive attitude, arms over her head, one knee bent to display her legs to best advantage.

"No fair," he said in a low tone, tugging at his tie. When the knot wouldn't come loose, he yanked it over his head. He tossed his jacket onto a chair.

"I'm waiting," Sharon murmured, trailing one hand languidly between her breasts.

"You're gonna get it." He unbuckled his belt.

"I hope so."

He pulled off the rest of his clothes and dropped next to her on the bed. She rolled onto her stomach playfully, feigning resistance, and he trapped her quickly. She could feel him, hard and urgent, against the back of her legs. He planted kisses along the ridge of her spine, moving her arms up to slide his hands under her breasts.

"Oh, I like this," he said softly. "Don't move."

"I'm not going anywhere," she whispered, closing her eyes.

He positioned her carefully and said, "I hope you realize I'm trying to get you pregnant."

"If you can't do it, nobody can," she answered, sighing with satisfaction as he entered her.

Conversation ceased as they became lost in each other.

Tay was sleeping as Sharon slipped from the bed an hour later. She was very thirsty. Her meal had been highly spiced, and she remembered a pitcher of iced tea Rosa had left in the refrigerator.

She picked Tay's shirt off the floor and thrust her arms into the sleeves; the tail hung down to her knees. She was heading for the kitchen when she spotted a pile of mail that Rosa had deposited on the hall table. One of the envelopes was addressed to her, with the Citrus Farms logo in the upper left-hand corner.

She picked it up and slit the seal with her thumbnail, then quickly perused the letter it contained. What she read gave her a sinking feeling in the pit of her stomach.

Citrus Farms was informing her that it had acquired a parcel of land on the far side of her half of the ranch. A stream flowed across it to Sharon's land through a long-standing easement. Citrus Farms was threatening to cut off her water rights, a serious matter in the arid valley.

So this was the latest scare tactic in the ongoing war to acquire the ranch. Without water, the ranch would be useless.

Tay was right. The developers were not just going to give up and go away.

Chapter 11

Sharon took the letter to her room and hid it in a drawer under a stack of clothes. She didn't want Tay to know about this latest problem. He'd gotten the loan to buy the Arabians based on the anticipated continuing success of the ranch. The down-payment money was gone, and he could be stuck with the horses and unable to keep them if Citrus Farms followed through on its threat.

Sharon didn't want to worry him. Her mind was racing; she thought she could solve the problem herself.

She went back to Tay's room and slipped into bed with him. He turned to her in his sleep, and she settled blissfully into the comforting warmth of his body.

She would deal with Citrus Farms on her own.

In the morning, after Tay had gone out to work, she showed the letter to Rosa.

Rosa read it quickly and looked up, her dark eyes mirroring her concern.

"Does Tay know about this?" she asked.

Sharon shook her head.

"Don't you think you'd better tell him?"

"I don't think I have to. He's got so much on his mind right now, it would be nice if I could solve this without telling him."

"Do you know what will happen if he finds out on his own?"

"I've got a call in to Pete to contact me when he gets back to the office. He knows a lot about real estate and his father knows more. I'm betting he can help."

"Pete? In view of his history with Tay, do you think he's the best person to ask?"

"He's the only person to ask. Besides, he and Tay made up before he left, you know that."

"But he's not going to be back until after his vacation."

"It will have to wait until then. It's only a few days. In the meantime I'm going to research the situation in the county records office. If I can arrange to get water from somebody else, the Citrus threat will be meaningless."

"How do you propose to do that?" Rosa asked skeptically, looking at her.

"Have a little faith, will you?"

"I'm trying to, but the only thing more precious than water around here is a guarantee of safe passage through the pearly gates."

"I'm a good lawyer. I'll come up with something."

"A lawyer who represents himself has a fool for a client," Rosa said dolefully.

"Rosa, if you start spouting aphorisms like my mother, I am going to scream."

"Just bear it in mind."

"I'm not representing myself. This isn't a legal case."

"Yet," Rosa said meaningfully.

That afternoon, with Rosa's words ringing in her ears, Sharon went to the records office and looked up the ownership of all the tracts of land that bordered her own in

Glendora. Most of it was in private hands, but she discovered that Sun City owned the tract that ran north of hers, a recent acquisition. It had an aqueduct fed by the runoff from the hills and, since Sun City was the direct rival of Citrus Farms, she instinctively knew that she might be able to use the information.

Pete Symonds called that night, fortunately while Tay was out with Miguel.

"Pete! Aren't you still on that coastal vacation? How did you get my message?"

"I checked in with the office and they told me you called. I must say I was surprised. I thought Tay would be keeping you too busy to make phone calls."

Sharon laughed. "He's been keeping me busy all right, but I managed to squeeze one in."

"So what's up?"

"Well, I'm getting remarried next week. To Tay."

"I thought it might be to Tay."

"He wants a real wedding. The one at the municipal building was kind of cold and formal, so we're going to do it at a church here."

"That's very touching, Sharon, and I cannot tell you how thrilled I am to hear it, but something tells me that's not the only reason you called me."

"True."

"Well?"

"I'm having a little problem with one of the developers trying to buy the ranch."

"What kind of a problem?"

"My father's will divided his land into two parcels, next to one another, mine and Tay's. Well, a stream flows onto mine from land on the side not bordering Tay's. Citrus Farms bought it, and I got a letter saying that they're going to cut off water rights from the stream easement."

"I see."

"Can they do that?"

"They can try. I doubt if a judge would let it fly if it would cut off your water supply completely, but they can sure make trouble for you, tie you up in court for a long time, cause you a lot of expense."

"That's what I thought."

"Sharon, you know how the system works."

"I know, I know. I have an idea, but I think it's going to be pretty expensive."

"As I recall," he said dryly, "your legal ideas are frequently expensive."

"Just listen, okay. I looked up the plot plans in the county office, and Sun City, which is Citrus Farms' biggest rival, just bought the tract north of mine. It has the water, too, an aqueduct fed year-round from melting snow."

"I know what you're thinking, and you're right. Expensive."

"What am I thinking?"

"You want to buy the tract from Sun City, right? You keep the water and tell Citrus to go scratch."

"Good idea?"

"What are you going to do? Threaten Sun City that you'll sell your half of the ranch to Citrus if they don't cave in?"

"Great minds run along the same channels."

"Where are you going to get the money?"

"That's the one small hitch in my plan."

"Nobody knows you out there. A local bank should finance it, but your husband is well-known. He would be able to swing it."

"I don't want to tell Tay."

There was a significant pause at the other end of the line. "Why not?" Pete finally said.

"He has a deal pending to buy a bunch of expensive horses. I don't want him to worry that it could fall through because of this. Besides, I can put my half of the ranch up as collateral for the loan without him."

"I hear what you're saying, and I can't tell you that you're wrong, but this has all the earmarks of a questionable situation. You know that. Tell Tay."

"Can you help me get the loan if I run into trouble?"

"How am I supposed to do that?"

"Pete, your father is wired into every real estate lending institution in the country. If he doesn't know somebody, he knows somebody who does. The ranch is a good bet, it's viable collateral, but I've never had a mortgage, not even a chattel mortgage. I have no credit history. A good word in the right ear could do the trick. You know how these things work."

Pete sighed audibly. "All right. Set it up. See the Sun City people and make the offer, go to the best bank and make the loan application. Keep in touch, let me know how it's going. I'll help if I can."

"Pete, you're an angel."

"I'm an idiot. If this thing falls the wrong way, your husband is going to kill me."

"No, he's not. That I can promise you. This is my party and I'll take responsibility for it."

"Hah." Pete remained unconvinced.

"You've been a big help."

"That's my job."

"Have you met anybody on your vacation?" Sharon asked, a smile in her voice.

"I have a couple of possibilities."

"How's Big Sur?"

"Big."

"And Monterey?"

"Everything the travel poster says it is."

"Good. I hope you're having a fine time."

"Your small-talk obligation has been discharged, Sharon. You can go now."

"Thanks."

"Bye."

"Goodbye." Sharon hung up with a feeling of elation. It was possible; it was even probable with Pete's help. She could pull this off and Tay would never know.

She stood and ran happily into the living room to make her plans.

During the next week Sharon negotiated with Sun City for the purchase of the land, telling Tay she was going shopping when she went to talk to them. When they agreed upon a price, she went to a Los Angeles bank for the financing, fearing that a Glendora loan officer might alert Tay to what was happening. She also thought that Pete's father would carry more weight with a larger, more cosmopolitan outfit.

The loan was in the works on the day of her second wedding, or so she thought of it. Rosa had helped her pick out an off-white cocktail-length dress with a beaded bodice and a bell-shaped embossed silk skirt. She wore it with a short veil suspended from an off-white bow of the same material as the dress, and she carried a nosegay of white roses. Everyone said she was a beautiful bride.

Her mother mercifully decided not to show up; Sharon wanted at least a year with Tay and a course in family counseling before she had to deal with a meeting between that formidable lady and Sharon's husband. Sharon's mother sent a set of china and an elaborate floral piece, both of which Rosa deposited in the living room like trophies.

After the candlelit ceremony they had a reception at a restaurant in town for the ranch people and some of Tay's friends. Sharon enjoyed herself immensely, convinced that she was on the right road at last. The loan would come through, Tay would get his horses, and all would be well.

Tay insisted on a short honeymoon at the most elaborate hotel in Los Angeles. It was almost midnight as he carried her across the threshold and into an elaborately decorated sitting room. The bedroom was beyond, the bed curtained with a fringed canopy.

"Do you believe this place?" she said to Tay as he took off his jacket. "There's a private bar stocked with everything over here in the corner, and a fruit basket on the coffee table."

"Champagne," Tay added, indicating the bucket standing next to the cherry secretary by the door.

"Did you arrange all of this?"

"Some of it. But a lot comes with the bridal suite—nothing but the best."

Sharon threw her arms around his neck. "What a guy I married."

"Twice," he reminded her.

"I liked the second wedding a lot better than the first."

"Me, too," he said, kissing her briefly. He held up her left hand, on which sparkled a new gold band. "Do you like the rings?"

"I love them."

"Rosa helped me pick them out. She has great taste."

"I wonder some smart guy hasn't come along and snared her," Sharon observed.

Tay shook his head. "She told me that after her husband died she didn't want anybody else. I think she's a one-man woman."

"I know another one of those," Sharon said, taking the studs out of his shirt.

"Yeah?"

"Yup. How do you untie this cummerbund?"

"It unhooks at the back."

"Then turn around."

He reversed position obediently. She removed the sash and pulled his shirt out of his pants.

"May I help you?" he asked, smiling over his shoulder at her.

"I wish you would. You're being about as cooperative as a Barbie doll."

"A Ken doll, please." He began to undress but stopped when Sharon reached behind her neck for her own zipper.

"I'd rather undress you," he said. He removed her clothes swiftly and led her to the bed.

"I feel like Marie Antoinette in this contraption," Sharon said, glancing up at the canopy.

"Wrong period. This is a Regency bed," Tay said, removing her underwear.

"Lillie Langtry then. How do you know it's a Regency bed?"

"Because this is the Regency suite," he replied, pushing her back on the bed with one hand and unzipping his pants with the other.

"Oh. Well, you booked it, you should know."

"Do you think you could stop talking for a moment, please?" he said, sprawling next to her.

"You should get used to this," Sharon said. "Sometimes I chatter."

"And sometimes you should shut up " he replied, covering her mouth with his.

And so she did.

During the following month, Sharon waited for final approval on her loan and tried to survive the blazing dry inferno of a San Gabriel August. In the beginning she worried that Tay would find out about her scheme, but she made sure she got the mail first and took all calls. Since Tay was out of the house most of the time that wasn't difficult. The waiting was tough, but as Pete's father had put in a good word and she had met the loan criteria, she was confident she would get the money.

The heat was really bothering her. Sharon insisted on air conditioning all the time and began to feel unwell. Everything irritated her, and Rosa told her to make an appointment with a doctor. She called the same clinic Tay had gone to for his cracked ribs and went one afternoon when Tay was at an auction with Carlo.

The doctor was the same cute number who had seen Tay.

"Braddock?" she said, knitting her finely arched brows. "I saw a Braddock a while ago, cracked ribs, I think. Tall, dark-haired guy, mid-thirties."

Sharon was not surprised that she remembered Tay. "My husband," she said pointedly.

"I didn't know he was married."

I'll bet, Sharon thought.

"So what are your symptoms, Mrs. Braddock?" the doctor said.

"I feel queasy and irritable all the time, and I'm exhausted. I'm falling asleep on my feet."

"Missed any periods?"

"I'm ten days late." No flies on this lady; having met Tay, she considered pregnancy as the first possibility.

"Have you been using birth control?"

"No."

"So you want a child?"

"I'd like one, yes."

"Well, let me examine you, then we'll run the tests."

The examination was brief but thorough. It transpired that Sharon's pulse and blood pressure were normal, her lungs clear. She didn't have a temperature or an intestinal obstruction.

"So am I pregnant?" Sharon asked as they were sitting again in the doctor's office.

"You could be. I'll call you when the results are in."

"How long will that take?"

"A day or so."

"Can you tell this early?"

The doctor nodded. "Oh, yes. Your hormone levels are already changing. It will show up on the tests."

"Do you think I'm pregnant?" Sharon said.

The doctor hesitated. Sharon could tell that she did, but she wasn't going to say so.

Sharon stood; she felt a little shaky but awed at the same time. How wonderful it it were true.

"Please let me know as soon as you hear," Sharon said.

"I will." The doctor followed her out with her eyes and called, "Say hello to your husband for me."

Oh, I certainly will, Sharon thought dryly.

At home Rosa was waiting for her.

"Well?" she said.

"The doctor thinks I'm pregnant."

Rosa nodded. "So do I."

Sharon grinned. "You're practicing medicine now?"

"You were nauseated yesterday morning."

"I was just nervous about Tay's hearing. I wasn't sure it would go as well as it did, and I wanted the whole episode to be over and settled."

"He's on probation now?"

Sharon nodded. "Six months. There will be no further incidents, you can rest assured on that subject."

"You don't seem very thrilled about the baby," Rosa said.

"Rosa, I want to be, but I can't bear getting all excited about it and then finding out it isn't true."

"It's true."

"What if I just have a bug or something?"

"What's the matter with you? Can't you believe that you're getting what you want?"

"I guess that's it. I'm afraid to believe it. Everything is falling into place so nicely, it's like a dream."

"So you've heard about the loan then?"

"Not yet, but Pete says if they're going to turn you down you hear fairly quickly. It's a good sign that it's taking longer."

"Uh-huh," Rosa said.

"Is that your inscrutable Latin face?" Sharon asked archly, observing Rosa's expression.

"It's not inscrutable. I think you should tell Tay about the loan. That's what the face means."

"It'll be arranged soon. Relax."

Rosa said nothing.

Sharon went into her room to change for dinner.

The next day Rosa was off and Sharon went into town to the grocery store. Tay came into the empty house for a drink and was examining the contents of the refrigerator when the phone rang. He picked it up on the third ring.

"Hello?"

"Peter Symonds's office calling for Sharon Braddock," a feminine voice said.

What did he want? Tay thought. "I'm her husband, I'll take the call," he said. "Put Symonds on the line."

"Mr. Symonds is not in, but I was instructed to talk directly to Mrs. Braddock."

"She's not here, I'll take a message."

The secretary hesitated. She tried to follow directions exactly, but she was very busy and she'd been dialing the California number for hours and getting no answer. She didn't want to waste any more time on this trivial matter.

"I suppose that would be all right, if you make sure Mrs. Braddock gets it," she said.

"What is it?" Tay said impatiently.

"Please tell Mrs. Braddock that her loan has been approved. The officer at Union Bank called Mr. Symonds senior this morning."

"What loan?" Tay said, bewildered.

"I have no idea, sir, that's all I was instructed to say. May I complete the message?" the secretary stated crisply.

"Go ahead."

"Mr. Symonds will assist in closing the deal with Sun City as soon as Mrs. Braddock inherits."

There was a strained silence before Tay said in a deadly quiet voice, "Is that all?"

"That's it. Will you see that Mrs. Braddock gets the message."

"I will," Tay replied mechanically and set the receiver in its cradle.

He slumped against the wall, his face blank with shock.

What the hell was going on? He didn't want to think what he was thinking.

Had Sharon been negotiating behind his back to unload her share of the ranch?

Had she been leading him on to buy time?

No.

It wasn't possible.

But then why was Symonds involved? Had they conspired together to get Sharon's parcel? Was she going to divorce him and then get together with Symonds after the will was probated?

He couldn't believe it. He closed his eyes, his body trembling, and he grabbed the keys to his truck and dashed out of the house.

Chapter 12

Tay ran for his truck as if chased by a league of demons. He jammed the key into the ignition and tore down the road away from the house, blinking rapidly to clear his blurring vision.

What a fool! he thought despairingly. He had believed everything she said; every lie, every manipulation he had accepted as the truth. Of course she was an excellent actress, and he a most willing subject. He desperately needed to believe that she loved him and wanted to be with him, so he was gullible. He went over the secretary's words in his mind, and they were like slivers of ice cutting him to ribbons.

She had planned this with Pete Symonds all along, and somewhere inside he'd known it. He'd fallen for her boyfriend's phony apology and graceful exit, the whole bit as polished as a vaudevillian's routine. Sharon was going to dump him as soon as the will was probated and go back to her lover, who was negotiating some kind of deal in her absence.

He wondered briefly what Symonds was up to, what loan the secretary had been talking about, and decided that it didn't matter. Sharon was planning to sell her parcel to Sun City; that was the only "deal" she could possibly have with them.

Tay remembered how she had felt in his arms, how she had responded so eagerly to his kisses, and he ground his hands into the wheel. It was a joke. Their love, their marriage, their plans for the future, all of it a farce perpetrated to lull him into a false sense of security. She knew his nature. If she had announced her plans to sell right from the beginning, he would have fought her. So she had pretended to reciprocate his feelings. She had even put up that smoke screen of talking to the developers and then changing her mind out of her concern for him. Oh, she was very clever, but this little accident with the telephone message had tipped her hand. Once she had inherited the land, she was going to skip, and now he knew it.

Tay pulled off to the shoulder of the road, wiping his eyes with the back of his arm. He couldn't see well enough to drive, and he didn't even know where he was going.

Cars whizzed past him, and he realized that he was on the interstate, heading up into the foothills. Fine. That was as good a place as any to think. There were a lot of places where a man could get lost in those mountains, one of them a camping spot he had used years ago when he wanted to get away.

He waited until he was under control before he pulled into the lane of traffic heading north.

Sharon waltzed into the house, humming under her breath. She had stopped off at the clinic while she was in town and persuaded the nurse there to give her the test results as soon as they came into the office.

She was pregnant.

Rosa wasn't there and Tay was working; she was disappointed that she couldn't share her joy with anyone. She thought briefly of finding Tay outside and telling him but decided that a romantic dinner would be a better setting in which to deliver such a bulletin. She had bought the ingredients in anticipation of getting good news from the doctor, and so she was ready with steaks and baking potatoes and fresh strawberries for dessert. She had even bought a bottle of wine. She had remembered the name of one Tay ordered in a restaurant and purchased it at the liquor store in Glendora. She put everything away and glanced at the clock.

It was almost five. Time to bathe and dress before Tay came in for the evening. By five-thirty she was ready and had started dinner. He usually arrived around six-thirty, and he called if he was going to be late.

She set the table and put out the food, growing concerned only when seven o'clock passed and she hadn't heard from Tay. She telephoned the main stable and got Miguel.

"Hi, it's Sharon," she said. "I've been waiting for Tay and his dinner is getting cold. Could you put him on for a moment, please?"

"He isn't here," Miguel said. "In fact, I haven't seen him all afternoon."

"Really?"

"He went up to the house around lunchtime and never came back. We were supposed to go over to George Jensen's and pick up that roan he's been boarding, so I wondered what happened to him."

"Is his truck gone?"

"Yup."

Sharon felt alarm raising the tiny hairs on the back of her neck. "Do you know if anyone else saw him leave?"

"No. I've been asking around and nobody did." Then, as if realizing that he shouldn't scare her, he added, "I'm sure it's nothing. He probably just took a trip into town and forgot to tell anybody."

"Probably," Sharon agreed, but she didn't think so. He always let her know where he was.

Unless he didn't want her to find him.

"Thanks, Miguel." She hung up, staring at the wilting lettuce in the bowls on the table.

Something was wrong. She could feel it. She thought for a moment and dialed Rosa's home number.

"Hi, it's Sharon," she said when Rosa answered.

"What's up?" Rosa said. She was never one to beat around the bush.

"Have you seen Tay?" Sharon asked.

"No. Was he supposed to come here?"

"Not that I know of, but I thought he might have stopped by to see you."

"Sharon, he sees me almost every day." There was a pause. Then, "What's the matter?"

"Nothing's the matter."

"Don't give me that. You're calling here to find out where your husband is? You've been practically joined at the hip the last few weeks and suddenly you can't locate him?"

"He was supposed to come back for dinner and he didn't show," Sharon said, abandoning all pretense. "I called Miguel, and no one has seen him since noon. His truck is gone, too."

"I see. Did you have an argument?"

"No! Everything was going fine. In fact, I had some news to give him tonight that I thought would make him very happy."

"He's going to be a father, right?"

"Right."

"Congratulations."

"Thank you. I wish I could be happy, but I'm too worried right now."

"You're sure you didn't do or say anything to upset him?"

"Rosa, I'm telling you, he went out of here smiling this morning. I went to town for a few hours and haven't seen him since I got back."

"Then something happened while you were gone. You know he always took off when something was bothering him."

"I thought those days were past."

"Apparently not."

"Can you think where he would go?"

"He always used to go into the foothills when he was upset."

"Any special place?"

"I know of one, but I'd have to give you directions. And I forbid you to go there at night, you'd get lost. If he's not back by morning, you can drive up there and see."

"All right." At an earlier time she would have gone immediately despite Rosa's warning, but she was very conscious of the new life she was carrying. She didn't want to take any chances with it.

Rosa gave her the directions, and Sharon copied them down on the notepad she kept by the phone.

"Let me know what happens," Rosa said.

"I will."

"Sharon, do you think this has anything to do with that Sun City deal you're planning?"

Warning bells went off in Sharon's head. She hadn't thought of it until that moment. "I don't know," she said.

"He wouldn't be happy about your going behind his back if he found out about it."

"But he wouldn't run away from home, either, would he?"

"Who knows? Don't forget what he used to be like. He could revert very fast if he were threatened."

"With what?"

"Losing you, maybe."

"Losing me! That's ridiculous!"

"Maybe he doesn't think so."

"Should I call the police?" Sharon asked, really frightened now.

"No, no. He'd never forgive you, and he can take care of himself. I don't think anything has happened to him, I just think he's taken off to be alone."

"To get away from me, you mean."

"Same thing."

"Oh, Rosa."

"I know. You'd better get off the phone in case he's trying to call you. And wait until tomorrow to look for him. He may show up later tonight with a perfectly reasonable explanation."

"All right." Sharon hung up, carefully wrapped the food she had prepared and put it into the refrigerator. Then she sat and stood, paced and walked, for the rest of the night, waiting for Tay to return. Around three in the morning she fell asleep on the living room sofa, and when she woke again the sun was rising.

She showered, dressed quickly and left the house, taking the keys to her father's car and the directions Rosa had given her. She realized that Rosa could be wrong about what had happened to Tay, but at least this way she felt as though she was doing something. If she couldn't locate him today, she would call the police, no matter what anyone said.

The sun was high by the time she found the mountain road Rosa had indicated, shown by a squiggle on the map. The going was rough, and she bumped along grimly, looking for the cabin Rosa had described.

She spotted it through the trees as she came around a bend in the road, and with a grateful lurch of her heart she saw that Tay's truck was parked behind it. She pulled her car in next to the pickup, got out and went over to the cabin. Hesitantly, she knocked on the door, which was ajar.

When there was no response, she pushed it inward. To her extreme disappointment the cabin was empty.

She thought for a moment, and realized that Tay had to be nearby. If she couldn't locate him, she would just sit down and wait; he would have to show up eventually. She wandered outside and listened closely, thinking that she heard the gurgle of water in the distance. She listened again; it sounded like a stream. She followed the sound and it got louder until she could see the gleam of water through the underbrush. She pushed on and finally broke through the trees, coming to a clearing where Tay was sitting on an outcropping of rock, staring into the distance.

She sagged with relief and watched him for a while, until he felt her gaze and turned to look at her.

"What are you doing here?" he said curtly.

Not exactly the lover's greeting she had been longing to hear. "I came to find you. Rosa told me where you might be."

He watched her as she picked her way to him, climbing over rocks and fallen tree limbs. He made no move to get up and help her. When she was standing next to him, she said, "Tay, what's going on? You didn't come home last night, I've been out of my mind worrying about you."

"I'll bet," he said acidly, looking away from her. He hadn't shaved, and his beard was dark on his cheeks and chin. He was wearing the same clothes he'd had on the previous day.

"Have you been sitting here all night?"

"What difference does it make?"

"Tay, don't you think you'd better tell me what this is all about?"

He considered her for a moment and said, "Fine. The game is over. You can stop pretending that you love me and will stay married to me. I know all about your clever scheme."

"What scheme?" she said, stunned. "What on earth are you talking about?"

"I have a message from your boy Pete," he said.

"Pete Symonds?"

"Do we know any other?"

"He called you?"

"His secretary did. Or rather she called you, but I took the message."

Sharon's expression changed, and he noted it.

"Yeah," he said sarcastically. "She blew it sky-high. When old Pete finds out about this, I don't think she'll be on the payroll too long."

"She spoiled the surprise," Sharon said, her shoulders sagging.

"Surprise?" Now it was Tay's turn to look dumbfounded. "Oh, it was a surprise, all right. The message was that he will assist you in closing the Sun City deal as soon as you inherit the ranch property."

Sharon looked at him, understanding everything in a second, unsure how to proceed.

"Nothing to say?" Tay asked, raising his brows.

"Tay, I think you misunderstood the message."

"It was pretty clear. You've been planning all along to dump me and sell your half of the ranch to Sun City."

"Wrong."

He stared at her. "What? You think I'm going to fall for some new lie you've dreamed up? Hell, Sharon, I know you think I'm stupid, and I can't say I blame you after the stuff I've swallowed during the last few weeks, but give me credit for some brains, at least."

"Tay, listen to me. I'm not going to sell my share of the ranch. Pete was talking about a different deal."

"A different deal," he said, shaking his head. "I can't wait to hear this one."

Sharon told him about the letter she'd received from Citrus Farms, and how she was planning to buy the northern tract from Sun City. While she talked, she could see his attitude change as he began to understand, and he finally interrupted her to say, "Why didn't you tell me about any of this?"

"I wanted to solve it for you, not bother you with it. You were buying those horses and you'd already put up the money...." Her voice trailed off into silence. She added, "Rosa told me to bring you in on it."

He sighed. "Rosa was right. God, Sharon, do you know what kind of night I just spent, thinking..."

"I know what you were thinking." She took a step closer to him. "Tay, maybe I was wrong not to tell you, but how could you jump to that conclusion?"

He shrugged, and shook his head.

She moved over to sit next to him and said quietly, "Darling, are you ever going to believe that I love you?"

He put his arm around her. "You just keep showing me, and I will."

"I have something important to tell you."

"What is it?"

Sharon kissed him as she told him her news, and he responded, drawing her down with him to the carpet of grass on the edge of the stream.

Epilogue

"Danny, stop banging that spoon on the table and eat your lunch," Sharon said.

The dark-haired four-year-old took one bite of his sandwich and started tapping the spoon on his plate.

Sharon put down the kettle she was holding and took the spoon out of his hand.

"Where's Daddy?" Danny said.

"He'll be here in a minute."

"You said that hours ago." Danny's concept of time was a little vague.

"Just be patient."

"You always say that."

"It's good advice, especially in view of the genes you inherited from your father."

"What are genes?"

"Part of a chromosome that..." She stopped. "Never mind, take my word for it."

"Daddy's bringing me a horse."

"Daddy's bringing you a pony, but not today, please God," Sharon said fervently.

"When?"

"Soon."

"You said the baby was coming soon."

"That's right." She glanced down at her burgeoning stomach. In about a month, she thought.

The door opened and Tay breezed in.

"Daddy!" Danny screamed as if he hadn't seen him that morning.

"How's my boy?" Tay said, snatching the child out of his chair. He swung the boy into the air and kissed Sharon's cheek at the same time.

"Hi," she said. "Where's Rosa?"

"Outside talking to Miguel. She'll be inside in a minute."

"The doctor's appointment is at one-thirty."

"Relax, we'll make it." He grinned.

"Unless I have the baby right here," Sharon said in an undertone.

"Not planning on it, are you?" Tay asked.

"Baby! Baby!" Danny yelled.

"Attaboy," his father said.

"Where's my pony?" Danny said, encouraged by the approval.

"I told you that we would go look at some later this week," Tay said.

"Tonight?" the child asked.

Tay looked at Sharon. "I think he has a vocabulary problem."

"No, he just wants what he wants, like his daddy," Sharon said, going back to the stove.

"I beg your pardon," Tay said, putting his son on the floor and hugging her from behind.

"Baby-sitter's here," Rosa announced, coming through the door.

"I'm not a baby," Danny said.

"Get it straight, Rosa," Tay advised her. "Once the new arrival is on the scene, Dan will expect to be treated with the proper amount of respect, as befits a senior citizen."

"How's Pilar?" Sharon asked Rosa.

"Nervous."

"Remember not to make any plans for tomorrow night," Sharon said to Tay. "The recital at UCLA is at eight, and we're meeting my clients after that."

"I want to go," Danny announced.

"Only dance lovers over sixteen are permitted," Tay told him. "Mrs. Hendrix is coming to take care of you."

"She has a moustache," Danny said.

"Danny!" Sharon said reprovingly.

Tay turned away, smiling.

"You'd better get going," Rosa said to him.

Sharon picked up her purse and followed Tay out the door. "See you later," she called back, blowing her son a kiss.

"Mommy looks fat," Danny said to Rosa after his parents had left.

"That will change soon, *mijo*," Rosa said.

"Can we play the domino game?" Danny asked.

"Finish your sandwich first."

"Then can we play?"

"Yes," Rosa said, glancing out the window to see Tay helping Sharon into the car.

He bent over and kissed his wife as he closed her door, and Rosa smiled.

*   *   *   *   *

SILHOUETTE *Romance*™

Escape to a place where a kiss is still a kiss...
Feel the breathless connection...
Fall in love as though it were
the very first time...
Experience the power of love!

Come to where favorite authors—such as
**Diana Palmer, Stella Bagwell,
Marie Ferrarella** and many more—
deliver heart-warming romance and genuine
emotion, time after time after time....

Silhouette Romance—
stories straight from the heart!

Silhouette®
Where love comes alive™

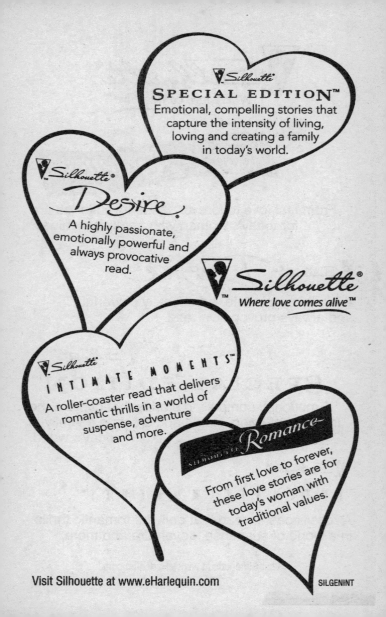

Silhouette
SPECIAL EDITION™

Emotional, compelling stories that
capture the intensity of living,
loving and creating a family
in today's world.

Silhouette®
Desire

A highly passionate,
emotionally powerful and
always provocative
read.

Silhouette®
Where love comes alive™

Silhouette
INTIMATE MOMENTS™

A roller-coaster read that delivers
romantic thrills in a world of
suspense, adventure
and more.

SILHOUETTE Romance

From first love to forever,
these love stories are for
today's woman with
traditional values.

Visit Silhouette at www.eHarlequin.com   SILGENINT

Where love comes alive™

From first love to forever, these love stories are
for today's woman with traditional values.

A highly passionate, emotionally powerful
and always provocative read.

SPECIAL EDITION™

Emotional, compelling stories that capture the
intensity of living, loving and creating a family in
today's world.

Silhouette®

INTIMATE MOMENTS™

A roller-coaster read that delivers romantic thrills
in a world of suspense, adventure and more.